THE OWL KEEPER

THE OWL KEEPER

CHRISTINE BRODIEN-JONES

ILLUSTRATIONS BY MAGGIE KNEEN

a YEARLING BOOK

Text copyright © 2010 by Christine L. Jones
Illustrations copyright © 2010 by Maggie Kneen

All rights reserved. Published in the United States by Yearling, an imprint of
Random House Children's Books, a division of Random House, Inc., New York. Originally published in hardcover in the United States by Delacorte Press, an imprint of Random House Children's Books, a division of Random House, Inc., New York, in 2010.

Yearling and the jumping horse design are registered trademarks of Random House, Inc.

Visit us on the Web! www.randomhouse.com/kids

Educators and librarians, for a variety of teaching tools, visit us at
www.randomhouse.com/teachers

The Library of Congress has cataloged the hardcover edition of this work as follows:
Brodien-Jones, Chris.
The Owl Keeper / Christine Brodien-Jones ; [illustrations by Maggie Kneen].
p. cm.
Summary: Eleven-year-old Max partners with an unusual girl, Rose, who shares his appreciation of the silver owls that the High Echelon wants to destroy, and together they make a perilous journey seeking to fulfill a prophecy.
ISBN 978-0-385-73814-9 (hc) — ISBN 978-0-385-90710-1 (glb) —
ISBN 978-0-375-89590-6 (ebook) [1. Fantasy. 2. Owls—Fiction. 3. Human-animal relationships—Fiction. 4. Magic—Fiction. 5. Prophecies—Fiction.] I. Kneen, Maggie, ill.
II. Title.
PZ7.B786114Owl 2010
[Fic]—dc22
2009027321

ISBN 978-0-385-73815-6 (pbk.)

Printed in the United States of America

10 9 8 7 6 5 4 3 2 1

First Yearling Edition

TO PETER,
WHO FIRST HEARD
THE OWLSONG

THE WAY TO THE OWL KEEPER
—from the silver prophecies

Owl in the darkness,
silver in the leaves,
Blind child comes leading
through the fog and trees.
Through the haunted forest,
beyond the aching hills,
Darker grows the eventide,
deeper grows the chill.

Silver and ice, silver and ice,
Silver owl will guide you,
with its golden eyes.

Ancient dark is rising
on the highest bridge,
Red-eyed wolves are running
on the distant ridge.
Beware the eyeless creatures
that would have your soul,
Choose the burning sunlight,
choose the path of gold.

SILVER AND ICE, SILVER AND ICE,
SILVER OWL WILL GUIDE YOU,
WITH ITS GOLDEN EYES.

JOURNEY TO THE MOUNTAIN,
FLEE THE FORTRESS OLD,
SILVER WINGS WILL SAVE YOU
FROM THE KILLING COLD.
TWO WILL MAKE THE JOURNEY,
OLD ONE GONE BEFORE,
TO THE ICEBOUND TOWER,
THROUGH THE CRUMBLING DOOR.

SILVER AND ICE, SILVER AND ICE,
SILVER OWL WILL GUIDE YOU,
WITH ITS GOLDEN EYES.

OWL KEEPER IS SUMMONED
ATOP THE FROZEN PLAIN,
OWLS AND SAGES GATHER
TO FIGHT THE DARK AGAIN.
TWO WILL MAKE THE JOURNEY,
SILVER OWL IN HAND,
SEEK THE MOONLIT TOWER
AS DARKNESS SWEEPS THE LAND.

SILVER AND ICE, SILVER AND ICE,
SILVER OWL WILL GUIDE YOU,
WITH ITS GOLDEN EYES.

CHAPTER ONE

When Max first saw the girl that night, standing beneath the owl tree, he thought she was a ghost or a vision, or maybe a comic-book character come to life. It didn't occur to him that she might be real. As far as he knew, nobody real had ever come to the owl tree before.

The girl tilted her head, peering sideways at him. That's no ghost, he told himself, pulling down the flaps of his woolen cap. He shivered, feeling feverish. This field of dry brown grasses was his territory, along with the owl tree that stood in the center. The river below was his too, with its muddy path and view of the forest on the other side. All this belonged to him.

Night after night, Max sat under the owl tree, to be alone to brood and think. He held a secret hope that the Owl Keeper might pass this way, but that had never happened—not yet, anyway—and for sure this girl wasn't the Owl Keeper. He wanted to say she had no right to be there, but the shivering went right through his lips and into his throat, locking the words inside.

He stared at the girl as she looked around in a defiant sort of way. She was tall—string-bean skinny, as Gran used to say—with an oval-shaped olive face. Hair fanned from her head in a burst of coppery orange, and leaves were tangled all through it.

Max had never seen anyone so disorderly. She looked moody and self-centered. Where had she come from? She couldn't be a Misshapen—they never left the forest—yet she was utterly unlike anyone he had ever known.

Without a word she whipped around, glaring at him with a haughty expression. Looking into those green eyes, too big for her face, Max could see that the girl was different in a scary kind of way. Those eyes had a lean, hungry look. Her woolly black coat hung to her ankles, a spider dangling from the hem. Sticking out from under it were long, bumpy toes. Nobody around here dressed in clothes like that, and nobody Max knew would dream of going barefoot in this damp climate.

Max had a nervous feeling in his chest. Clenching his teeth, he stepped forward, unsure of what to say. The girl drew herself up. Beneath the coat, her shoulders moved like frail wings. He noticed she was nearly a head taller than he was.

"You don't have any deathwatch beetles attached to your coat, do you?" he asked hesitantly. Didn't she see that spider hanging there? This girl, Max realized, was even more of an outsider than he was.

Her eyes flashed. "What's that supposed to mean?" She jutted out her sharp chin. Her coat smelled like wet leaves.

"Deathwatch beetles are bad luck. They foretell death—that's what my guardian, Mrs. Crumlin, says."

"Death doesn't scare me." The girl pointed to the top of the tree. Despite the cold air, she wasn't wearing mittens. "What's up there?" Her eyes traveled to a small silver-feathered owl, sitting on a high branch.

Max froze. No one knew about the owl. Since last winter he had kept her hidden in the owl tree, away from prying eyes. The problem was, silver owls didn't exist—not officially, at any rate. Silver owls had been declared extinct by the government.

"It's just an ordinary barn owl," Max lied. He hoped his owl hadn't heard that remark; she'd be terribly insulted if she had. "She lives in this tree. I call it the owl tree." This girl is acting so uppity, he thought, you'd think the owl was the intruder, not her.

Max adored owls—they were his passion—and he was endlessly fascinated with silver owls. He'd learned volumes about them from his gran. To have this small silver owl appear out of nowhere, he knew, was nothing short of a miracle.

The girl scrunched up her eyes. "I never saw a *silver* owl before," she said, her voice thin and scratchy.

Neither had Max—not until this owl turned up with a message in her beak. Fearful of her at first, he quickly realized that she was unique, with her heart-shaped face and golden eyes. He didn't mind that she was small and scruffy—her feathers gave off light, a luminescent glow that silver owls were famous for. It was the kind of light Max imagined at the center of the sun, if only he dared look at it.

"I told you, it's not a silver owl," he insisted. "It's a cousin or some distant relative."

The girl paid him no attention. She couldn't stop looking at the owl. Max wished he had a stronger voice. If his words boomed out, she might listen. She'd probably be impressed if he told her about the message; maybe she'd even help him decipher it.

But the message was his secret, and so was the mystery of his amazing silver owl. Telling this girl anything might be risky. What if the authorities had sent her to spy on him?

"Real silver owls don't exist," she said, her lips set in a fierce line. "That's what they want us to think anyway." She threw him an enigmatic smile.

Alarmed by her comment, Max looked away. How much, he wondered, did this girl know about silver owls? According to the textbooks, countless birds had perished during the Great Destruction. The books said that all the silver owls had.

But Gran had told Max that not every silver owl had been destroyed. Dispersed by the Dark Brigade, the silver owls had been weakened and were in hiding, waiting for the Owl Keeper to appear. One day, said Gran, they would fulfill an ancient Prophecy and bring their OwlSong back to the world. But as Max grew older he'd started to wonder if it was true—or had it just been one of Gran's made-up stories?

The bobble on his cap flopped over one eye and he knocked it back. "My owl eats mice and small birds—swallows them whole!"

He wanted to impress this strange girl and his words tumbled out before he could stop them. "Afterward she spits out a pellet with bones and feathers and fur inside. If you take one apart, you never know what you'll find."

"Know what I think?" said the girl, tilting her head at a funny angle. "I think this isn't any ordinary owl. I can tell by looking at it: this is a real silver owl." She paused dramatically. "It's the last silver owl on the whole planet!"

Her fiery eyes alighted on Max. He shifted from one foot to the other, feeling more anxious than ever. There was no way to trick this girl, he realized. She was too smart.

"You won't tell anybody, will you?" Max studied her solemn, pinched face, searching for a sign that she was trustworthy. The owl fluttered down onto his arm, blinking at him, her movements slow and stiff. He smoothed her soft feathers with the back of his hand, feeling her warmth, her tiny beating heart.

"She's got courage, you can tell." He breathed deeply, thinking if only he could be brave like his silver owl. "I found her last winter, up in this tree," he added proudly. "She had ice on her wings and white thistles stuck to her feathers."

He didn't mention how he'd been afraid at first, thinking the bird might try to attack him.

"That owl's wing is sticking out funny," said the girl. "And that eye worries me. Look how it only opens halfway." She wiped her nose on her coat sleeve. "Seems to me somebody tried to knock its eye out."

"Her wing's broken!" snapped Max, irritated with this girl and her comments. Why was she so critical? "Can't you see? She was in a fight!" He steadied his voice, trying to explain. "She can hardly fly at all. That wing of hers has to mend. I bring her mice and grubs—she's not able to hunt for herself."

"Then that bird's stuck here in this tree, isn't it?" said the girl, her eyes fixed on the owl. "It can't get away even if it wants to."

Max shrugged. He often sensed that his owl longed to fly off, swift and far, that she was just waiting for her wing to heal. But he didn't tell the girl that his greatest fear was one day she'd fly away and never return.

They stood in silence as the minutes ticked by. The girl fidgeted. Max could see her eyes wandering, taking in the tree, the owl, the high grasses all around them. He chewed on his fingernails, worried that he'd said too much.

"I won't tell anyone," the girl said at last. "Your secret's safe with me."

Max looked up, surprised and relieved. The owl fluttered awkwardly into the air, landing on a low branch next to the girl, hooting softly. Is the owl trying to tell me something? he wondered. Was she saying he could trust this quirky, peculiar girl?

"Who are you?" he asked. "Why are you here?"

The girl whirled around to face him, puffing herself up like an owl. "I'm named after the moon goddess Artemis! She was a free spirit who ran through the forest and shot her enemies through the heart with arrows. Nothing scared Artemis, the goddess of wild animals—she was totally fearless!"

Mouth open, Max backed away, startled by her fierce reply. He wondered if she was hiding any bows and arrows under that long coat of hers.

"I know about the myths," he said. His granny had read them to him out of a tattered leather book. He cast back in his mind for stories about a huntress.

"Artemis Rose Eccles, that's me," the girl huffed. Then her body seemed to deflate and she settled back down. "You can call me Rose; it's less formal."

Max gave a shy smile, thinking he had worried needlessly. The High Echelon would never hire anyone as unstable as Rose. "I'm Maxwell Unger. Max for short." He pointed across the field. "My house is at the top of this hill, behind that clump of trees. You can't see it too well in the dark. I live there with my parents at the end of a dead-end street."

Rose looked sidelong at him. Her eyes were the color of the moss around the tree. "What are you doing out here in the middle of the night?"

Max's face burned. "I've got my reasons." He tugged the earflaps on his cap, wishing she would stop looking so hard. "Besides, I could ask you the same."

"You could." Rose bent down and scratched her ankle. "But I asked first."

Max frowned, thinking how this wild girl had an answer for everything. "My parents don't know I come here at night," he confided. "If they did, they'd be really upset."

The silver owl hooted softly, so softly one might mistake it for the wind. It was the sound Max loved best in the world. Shoulders hunched, he dug his hands into his jacket pockets. How could he tell Rose that for the last five years the dark was all he had known?

CHAPTER TWO

"Is that you, Maxwell?" Mrs. Crumlin set down her knitting needles and heaved herself off the sofa.

Rubbing his eyes, Max stood in the hallway gazing into the dim parlor. He had been sleeping in his bedroom most of the afternoon. Unlike other boys his age, he never went outdoors in the daytime. Five years ago he'd been diagnosed with a rare and mysterious illness: he was allergic to sun particles.

For Max, only the night mattered.

The drapes were pulled tightly together, secured from top to bottom with clothespins so that no sunlight could filter in. Mrs.

Crumlin's lumpy shadow bobbed up and down as she stumped over to the radio, humming to a Top Ten song.

> Ancient dark is rising on the highest bridge,
> Red-eyed wolves are running on the distant ridge.
> Beware the silver darkness that would have
>   your soul,
> Choose the temperate city domes, with their lights
>   of gold.

Most of the popular songs these days were about the dome cities that were going up all over the country. Max found their lyrics totally inane. The Citizens' Dome Construction Scheme was nearing completion, which meant people would be moving out of the towns and into the new domes.

Why, he wondered, did the song include those scary parts? It gave him a feeling of dread, hearing that line about wolves.

Dressed in pajamas and slippers, he scuffed into the parlor. "I had another nightmare," he announced, tripping over his pajama cuffs. Nothing ever seemed to hang right on his small, skinny frame.

"Have a seat, Maxwell." With a look of concern, Mrs. Crumlin patted the sofa. Devoid of color or shape, her dress reeked of bleach and pickling spices. "I hope you're not having one of your funny turns."

Bleary-eyed, Max flopped down on the cushions. Shadows, thrown by sputtering flare lamps, leapt across the walls. He could smell burnt food, drifting in from the kitchen down the hall— Mrs. Crumlin's idea of home cooking, he joked to himself.

Max Unger was a pale-faced flannel-shirt sort of boy, with dark brown eyes and stringy brown hair. He had his father's straight nose, his mother's high cheekbones and a dash of freckles. His ears were slightly too big, but his mother promised he'd grow into them.

Mrs. Crumlin often remarked that Max's face had a look of permanent worry due to his insecure nature. True, he was often anxious and easily frightened. As a little boy he had been afraid of large dogs, fearful of spiders, terrified of loud noises. Even now, those things could make him jump.

"Breaking news," boomed the radio announcer. "In an emergency session last night the government passed the Sealed Borders Act, declaring that all borders will be closed until further notice. This action, they say, comes after threats from hostile countries as yet unnamed. Under this act, no one is allowed to enter or leave the country without High Echelon permission."

Puzzled, Max sat up, listening intently, but the announcer had moved on to the weather. Why would the government want to cut them off from the rest of the world?

"Why are the borders closed?" he asked.

"Not to worry, Maxwell, the High Echelon knows what it's doing. Remember, its job is to protect us." Mrs. Crumlin turned down the volume. "Puzzling, I'd say, the way those injections bring on those nightmares of yours," she said, changing the subject completely. "Would you like to tell me about your dream?"

"No," Max said, gnawing on a fingernail. "I wouldn't."

His mother often said that Mrs. Crumlin had a thankless job and that Max should see things from her point of view. But he resented the way she was always quizzing him about his dreams, pressing him for details.

"Very well." Mrs. Crumlin sounded a bit hurt. "Have it your way."

When Max was little, he'd had impossibly wonderful dreams that featured mysterious towers and enchanted trees and silver owls flying through snow. He remembered those as the Good Dreams. But when he turned seven, those dreams ended abruptly. Ever since, he had suffered from disturbing nightmares.

"Hungry, Maxwell?" asked Mrs. Crumlin, straightening a lamp shade. "I'll find something to munch on." She plodded off. "Try not to bite your nails, dear."

He leaned back on the cushions, pretending he hadn't heard that last, annoying remark.

Max's schedule was totally different from those of other kids his age. Because he spent his nights at the owl tree—a secret he'd kept from his parents for years—he'd gotten into the habit of sleeping through the day.

Mrs. Crumlin arrived each morning at seven sharp, lugging a tapestry bag stuffed with yarn, just as Max's parents were leaving for work. All day long she knitted and pickled and boiled up meals, singing nonstop to the radio. Every hour she inspected the house, clumping from room to room, checking that no sunlight filtered inside. When Nora and Ewan Unger returned each evening at six o'clock she rushed off, terrified of being caught out in the dark.

The Ungers' kitchen was a permanent disaster. Pots were burned, counters scorched, dish towels mangled, all on account of Mrs. Crumlin. Max's father said it was a marvel the house was still standing at the end of the day. Max didn't mind the chaos, the off-putting smells or even Mrs. Crumlin's inedible cooking. It was her constant niggling that drove him crazy, her disapproving looks, and the way she passed judgment on everything he did.

"You look peaky, Maxwell." Mrs. Crumlin set down a mug of hot cocoa and a plate of her sunfire cookies. "Everything all right? I'm willing to listen, if you'd like to discuss your dream. No need to be hypersensitive."

Mrs. Crumlin loved words like *hypersensitive* and *hyperfrenetic*, Max noticed. She used them every chance she got.

"I don't feel like talking," he said, running a hand through his limp hair. He could tell it needed a good shampooing. "My throat's scratchy." Max often woke from his nightmares with a sore throat, his eyes burning.

She made a sympathetic clucking sound that set his nerves on edge. "Your face is flushed, Maxwell. Let's hope you're not coming down with a fever. Drink up, now." She handed him the mug. "A pity you're so susceptible to germs. I do worry, since we'll be celebrating your twelfth birthday next month. Won't that be exciting? That's when the High Echelon will announce the details of your apprenticeship."

Max's mouth went dry. The thought of his upcoming apprenticeship filled him with dread. Under High Echelon law, children left school on their twelfth birthday and were assigned a field of study. Some were sent to institutions of learning, others apprenticed with Master Craftspeople, while an unfortunate few were sent to work underground.

"Don't look so glum, Maxwell," said Mrs. Crumlin in a chirpy voice. "The High Echelon has your best interests at heart. Rest assured it'll make an appropriate match."

Max had no idea what the High Echelon had planned for him. No one ever did. When he was small, he dreamed of a career tracking down silver owls and building them a sanctuary. If only owl tracking were one of the choices. But of course it wasn't— not when silver owls had been declared extinct.

Mrs. Crumlin plumped up his pillow. "Perhaps we need to speak to Dr. Tredegar about those bad dreams."

Max stiffened. Dr. Tredegar had been coming to the house to give him injections every week since he was seven. Never pleasant, the injections had become increasingly painful over the years.

"My mother already telephoned him." Max crunched into a sun-shaped cookie. It was hard as a rock, with a pungent odor. "Tredegar told her the nightmares are a side effect of the shots and there's nothing he can do." He took small bites, not wanting to be rude, trying to be tidy. Despite her messy kitchen, Mrs. Crumlin was a stickler about crumbs in the parlor.

"*Doctor* Tredegar to you, dear," she corrected. She was also strict when it came to good manners.

Even in the day, Max found himself haunted by the nightmares. Recently they'd become so intense that he often woke up in a cold sweat. What kind of medicine were they giving him? he wondered. What if they were rewiring his brain or something equally weird? Gran had always maintained that the government was doing secret experiments. Yet whenever Max asked questions, the doctor made silly wisecracks and his father mumbled clichés about stabilizing his condition.

Mrs. Crumlin shuffled over to the radio and turned up the sound. "Those bitten-down fingernails are *so* unsightly, Maxwell." The speaker crackled with static. "I am disappointed," she went on, fiddling with the antenna. "A boy your age should take pride in his appearance."

Ignoring her comments, Max stuffed the rest of his cookie beneath the sofa cushion. He knew Mrs. Crumlin wouldn't find it because she never bothered to clean under there.

Following Max's seventh birthday, Gran had died unexpectedly, and on a routine examination Max had been diagnosed by Dr. Tredegar with his rare condition. On the doctor's advice, the Ungers had taken their son out of school and arranged for a tutor and a guardian. The tutor, Professor LaMothe, was a whiskery old bloater with a potbelly and breath that reeked of tinned eels. Luckily for Max, he had modest expectations. A mild-mannered man, the professor lectured Max one day a week, barking out mathematical theorems and quoting paragraphs from the Constitution of the High Echelon.

Adapting to Mrs. Crumlin had been far more stressful. Her first week at the house, Max had caught her rummaging through his closet, digging out books he'd hidden at the bottom of his toy chest. He had shouted terrible things at her, but it hadn't done any good. He never saw the books again. His stuffed toy owl went missing at the same time.

Over the years, he'd put up with Mrs. Crumlin's mugs of bitter hot cocoa, her incessant nagging, her moronic board games and off-key humming. In the end, he'd resigned himself to her being there.

But Max had never resigned himself to Gran's being gone. He missed the dusty jumbled rooms of her house, the falling-apart books she was forever sorting through, the adventure tales she read aloud to him. He missed her impulsive hugs and silvery laughter, her amusing stories at the dinner table. His memories of that time were filled with light.

Mrs. Crumlin was the exact opposite of his grandmother. Gran had expressed endless curiosity about nature and imaginary worlds, and never toed the line when it came to government edicts. Unlike Gran, Mrs. Crumlin never hugged, rarely smiled and always kept her private life under wraps. Was there a Mr. Crumlin? Little Crumlins? Grand-Crumlins? Max didn't have a clue—and his parents had warned him not to ask.

"And this just in," came the announcer's staccato voice. "Three silver owls were tracked down and destroyed yesterday morning by the Dark Brigade in the Easterly Reaches area. This was in response to a new government edict calling for the eradication of silver owls, which were thought to be extinct. The Silver Owl Eradication Edict was passed after scientists found that the remaining silver owls carry plague and pestilence and may attack humans. Should you see a silver owl in your area, contact your local Dark Brigade immediately."

Max froze, sick with fear. If they sent him away for his apprenticeship, what would become of his beloved silver owl? Who would look after her and keep her safe? If the authorities caught her, he'd never forgive himself.

The theme song from *Flamingo Valley*, Mrs. Crumlin's favorite radio drama, started up. There was a single station, run by the High Echelon, and its mindless songs and broadcasts bored Max silly. He often wondered why there was only one. According to Gran, the airwaves had once crackled with numerous stations that offered poetry, music, drama, debates and political forums.

Back when Gran was young, no one had been afraid of the government. Back then, Max reflected sadly, silver owls flew wherever they wanted and people were free to speak their minds.

As the theme song to *Flamingo Valley* ended, Max curled up on the sofa and drifted off into a familiar nightmare.

Just like in his other dreams, he was transformed into a creature that was powerful and deadly. No longer human, he flapped two ragged wings, soaring unevenly through the night. Buoyed by winds and currents, his body weighed almost nothing. In real life he was nervous about heights, never daring to go too high in the owl tree. But when he flew in his dreams, his fears melted away.

He saw stars scrambled overhead, and two moons floating above the forest—the broken halves of the old moon, which had cracked in two during the Great Destruction. Beneath him churned the black, icy waters of the river, rushing into empty darkness.

In the distance loomed a plateau pulsing with a strange, un-earthly light: the Frozen Zone. For a moment Max lost his bearings. Then, righting himself, he saw the village of Cavernstone Grey with its twisting streets and barn-board houses, its outlying farms and factories. He circled the grounds of Cavernstone Hall, where his parents worked, and flew over a mysterious building called The Ruins.

He sniffed, smelling fetid creatures like himself. Scores of them were pouring out the windows of The Ruins. As he glided down, the cold rush of the river filled his ears. His heart thudded and a reckless thrill surged through him.

He spotted an ancient tree in the middle of a field and swooped toward it, skimming the tips of the branches. Hunger gnawed at the pit of his stomach. His ears pricked at the sound of a low, sad hooting.

When he saw the silver owl high on a branch, head tucked beneath one wing, a warm glow spread through him. But the warm feeling quickly gave way to rage. A bitter taste filled his mouth and a dark, primal craving washed over him: the urge to destroy.

Then, as always happened, the silver owl looked up, her eyes wide with fear. For an instant her heart-shaped face reminded him of Gran's. Behind his eyes the blood thickened and boiled, blotting out the image. A ravenous hunger took hold of him.

With a triumphant shriek, Max flew toward the owl.

CHAPTER THREE

Stepping off the back porch, Max ducked beneath the hooded flannel shirts and long underwear snapping on the clothesline. Mrs. Crumlin had hung them after breakfast and forgotten to take them down. On top of the line sat three fat sleeping ravens.

Against the bleak night sky, his house stood silent and shuttered. Like the other houses at the edge of town, it was solid and ordinary, with a tilting roof, unpainted shingles and porches at the front and back.

His mom and dad had gone to bed at their usual time of eight o'clock. Because Max only saw his parents at dinnertime, it was difficult to be close to them. Nora and Ewan Unger worked long hours, six days a week, arriving home each evening exhausted. The High Echelon had put an end to vacations and sick time, and missing work for any reason was frowned upon. On their day off they were required to attend Dome Commission meetings.

Each night Max waited to make sure his parents were asleep, then sneaked out through the back door. The darkness drew him like a magnet: he could never resist the night.

Grasses crackled as he thumped across the dark field to the owl tree, trying to forget his nightmare from the afternoon. He knew he was a bird of prey in his dream—but what kind? A raven? He didn't think so, because ravens were languid and dozy.

Why would he want to attack the silver owl? She was like a secret treasure, more precious to him than anything in the world. Max wound his scarf tighter around his neck. Calling up those dreams upset him terribly, leaving him anxious and confused.

Beneath his fleece-lined jacket, he wore three sweaters, knitted by Mrs. Crumlin from surplus wool. His leather boots had been shipped from a mail-order house and had extra-thick treads. He'd gotten them for his eleventh birthday, though it had taken nearly a year for his feet to grow into them.

When he was young, Max would sneak out of the house with Gran at night, setting off on all kinds of adventures, exploring marshes and tramping across grasslands. He was scared of many things, but the night had always felt safe to Max, wrapping itself like a magical cloak around his grandmother and him.

Gran knew where to find dryad beetles and turtle eggs and a fungus that glowed in the dark. They searched for silver owls, though they never found one. Silver owls were a rare breed of warrior owl, Gran explained, and they possessed a fierce and terrifying magic, called OwlSong.

As a little boy, Max would clutch his blanket and stuffed toy owl and Gran would sit on the bed next to him, telling him his favorite story before he fell asleep, the tale of the Owl Keeper. It began in the ancient city of Silvern, high on a wintry plateau, with a strong-willed, independent girl named Fuchsia who lived in a tower and tended bees.

In Fuchsia's twelfth year, the evil group Alazarin Oro invaded the country, overthrowing the benevolent Circle of Sages. The Sages fled, braving snowstorms and hiding in the forests, until they reached Silvern. There they met Fuchsia, who offered them refuge in her tower. Inside they discovered hundreds of stone owls carved into the walls, which the Sages recognized at once as silver owls (Max's favorite part of the story), turned to stone by the Alazarin Oro. The Sages unlocked the dark spell, earning the owls' undying loyalty, and Fuchsia became the first Owl Keeper.

Once freed, the silver owls emitted their powerful OwlSong—not so much a song, explained Gran, as a vibration, rippling across the land, creating an energy force that shifted the balance away from evil, restoring peace once again.

But, as centuries went by, the dark forces gained momentum. Sages and owls were scattered and Silvern fell to ruins. Yet there was a prophecy, written in the Silver Scrolls: in times of darkness an Owl Keeper would appear, to unite silver owls and Sages against the powers of evil. The time of the Owl Keeper, Gran would say, is coming soon.

As he approached the owl tree, Max saw the outline of the girl: mammoth black coat, beaky nose, hair flaming around her head. Beyond her, in the distance, he could see the dark haunted waterway that was the river, and the forest on the other side.

He balked when he saw Rose's tough-girl stance. Her aggressive style intimidated him. Rose was a reckless type, Max could tell, and that made him nervous. He liked his life orderly, with everything in its place and nothing left to chance. Artemis Rose Eccles was just the opposite. She was messy and impulsive, a risk taker who scrambled everything up.

"I guess you're not scared of the dark," he said, walking over to her as if he weren't afraid.

Rose stood on her toes, reaching for a branch. "Obviously you weren't listening." Her voice was high and know-it-all. "*Scared* isn't in my vocabulary. I'm not afraid of anything, and that includes the dark." She hoisted herself up. "*And* the Misshapens."

"You don't have to worry about them," said Max irritably. "We're safe here because they hate open spaces."

"I know that." Her smug voice drifted down.

Max had heard rumors about the Misshapens all his life. They were the government's botched experiments: laboratory-made creatures cast off by the High Echelon and set free to roam the forests. Some nights he sat in the owl tree, looking across the river, and saw their eyes glowing through the trees. Gran said the Misshapens would never cross over because they'd been pro-grammed to stay in the forest.

Max heard Rose giggle. She was making faces at the silver owl from her perch on a branch. The owl puffed up her feathers, basking in the extra attention. Then she hopped from limb to limb, nursing her crooked wing, trying to get closer to Rose.

Max caught the owl as she tumbled off a low branch. Some-times her timing was a little off. The owl clung to his sleeve with sharp claws, carefully trundling up to his shoulder. She seemed to know he would be in trouble if his jacket got torn.

He turned his head sideways and the owl swiveled her head right around. They blinked at each other and the owl nuzzled her head against his cheek. Max was always surprised at how delicate she was, how warm to the touch.

"See, Rose, this is her way of saying hello. It's owl talk." He never tired of petting her sleek feathers or breathing in the grassy sweetness of her breath.

"You should know," said Rose, hanging upside down. "I never had a pet owl." She swung herself up and sat on the branch. "Tell me about your parents, Max," she said, catching him by surprise.

Max couldn't think of anything impressive to say. Gran always described his father as the kind of man who liked his bread white and his hedges straight. His mother wore bifocals and was in the habit of falling asleep at the dinner table. Dr. Tredegar prescribed pills for her nerves.

Then he brightened. "My mom and dad both work at Cavernstone Hall. It's a chocolate factory where they make high-end chocolates and gourmet cocoa mix," he said importantly. "They have high-ranking jobs and they use smart cards to get in and out. And, oh yeah, my dad won an award for perfect attendance."

He didn't tell her that he had no idea what his parents did there. It made his stomach knot up, thinking how distant and quiet they'd become, especially since Gran died. Sometimes his heart ached for them. If only he could tell his parents about Rose and the silver owl—but how could he? They lived in constant fear of the High Echelon and its tedious rules.

"What kind of jobs?" demanded Rose.

"Umm . . ." Max groped for words that would sound important. "Management, computers, that sort of thing." Why was she always quizzing him?

Soft silvery sounds came from the owl's throat and Max stroked her iridescent wings. "I know lots of things about silver owls," he boasted, eager to change the subject. He tried to recall owl facts that would impress Rose. "Mostly they see in black-and-white, but they sometimes recognize the color blue." His voice caught as he remembered that blue was the color of Gran's eyes. "And they can turn their heads right around, two hundred and seventy degrees."

There was no comment from Rose; she was too busy swinging on the branch. Her wiry frame and quick movements reminded Max of a tamarin monkey. He'd seen pictures of tamarins in Gran's book on rain forests.

Why didn't Rose say anything nice about his silver owl?

Couldn't she see how intelligent the owl was? How extraordinary and elegant? Max considered his owl perfect in every way. He sighed, thinking how his words were lost on Rose. She obviously thought owls were boring.

"I guess you're wondering who this weird kid is who talks to owls," he said bravely. "Right?"

Rose swung down. "Wrong," she said, dusting off her hands. "I don't think you're weird. I think you're *mysterious*." She looked Max over and nodded to herself. "Yep, there's a whiff of mystery about you. Something along the lines of . . . *spellbinding*."

"Really?" Max was astounded. He had never thought of himself as mysterious before—not with his dull brown eyes and stringy hair, his skin the color of paste, and his habit of breathing out of his mouth instead of his nose.

"You don't see things like ordinary people, do you, Max?" Rose pushed her face up to his. Her hair had a sticky smell, like tree sap, and for a moment her eyes seemed fathomless. "You're like that owl. She's mysterious too."

Max smiled to himself. Maybe Rose had noticed his owl's special qualities after all.

"You still didn't answer my question from the other night," she persisted. "What are you doing out here in the dark?"

Max thought a moment. "Ever since I was little, I've loved the dark. My gran and I used to sneak out of the house at night and go looking for owls." He felt a familiar sadness inside his chest. "She said if you look into the dark long enough, you'll see things that others don't."

"She sounds like one smart granny." Rose glanced over at the silver owl. "That's one smart owl, too. She understands everything we say, doesn't she?"

"Yeah, she does. And sometimes I understand her, too!" said Max enthusiastically. "I'd give anything to speak owl language." Gran once said that, long ago, people called Night Seers knew how to converse in the language of owls. What a remarkable talent, he thought dreamily, wishing he'd lived back then.

The owl was quiet, fixing them in her silver gaze. Maybe I should listen more closely to my owl, Max told himself. I think she wants me to like Rose, even though she's kind of bossy.

Then again, he thought, should he trust this odd and unpredictable girl?

"I found a message in her beak!" he blurted out, surprising himself, because he hadn't meant to say it. "It was folded up and wet with snow, but she let me take it and I hid it in my room. I think she was headed for the coast, because the message talks about ships and silver treasure. But she never made it to the sea because she was attacked, and whoever did it broke one of her wings."

"A secret message?" breathed Rose, and for a moment Max regretted telling her. What if she couldn't keep quiet about it?

"Hey, maybe it was meant for pirates!" Rose went on, waving her arms around. "Or diamond smugglers! Black-market gangsters! Who knows?" She reached out and patted the owl's head. "I think this owl has lots of secrets." Max watched her finger slide down the curve of the owl's beak. "And I think you do too, Maxwell Unger."

Her eyes flicked over to him and he looked away. A shiver of anticipation slid down his back. This girl was complicated, he thought, but in a good way. Suddenly he saw in Rose a kindred spirit.

Something shifted deep inside him, like the snick of a key, springing open a door. Out tumbled thoughts, ideas, emotions and dreams that had been locked away for five long years.

"My mom and dad don't even know I come here!" he told her. "They think I'm in my room at night doing homework; they don't know I sneak outside after they go to bed. I think Mrs. Crumlin suspects, but she never says anything. I get restless and bored being indoors all day. That's why I come here in the night—I have to be in the dark!"

Rose's eyes went wide. "Why don't you go outside in the daytime?"

"I can only leave my house when the sun goes down," he confided. Then, before he could stop himself, the words were spilling out. "I'm allergic to sun particles! If I stay one minute in the sunlight, I get seriously ill! If sun particles touch my skin, I'll burn up! I could die, that's how bad it is."

Rose's eyes grew even bigger. "Would your eyeballs sizzle in their sockets?"

"Sure they would! My hair would catch fire and my skin would bubble up like fried chicken!" Max pulled his cap down over his ears. Mrs. Crumlin and Dr. Tredegar had explained the worst-case scenario in excruciating detail. "I developed the condition when I was seven, and now the dark is the only place I can be. It's a disease and it won't ever go away. I take medicine to keep it under control."

Had he said too much? he wondered.

Rose didn't say a word. But she didn't laugh, either, the way he feared she might.

"I hope I don't catch what you've got," she said at last.

"You won't," said Max. "Dr. Tredegar says it's in my genes. That means I was born with it."

Rose stared at him with that solemn, haughty gaze. Any minute now, he thought, she's going to take off into the night and never come back. He couldn't blame her. Why would she want to be friends with a pale sickly kid who was deathly afraid of the sun?

But Rose didn't go anywhere.

"Look," she said, pointing to the tree. "That silver owl is getting ready to fly."

CHAPTER FOUR

Seated at the kitchen table with Mrs. Crumlin, Max yawned through an hour-long game of Dark Hearts and Winding Shrouds. Mrs. Crumlin was winning as usual, cackling with glee each time she captured one of his pawns.

Mrs. Crumlin was manic about board games—Echo Magicians, Dome Delirium, Skeletons in the Cupboard, you name it. She was a big fan of jigsaw puzzles too. For months she had been constructing a 1,001-piece puzzle in the parlor.

As the game wound down, Mrs. Crumlin turned up the radio and Max heard a voice warble:

Through the haunted forest, beyond the aching hills,
Darker grows the eventide, deeper grows the chill.
No longer fear the darkness, build your shining
    domes,
You'll be warm and safe there, in your perfect
    homes.

"Eerie, those beginning lines. They take me to another place altogether." Mrs. Crumlin tapped the game board with a pencil. "What do you make of them?"

"Weird," answered Max with a shrug.

"I do wish you wouldn't talk in monosyllables, Maxwell. Try to exercise your vocal cords a bit more."

He sighed. She was always trying to weasel information out of him: details of his dreams, opinions on songs. But Max never gave straight answers; he liked to keep her guessing.

According to his grandmother, the High Echelon had purposely trivialized the Silver Prophecies, reducing them to mindless jingles, songs and nursery rhymes, distorting the ancient words beyond recognition. The reason they did this, she said, was to make people forget the true Prophecies and discredit the Sages who had written them.

"And this reminder from your friendly High Echelon, here to serve your every need!" barked the radio announcer, breaking into the end of the song. "Remember to report any treasonous statements or suspicious actions by fellow citizens, no matter how insignificant they may seem, to your local Dark Brigade. Failure to report may result in a lengthy prison sentence—so don't delay!"

Max stared down at the game board, wondering what kind of suspicious actions the announcer was talking about.

"Game's over, I won!" crowed Mrs. Crumlin.

"Here's a bright spot on the horizon," the announcer continued. "The newly constructed Children's Prison will open its doors in the Eynhallow Hills tomorrow at twelve noon—"

Max sat rigid in his chair, shocked by the announcement. Mrs. Crumlin leaned over and clicked off the radio.

"What did he say?" asked Max. "A prison for *kids*?"

"Yes, of course," snapped Mrs. Crumlin. "Haven't I always said the High Echelon believes in punishment for all ages?"

There was a knock at the front door and Max jumped up, knocking his game pieces onto the floor. For a split second he imagined Rose standing on the porch in her muddied coat, hair sticking out every which way. He glanced at the clock: seven minutes past three. Of course it wasn't Rose. A classmate named Einstein Tredegar stopped by this time every afternoon to deliver his homework.

Mrs. Crumlin threw Max a stern look and lumbered to her feet. "Stay in the kitchen, Maxwell, you could get a chill! I'd never forgive myself if you were poorly again, the way you were last winter, inhaling vapors for weeks on end. Remember?"

Max remembered, all right: he had been stuck in bed for a month drinking her disgusting oxtail soup.

She shambled across the linoleum and out of the kitchen. Max curled around the doorframe, peering down the hallway as Mrs. Crumlin opened the door. Einstein stumbled into the house, folders and books flying out of his red and yellow book bag.

"Oops, sorry," he said, unzipping his red bomber jacket. "Hallo, Max!" he shouted.

Max hurried down the hall to greet him. Above the jacket's sun logo, Einstein sported badges that read DOMED CITIES— COMING YOUR WAY! and YOUR FRIENDLY HIGH ECHELON: BUILDING A BRIGHTER FUTURE. They were illustrated with the face of a cartoon hero, Dudley Dome.

Max always looked forward to hearing Einstein's stories about the dour, prune-faced teachers; the brutal fistfights on the playground; the global emergency drills where students crawled under their desks while sirens wailed. Einstein was his sole link to the outside world, since none of the other kids in Cavernstone Grey bothered with Max.

"Making headway with that puzzle of yours, Mrs. Crumlin?" asked Einstein. Max noticed that Einstein was always extra-polite and attentive to Mrs. Crumlin, probably because she was friends with his uncle, Dr. Phineas Tredegar.

"Oooh, coming along nicely, thank you! I'm three-quarters finished."

Einstein gave a low whistle, as if he were truly impressed. Max knew it was an act, but he had to admire Einstein's talent for flattery.

"It's a lovely picture of a dome, you'll be pleased to know." Mrs. Crumlin glanced at her wristwatch. "Goodness, time for *Flamingo Valley*!" She bustled across the hall and into the parlor.

Some days Max would give Einstein a rundown on what he'd learned from Professor LaMothe, but the lessons rarely amounted to much. Although the two boys never officially hung out together, they had formed an easy friendship over the years.

"Where have you been?" Max wanted to know. "I haven't seen you since last week!"

"Sorry about that," said Einstein, removing his red and yellow gloves with the fingertips cut off. "I caught the flu and missed a week of school. Now I'm playing catch-up."

Max took a step back. The last thing he wanted was Einstein's germs. Germs were his worst enemy, the doctor had warned, and a fever could land him in bed for weeks on end.

"Wasn't too bad," said Einstein with a grin. "I got to eat stewed cusklets in bed and listen to dome jingles all day. That kept my spirits up."

Max grinned back, though secretly he felt sorry for Einstein. His relatives were gung-ho High Echelon supporters, and Einstein had been exposed to their fanatical hype since infancy. Max sometimes suspected that they'd scrambled Einstein's brains.

"Guess what, our school's having a jingle contest to name Cavernstone Grey's new dome!" said Einstein excitedly.

Max stifled a yawn.

"The dome will be ready in a few weeks! Is that exciting or what? Here, have a look." Einstein snatched one of the books he'd dropped on the floor. Holding it under the flare lamp, he thumbed through the pages, flipping to sketches of domed cities and diagrams on how to build them.

Einstein's obsessive chatter about dome construction unnerved Max. What was so wonderful about domes anyway? he asked himself. Why didn't their textbooks discuss weightier issues, like how the High Echelon had overthrown the peaceful government of Simone de Kafka in a violent coup? Not one history book dared to explain how the High Echelon's secret weather experiments had caused the Great Destruction of 2066. Instead, everyone was taught that de Kafka's government was responsible for the catastrophe.

Now it seemed things were going from bad to worse, thought Max: an edict against silver owls, the borders closing overnight and a prison for kids. He'd listened through his parents' bedroom wall and heard them talking about people disappearing and not being seen again. But he was too timid to voice any of these concerns. He knew there was a chance that Einstein might report him.

"Look, Max, this one's got a fake beach with waterslides and an imitation volcano!" Einstein held up a sketch of a bubble-shaped structure with LEISURE DOME written under it. "This is our future!"

Not wanting to hurt his friend's feelings, Max managed a weak smile. "Fantastic."

"I really want to design domes." Einstein closed the book, staring at it with an expression of reverence. "That's my big dream, to be chosen for an engineering apprenticeship. Think of it, Max, we'll have light twenty-four hours a day and perfect temperatures all year round!"

Max frowned. He didn't want to think about a world without darkness, a world where there was no chance that silver owls and kids like him could survive.

"Guess I'll have to find an underground bomb shelter to live in," he said, feeling gloomier by the minute.

What was going to happen to him when everyone moved to the domes? What would happen to his owl? He could never live in a dome because they relied on solar power to generate artificial light—and that meant sun particles. His parents always sidestepped his questions when he asked about his future, but he could tell they were as worried as he was.

"I could build a yurt," he joked, "and set it up inside a cave."

"A yurt?" Einstein threw him a quizzical look. "What's that?"

"Ah, um . . . nothing." Max stared at the floor. "I made it up." He shouldn't have mentioned it. Yurts were probably on the Banned Cultural References list. He'd read about yurts in one of Gran's books: they were tents used by nomadic peoples in a place called central Asia.

"What else is new at school?" he asked, anxious to change the subject.

"Except for the jingle contest, it's the usual mind-numbing stuff." Einstein crammed more books into his book bag. "Oh, we've got a new kid in our class."

Without thinking, Max blurted out, "Is she tall and skinny, with red hair sticking out every which way? Beaky nose? And real bossy, right?"

"His name's Harvey. He's got yellow hair and a busted front tooth." Einstein scratched his head. "I don't know about any new girls. What's her name?"

Max caught a whiff of pickling spices and turned to see Mrs. Crumlin peeking through the parlor door. She'd make a pathetic spy, he mused.

"What am I thinking?" Max smacked his forehead with the

palm of his hand. "That was something I dreamed!" He gave a strangled laugh. "Happens all the time when I get a fever." He faked a cough.

Einstein stared at him. "You okay, Max?"

"Bad throat," he rasped. "I'm fighting off germs and the midwinter blahs. Happens every year."

"Maxwell Unger!" bellowed Mrs. Crumlin. "What's this talk about germs and fevers?"

Max hung his head. He hated Mrs. Crumlin talking to him that way in front of Einstein.

"Got ears like a bat, don't she?" whispered Einstein, a clownish grin spreading across his face. "No worries, Mrs. Crumlin. Max is telling me about his weird dreams."

"I *know* about the dreams," snapped Mrs. Crumlin, her tone frosty. "It's the fevers I worry about. What with the mold and rising damp, one can never be too cautious."

"You're absolutely right, Mrs. Crumlin—it's a scary world out there!" said Einstein with a wink at Max. He hoisted his bag over one shoulder. "See you, Max."

"So long," murmured Max, feeling a bit dejected to see Einstein go. It was always a letdown when he found himself alone again with Mrs. Crumlin.

He headed up to his room, trying to imagine, as he often did, life at Cavernstone Grey School. Rows of wooden desks, a red and yellow flag draped over the blackboard, pupils with heads bowed copying down slogans or writing essays on "Why I Admire the High Echelon." He imagined kids in the bleachers waving banners with government mottos, throwing straws and apple cores in the lunchroom, being locked inside the coat closet as punishment for bad behavior.

Somehow he couldn't picture himself in such an absurd setting. He couldn't imagine his silver owl there, either, and certainly not Rose.

Mrs. Crumlin's no-nonsense voice floated up: "I'll bring you a hot-water bottle soon and, oh yes, your cough medicine!"

Max flung himself onto the bed. What an idiot he'd been. He'd almost told Einstein about Rose! And that silly excuse about fighting off a fever. Now he'd have to suffer through Mrs. Crumlin's nauseating home remedies.

He told himself he didn't care about hanging out with Einstein and the other kids. He was no good at cracking jokes. Playing sports made him dizzy and out of breath. And, judging from what Einstein wore, Max's clothes were ridiculously out of date—not surprising, since they were all made on Mrs. Crumlin's antiquated sewing machine.

At Cavernstone Grey School, kids who were a bit different were always laughed at, and considered outsiders. Max knew that the students made fun of weaklings and worrywarts. And, unfortunately, he fitted perfectly into both those categories.

Early the next morning Dr. Tredegar buzzed the front doorbell. Mrs. Crumlin called Max down to the parlor in a cheery voice, as if his weekly injection were the most fun-filled event in the world.

"Be down in five minutes!" shouted Max.

As always, Mrs. Crumlin instructed the doctor to tie his

shaggy black hound to the porch rail because she worried that it would set off Max's allergies. Max never said anything, but he was afraid of dogs, especially big ones.

"That creature is far too skittish," Mrs. Crumlin always complained. "I can tell by looking that it's a biter."

Although there was a government ban on owning pets, wealthy people were allowed guard dogs, and doctors could own rescue dogs—not that Dr. Tredegar's high-strung hound was capable of rescuing anything, thought Max, leaning over the rail to eavesdrop.

"Anything to report on the dreams?" asked the doctor in a low tone.

Mrs. Crumlin shook her head and mumbled something Max couldn't hear.

"What about his memory? Do you think he's more confused about the past, forgetting more details?"

"Definitely," came the reply. "He—" Mrs. Crumlin's head whipped sharply around and she stared straight at Max. "What do you think you're doing?" she snapped. "Snooping, are you?"

"Good day to you, Maxwell!" Always pleasant, Dr. Tredegar flashed his toothy smile. "Come on down then. Time for your injection." Max could see a red leather medicine bag embossed with the High Echelon's yellow sun hanging from the doctor's arm. The bag's official colors and logo meant that Dr. Tredegar was a high-up government employee.

Max shuffled downstairs, trying to work out the conversation he'd overheard. Why was the doctor so interested in his dreams and memories? In recent months Max had been having problems remembering things—especially his early memories of Gran. It worried him too that he was often confused about real things that had happened in the past.

But how did Dr. Tredegar know about his memory problems? Max hadn't told anyone about them.

He entered the parlor, where Mrs. Crumlin was sinking into her favorite soft chair, the one with doilies on the arms. He perched on the rocker by the window, from which he could see the dog tied up on the porch, yipping frantically.

Dr. Tredegar, a tall, stooped man with square teeth and oily hair, favored red and white striped blazers, paisley shirts and red alligator shoes. He clicked open his bag and plucked out a glass vial. The blackish purple liquid inside was thick and sludgy, flecked with bits of red. It gave off a sharp, metallic smell that shot right up Max's nose.

His insides rolled around like marbles as he watched the doctor transfer the liquid to the InjectaPort. The InjectaPort, which Dr. Tredegar had designed, was a medical device made of titanium; two inches long, it consisted of a small barrel inside a larger barrel. At one end was a plunger, and at the other were five short needles designed to inject just below the skin. Max had never gotten used to the injections, and in recent months they'd become horribly painful.

"Why don't we skip my injection today?" he said. A rebellious feeling stirred inside him. "It left a big bruise last time and my arm still hurts."

Dr. Tredegar chuckled, flicking his finger against the side of the InjectaPort. "Nice try, son, but that's not really an option."

"Wouldn't want you to regress, would we, Maxwell?" chortled Mrs. Crumlin. "We have your future to think of."

"But it hurts. It *really* hurts!" insisted Max. Why didn't they ever listen to him?

"You needn't raise your voice, Maxwell," reprimanded Mrs. Crumlin. "We know it stings a teensy bit, but you're a big boy now."

He hated it when she used that condescending tone. With a sigh, he held out his arm and pushed up his sleeve. He didn't have the strength to fight both of them.

"Rick rack ruin," sang Dr. Tredegar. "Over before you can say—"

Max shut his eyes, wincing at the sound of the doctor's twangy, nasal voice. He braced himself for the pain.

"Crimson moon!" Dr. Tredegar jabbed the InjectaPort into his arm.

Max flinched, blinking back tears.

"There's a brave boy." Mrs. Crumlin plucked a doily off the floor. "See, it wasn't so bad, was it?"

Muttering to himself, the doctor fumbled through his bag. "Now, where did I put that prescription pad?"

Clutching his arm, Max staggered out of the parlor and up to his room. He could feel the medicine moving inside his veins, spreading like a slow dark fire all through his body.

Lying on his bed, he gazed up at the wallpaper, a design that went back to his childhood: gray and blue ships sailing across the walls on crystal blue waves. The paper was so brittle it had started to peel, but Max didn't mind. He always found the ships comforting.

He rolled onto his side and drifted off, knees drawn to his chest, into a familiar nightmare. In the dream, Mrs. Crumlin handed him a red mug with yellow suns around the rim. He knocked back the steaming cocoa in one gulp, leaving a purplish black sludge at the bottom.

He felt his fingers go cloggy-soft; the mug fell, smashing on the floor. Slobber gushed from his mouth. His back splintered and cracked open as thin ragged wings tore through. Beneath his slimy skin he could see a web of pulsing veins.

Wings outstretched, he soared into the sky, high above The Ruins. Dark shapes poured out through the windows, flapping off in uneven lines. Their hot breaths smelled like week-old garbage. He could see they were unfinished and half-made: frightening jellyish creatures, hissing and drooling.

On a branch the silver owl sat motionless, emitting soft silvery sounds. Her plumage sparkled in the moonlight. The tufts on her head fluttered in the breeze.

Where am I? thought Max. What am I doing here?

Rage shook his body, erasing all thought, and he dove earthward, shrieking, as the eyes of the small owl grew wide with fear. Talons outstretched, he snatched the trembling bird from her perch.

Max opened his mouth and crunched down, sinking his needle-sharp teeth into the owl's feathers. He could hear the tiny bones snap. The owl fell to the ground, where the others waited hungrily at the base of the tree.

After they had finished, Max spiraled down, settling on a branch at the bottom. All that was left of the owl was a frail, hollow bone, broken in two, lying on top of the moss.

CHAPTER FIVE

Some nights the girl was there beneath the owl tree and some nights she wasn't. Max never knew when to expect her. He liked it that way, since it meant something in his life was unpredictable.

"Silver and ice," he sang, tramping through the field, *"silver and ice. Silver owl will guide you, with its golden eyes."*

What had Cavernstone Grey been like when summer existed? He tried to imagine the heat rising up from the earth, the hum of insects in the waist-high grass. Before the Great Destruction, there had been fish called trout swimming in the river, and silver owls in the trees. Just seeing a silver owl, it was thought, brought good fortune. Back then, no one feared the forest, because Misshapens hadn't been invented yet.

Max's eyes watered from the cold. He pretended they were owl eyes, x-raying the dark, taking in every fern and blade of wheat, every dead insect, every crumpled leaf. If he concentrated, he could see pale greens and golds, muted shades of red.

He studied the vast overarching sky, where clouds scudded past the two moons—one a pearl gray, the other crimson. From a high, distant plateau gleamed the Frozen Zone. Max's stomach churned whenever he looked at it. A dead city ringed with ice, the Frozen Zone had been climate-damaged during the Great Destruction. The High Echelon declared it off-limits, citing public safety reasons, and warning that instant death awaited anyone who went there.

Max had vague memories of Gran telling him about the Frozen Zone. When Absolute Dark fell over the land, she had said, they must make their way to the high plateau. He seemed to remember there was an ancient tower there—or was that something he'd seen in a book?

He was sure Gran had mentioned the Owl Keeper, and the silver owls, but the details were sketchy. What exactly was Absolute Dark, he wondered, and why would anyone journey to such a cold, terrifying place?

As Max approached the owl tree, he saw Rose standing beneath it and his heart gave a small skip. One arm outstretched, she was swinging something small and dead. Her moth-eaten coat flapped in the wind, and on her feet were a pair of huge green boots.

"Here's your dinner, mister owl!" she shouted up into the tree. "Come get this fat, juicy mouse!"

Blinking, the owl flitted down to a low branch. She blinked twice more, then flipped her head back and swiveled it around. Max loved to watch her do that, because it was a talent only owls had.

"She's not a mister," he told Rose, "and she doesn't want your old mouse."

Rose spun around, tipping sideways in her big boots. "Well, why not? Why is that owl so fussy? Doesn't it want a yummy midnight snack?"

"Owls eat fresh mice, not dead ones," said Max.

The silver owl hopped onto his shoulder, rubbing her beak against his cold cheek, warming him, and he thought how amazing it was that he'd found her. Where had this little owl come from? he wondered for the hundredth time. How lucky he was she'd chosen his tree to land in!

With a look of disdain, Rose tossed the dead mouse into the high grass. "I guess you're the authority when it comes to owls."

"Owls were my granny's specialty," Max said with pride. "She studied owls all her life and collected hundreds of books about them." He bit down on his lip. Why was he telling Rose things that could get him into serious trouble?

"Books? But they're illegal!" Rose narrowed her eyes. "The High Echelon only allows comic books with heroes who fight the silver owls—and, of course, boring textbooks with government stamps of approval."

"I know that!" he snapped. Why did Rose have to act so

superior? "I know the High Echelon punishes anyone who goes against their edicts—including kids like us," he added, thinking of the Children's Prison. He smashed a clod of earth with the heel of his boot.

This was too hard, he thought—how long could he keep all his secrets bottled inside? He felt a sudden desperate need to confide in Rose. "Gran hid the books," he said in a low, shaky voice. He knew he was taking a chance, telling her. "She felt it was her duty because she was a Sage. Nobody knew except me."

"Your granny's a *Sage*? Wow, I'm impressed!" Rose grabbed a branch and swung back and forth, tendrils of dark hair flying about her olive-skinned face. Then she went quiet and it struck Max that maybe she was meditating, the way Gran used to do.

The owl snuggled against the scarf Max had wound tightly around his neck. "See how her feathers are fringed?" he said admiringly. "They muffle her wingbeats so that small animals don't hear her coming."

Rose stopped swinging and looked up. "Can I meet your grandmother, Max? Please?"

The old sorrow rushed through his body, weighing down his limbs, like blight spreading through a tree. "You're too late," he said. "My gran died."

"Oh." Rose's face crumpled a little.

"I was only seven. It happened real sudden." He furrowed his thick brows, remembering. "Afterward the authorities came and emptied out her house—they packed all Gran's things into an official van. She didn't own much except her books. Then a bulldozer came and flattened the house like a griddle cake." He chewed on his lower lip, trying to hold back tears. "Nothing was left."

The owl nudged his hand and dropped something into it—a white thistle—and Max knew she was trying to cheer him up. He wondered if the thistle belonged to some mysterious other world, a world where silver owls lived happily.

"I always wondered what happened to her books," he said wistfully.

"Simple," said Rose in that brassy, self-confident voice of hers. "The High Echelon burned them, just like they burned all the books when they shut down the libraries and universities! They closed museums and rewrote history books to cover their tracks and put those dopey songs on the radio! Now the borders are sealed and people are disappearing left and right!"

Max looked nervously over his shoulder. They weren't supposed to be discussing the Great Destruction or criticizing government policy. If the High Echelon heard them, or found out that he was harboring a silver owl, there would be serious consequences.

"Keep your voice down, okay, Rose?" he whispered.

She ignored him. "We lost spring and summer because of their bungled experiments! Nature crashed and burned: tremors, plagues, the moon cracked in two! They wiped out animals and fish and birds!" She pounded her fists against the tree. "The worst environmental disaster in the history of our planet!"

Max was shocked to hear her criticize the government. Only Gran had ever dared to do that. Referring to the High Echelon, Gran had often said: "If a government can't tell the truth, then it rewrites it." The people he knew either praised the authorities or said nothing. But here was Rose, ranting and raving, not even worried that someone might hear and report her.

Still, he knew that everything she said was true. Gran had told him how the High Echelon, grasping and overconfident, had tried to tweak the weather to create longer growing seasons. Their reckless experiments with fog banks and solar flares caused the Great Destruction of 2066—a cataclysm that shifted the earth on its axis, altering tides and magnetic fields, triggering atmospheric explosions, exploding nearby planets. Plagues were unleashed, wildlife vanished and thousands perished.

Looking distraught, Rose reached over and petted the owl's silver wing. "Nice owlie," she said, and Max could tell she was trying to calm herself. He smiled, thinking Rose must like his owl after all.

"Hey, go easy, that's her bum wing!" he told her.

"Oh yeah. Sorry." Rose patted more gently.

Max beamed. "Isn't she incredible? Look how her feathers sparkle. Like diamonds!"

"Her eyes are like two gold pirate's coins," murmured Rose.

"Remember I said I found a message in her beak?" Max blurted out. He couldn't keep it a secret any longer. "It's just two lines, but look—it was written by hand, with old-fashioned ink!" Excited, he pulled a folded-up paper out of his jeans pocket.

Rose gasped and leaned forward. "Read it, read it!" she urged. The owl hooted, flapping one wing and scurrying across the branch.

The paper crackled in his hands. Max cleared his throat and

read: " 'Tear down the sails of the eastbound ship, steering into the darkest port, and beneath you will find the Silver Treasure.' See here? 'Silver Treasure' is capitalized." At the edge of his vision he saw the owl, hopping on one foot, blinking her one good eye.

"That's it?" said Rose, sounding disappointed.

Max gave the kind of heavy sigh his father did whenever Max annoyed him. How could she be so dense? "It's a riddle, Rose, a secret message! It's not meant for just anybody."

"Well, that owl's taking a big risk just to deliver two measly lines. I thought silver owls were special, not everyday delivery owls."

"She *is* special," bristled Max. "She's the last of the silver owls! There's no other owl like her in the world!"

Rose, as usual, was distracted. She dropped down from the tree, her boots making a hollow thud on the ground. "Oh no!" she shouted, leaping past Max, nearly knocking him down. "Deadly purple sphinx!"

He watched, confused, as she dove onto the ground, landing next to a spindly-looking flower.

"Cousin to deadly nightshade! I don't believe it!" She smiled up at him, showing her small shiny teeth. "Don't tell me you've never seen this flower before?"

Max shook his head. Why was Rose so ecstatic over a puny little plant?

"Deadly purple sphinx only opens at night!" Her voice fell to a melodramatic whisper. "It's like you and me, Max! It loves being outside in the dark!"

He squatted down to examine it, noting how the flower struggled up valiantly through the moss and trampled ferns. Its petals were bruised and fragile, as if cut from crushed velvet. He had never seen so delicate a plant.

As he reached for it, Rose knocked him over. "Don't you know anything? That flower will kill you in seconds flat! They make poisons out of it! Why do you think it's got 'deadly' in its name?"

Max picked himself off the ground, brushing mud from his jacket. Why was Rose so jumpy and wild? "You mean if I touch it I'll die?" It sounded like advice from a witch in a fairy tale.

Rose gazed at him in that haughty way of hers. "My dad learned things like that at spy school. He knows how to mix up potions using stems and leaves and dried-up bugs. Tinctures of henbane and foxglove, syrup of squill! Deadly nightshade, belladonna! His recipes are positively lethal—they could bring down a diplodocus."

Max frowned. He wasn't exactly sure what a diplodocus was. And did spy schools really exist?

"Add it up, owl boy, my dad's a secret agent! Everything he does is classified with a capital *C*." Rose looped her leg over a branch and hoisted herself up next to the owl. "Sometimes murder is the only option."

"Your father *murders* people?" A chill went through Max. *Murder* was one of those extreme words that made his flesh creep.

"The key word here is *exterminate*. Ex-ter-mi-nate. Like what you do to rats." Rose stroked the owl, a little too gingerly, Max thought. "My dad exterminates people because the High Echelon tells him to; it's all hush-hush, top-secret stuff. His name is Jackson Branwell Eccles, but mostly he uses made-up names. He's got a PhD in undercover surveillance—a real egghead, you know?"

Max swallowed. All this talk about spies and murdering people was making him feel anxious and overwhelmed. A hundred questions tumbled through his head. What exactly was an egghead?

"Hey, Max." Rose sat on the branch swinging her legs. "What's that song I heard you singing?" She leaned down, smelling of honey and wild grass. "You know, the one about ice and silver?"

Didn't Rose ever stop asking questions? Max wondered. "It's the Owl Keeper's song," he said. "My granny used to sing it to me."

"What's an Owl Keeper?"

"Keeper of the silver owls," he replied, feeling a bit superior to know something Rose didn't. "There's a prophecy that in times of Absolute Dark an Owl Keeper will appear to gather the silver owls and Sages, uniting them to defeat the evil forces."

Rose gave an imperious sniff. "Too bad the Owl Keeper's not real. We could use somebody like that around here. And too bad about the owls, too."

"The Owl Keeper's real!" said Max, annoyed by her flippancy. "He's coming this way soon."

"Well, he'd better hurry up, that's all I can say. What's Absolute Dark?"

Shivering, Max gazed at the moons overhead. He didn't really know the answer, so he improvised. "I guess it's when things get very bad and everyone loses hope." He could feel the damp seeping in through his sweaters. "I have to go now." Spending time with Rose, he realized, was exhausting.

"First sing the song," ordered Rose.

Max looked up, startled. "My voice is no good." He could feel himself blushing.

"Go on!" she said. "I promise not to laugh."

He gave a sigh and, in his froggy voice, began to sing:

> *"Silver and ice, silver and ice,*
> *Silver owl will guide you, with its golden eyes. Owl*
>   *in the darkness, silver in the leaves,*
> *Blind child comes leading through the fog and trees.*
> *Two will make the journey, old one gone before,*
> *To the icebound tower, through the crumbling door.*
> *Silver and ice, silver and ice,*
> *Silver owl will guide you, with its golden eyes."*

He frowned. "I can't remember the other verses. I get them mixed up."

"That was fantastic." Rose fluttered her lashes and looked straight at him. "It sounded kind of *otherworldly*."

Max felt the tops of his ears go red. Nobody had ever called his singing otherworldly before. Mrs. Crumlin always said he couldn't carry a tune in a bucket.

Rose smiled. "It's a song about your owl, too!"

Max smiled back. Rose had called the silver owl *his* owl! He pointed to the owl, sleeping peacefully on a branch. "See the light from her feathers? It's ethereal, like the light from the moons."

"That's called an aura," said Rose knowingly. "Your owl's got an aura."

CHAPTER SIX

M ax sat at the kitchen table, looking dubiously at a cake sprin-
kled with coconut flakes, leaning to one side. Today was Tuesday,
Mrs. Crumlin's day for baking cakes. He groaned inwardly. This
was no doubt one more of her over-the-top, sickly sweet creations.

"Good timing," she twittered. "I've just popped this lava cake
out of the oven. What do you think of the icing? Maxwell, you're
mouth-breathing again."

Max closed his mouth. Why did she have to criticize every little thing? A tinny voice was singing on the radio and Mrs.
Crumlin hummed along:

"Flee the icebound mountain, flee the fortress old,
Flee the deadly Frozen Zone and its killing cold.
Journey to the city domes and their perfect light,
Never fear the dark again, never fear the night."

Max watched her lumber about, boiling up fava beans for the evening meal. Her bulky shape seemed to fill the kitchen. She reminded him of an extinct animal—a whale, maybe, or an elephant—Max had seen pictures of both in Gran's books.

When Max was small, his favorite book was the story of an elephant king. He never tired of hearing Gran read it aloud. Snuggled on her lap, he would breathe in the musty pages. The heady scent of old books was his favorite smell in the world.

A few days after Gran died, Mrs. Crumlin had arrived at the front door clutching a tapestry duffel bag and promising to set the house in order. When she discovered the books in Max's toy chest and under the bed, she had dumped them into her bag, exclaiming, "What on earth was your grandmother thinking? These are banned books! They go against all the rules!"

It had been a shattering experience, seeing those books disappear. Mrs. Crumlin swore she'd never set eyes on his toy owl, but Max knew she'd taken it. He had cried for weeks afterward. She offhandedly dismissed his tears, saying books could be dangerous if they fell into the wrong hands. Max had never really forgiven her.

Only *Owls of the Wild* had survived, because he had hidden the book under a closet floorboard, next to a small seashell. The book and shell were all he had left from his grandmother.

"You're daydreaming, Maxwell." Mrs. Crumlin slammed down a slice of cake on a chipped plate.

He felt his stomach seize up. He could see that the cake was runny in the middle, with crunchy bits all through it. Why didn't she stick to simple things like instant pudding?

She sat down opposite him at the table, waiting for him to take a bite. "I heard the recipe on a radio cook show." Her sausage-shaped fingers rearranged the salt and pepper shakers. "Always fun to try something new."

"Breaking news!" barked the radio announcer before the song had finished. "Six citizens, believed to be members of the radical organization Silver Sages, were captured outside Barleygate Headlands Lighthouse and taken into custody by the Dark Brigade! As of midnight last night all Sages have been declared enemies of the state."

"Enemies of the state?" echoed Max, a cold hand closing around his heart. He turned to Mrs. Crumlin with a puzzled look. "The Sages? But what did they do wrong?"

"If you slept less and listened to the radio more you would know!" she snapped. "The No Tolerance for Dissenters Edict went into effect overnight. Sages have been stirring up trouble for years. They're radicals, disloyal to the government! The High Echelon has taken a stand against them—and not a minute too soon, I might add."

"But my—" Max was about to say his grandmother had been a Sage, but quickly thought better of it.

Mrs. Crumlin's gloating expression unnerved him. Hadn't the

Sages belonged to a circle of wise scholars who fought for peace and equality?

"Eat up, Maxwell." Mrs. Crumlin pointed to the cake.

He took a forkful and nibbled at it. The runny part was loaded with sugar and the crunchy bits had a tart flavor that made his lips pucker. But he knew if he didn't eat the cake she would be insulted.

"Tasty, isn't it?" she asked.

"Mmmm," he replied. He could never figure out why her desserts always smelled so delicious but never tasted quite right. "Why don't you try a piece?" Max had noticed that Mrs. Crumlin never went near her own desserts.

"Dear me no, not at my age! Now then, you haven't seen a pair of boots anywhere?" She scratched the scalp beneath her thinning hair. In times of stress, Max knew, she suffered from rashes and dry skin. "Green rubber boots, brand-spanking-new, from the same mail-order house as your boots. I left them on the porch, but last evening I went to fetch them and they were gone. Strange, isn't it?"

The cake lodged halfway down Max's throat. His face burned as he pictured Rose in those huge green boots.

"I didn't see any boots," he lied, hoping Mrs. Crumlin didn't notice his ears go red. He crammed a piece of cake into his mouth, trying to keep his face blank and his brain neutral. Sometimes he suspected that she could read his mind.

"Goodness, this vinyl needs sponging." Mrs. Crumlin smoothed the tablecloth with her beefy hands, then jumped to the next topic of importance. "Shall we have cusklet loaf tonight, or fava bean soufflé? What's your preference?"

These were the kinds of inane questions she asked day after day, with such intensity one would think the fate of the world hung in the balance. Max could only take so much of her mindless chitchat.

He pushed away his plate, feeling bloated and ill. Everything Mrs. Crumlin cooked ended up charred to a crisp, so the menu didn't really matter.

"Either's fine," he told her. Then, without thinking, he blurted out: "Do you think the High Echelon plans to make me a special agent? I could deliver secret messages and stuff like that!" Oh no, he thought, why do I always say things that could get me into trouble?

A bristly eyebrow shot up. "You? A special agent?" Mrs. Crumlin sounded out the words as if speaking a foreign language. "Heavens no, Maxwell, you're far too frail for that sort of work." She marched over to the sink and turned on the tap.

Max clenched his jaw. He detested her belittling tone. "But if they trained me to be a spy, I could sneak around in the night," he argued. "It would suit me, because of my condition and everything." It would also mean he could take his little owl with him. Maybe he'd keep her hidden inside his secret-agent briefcase.

"Patience, Maxwell, the High Echelon is aware of your condition. It will decide on an appropriate career." She emptied half a box of soap flakes into the water. "Hmmm. Perhaps I should contact the police about those missing boots. I'd hate to think we have thieves lurking in our woods—or worse." She plunged her arms into the dishwater. "It's disturbing to think the Misshapens are growing bolder. Perhaps they're venturing farther afield."

"They'd never do that," said Max. "They hate open spaces." He remembered Gran telling him the Misshapens were bound to the forest—something to do with their inner wiring—and could never go beyond its natural boundaries. Anxious to change the subject, he asked, "Have you ever been to The Ruins, Mrs. Crumlin? What's inside them?"

"You mean that heap of derelict buildings on the other side of town? They're empty as old eggshells." She stood scrubbing a pot as if her life depended on it. Max noticed that her voice had a nervous edge, and she was talking faster than usual. "The High Echelon boarded up The Ruins ages ago, for safety reasons. They could collapse at any moment."

Max sat, chin in hands, wondering what Mrs. Crumlin was hiding. "What are The Ruins, anyway?" he asked. "Did the tremors knock them down?"

Mrs. Crumlin ignored him—her way of putting an end to the conversation. No surprise there, since she always kept to safe topics like recipes and radio song lyrics. He was tempted to ask more about the Sages, but he'd probably be skating on thin ice, as his father liked to say. His parents had cautioned him never to question Mrs. Crumlin about politics or her personal life.

"Time to fix you a mug of hot cocoa, young man," she said, her voice husky. "We don't want any tummy upsets or congested noses."

She retrieved a yellow box from the cupboard, the same one

she pulled out every day. Printed on the box was the motto CAVERNSTONE GREY HOT COCOA—JUST LIKE GRAMMA USED TO MAKE, and below that was an illustration of a refined-looking lady with half-moon glasses and wavy gray hair. Wavy Gray was Max's secret name for her. He often wished Wavy Gray could be his guardian, instead of fussy old Mrs. Crumlin.

Max hated being sickly. Mrs. Crumlin put it down to bad luck, saying he'd inherited his timid nature as well as weak genes for extra-soft teeth and limp hair. "Such a frail, uncertain child," she would remark to Dr. Tredegar, "and dull as foggy weather." But why did he catch fevers and colds so easily? Why couldn't he fight off germs like ordinary kids did?

Then there were the terrifying dreams, jolting him awake in the middle of the night. What were the grotesque creatures that flew in and out of The Ruins—hairless and jellyish, with half-formed faces? Why did he fly with them and hunt down his silver owl?

Did these things really exist, he wondered, or had he unconsciously invented them? It rattled him to think his mind had made up such disgusting creatures. Maybe, he told himself, they were half-digested memories from scary books he'd read, or illustrations from one of Gran's medical texts.

Steam rose from the mug, warming his face, blotting out Mrs. Crumlin, who was nattering about the latest knitting patterns. Her empty words floated through his head, light as cotton candy.

"Citizens will be pleased to hear that the Citizens' Dome Construction Scheme remains on schedule," announced the news reporter. "The target date is July seventh, the day citizens will be transported from their local cities and towns to the government's all-modern, temperature-regulated, darkness-free domes!"

"Fancy that, Maxwell, the domes are opening the same day as your birthday," said Mrs. Crumlin, clucking her tongue.

Ignoring her, Max glugged down the hot cocoa. He didn't want to think about the domes, or what it would mean to turn twelve. The drink was chalky as usual, with a bitter aftertaste. Hot cocoa always made him feel groggy, disembodied, as if the world around him were slowly slipping away.

Don't worry, he told himself, Mrs. Crumlin is at the helm. All you have to do is obey. Forget the High Echelon and the domes and Gran's lost books, forget the stolen boots and the silver owls. Forget the Owl Keeper and Sages and the myths surrounding them. Forget Rose's father, exterminating people with his creepy toxic plants.

"Try Cavernstone Grey Premium Gold-Foil Truffles!" came the soothing voice of a female announcer. "You can rely on Cavernstone Grey: the finest chocolates in the country!"

Little by little, Max's stomach stopped its relentless churning. He closed his eyes, thinking how the cocoa never failed to comfort him, damping down all those unsettling thoughts, wrapping him inside a pleasant, airtight cocoon.

CHAPTER SEVEN

Max took one bite of Mrs. Crumlin's singed fava bean soufflé and reached for the sliced bread. In the flickering candlelight, he noticed his parents looked pale and sleep-deprived. They had arrived home late from work, so Mrs. Crumlin had stayed longer than usual, coaxing Max into a tedious session of Skeletons in the Cupboard. She'd left the moment his parents walked through the door, anxious as always to be home before the sun went down.

Max watched shadows move across the geometric patterns of the wallpaper. Outside the shuttered windows of the dining room a northerly wind was howling. It was, he reflected, the kind of wind that Gran used to say set her pulse racing.

"Well, well, Mrs. Crumlin has done it again." Mr. Unger leaned back in his chair, patting his stomach. "A thoroughly delicious meal."

"Why do you always say that, Dad?" said Max, annoyed. "That burnt bean dish is totally disgusting. Mrs. Crumlin is the worst cook in the world!"

"The old dear tries hard," murmured Mrs. Unger, pushing her food around with her fork. Max noticed her hand trembling slightly. "Put yourself in her shoes, Max. Day in, day out, she's baking, cleaning, knitting, keeping the house dark, protecting you from germs."

"Yeah, but what about you and Dad? You work way harder than she does!" Max looked at the two of them, noticing the deep circles beneath their eyes. "Why were you late tonight?"

His parents exchanged a look. As usual, he found it impossible to read their veiled expressions.

"They announced an important meeting after work." His father's voice was curt. "Attendance was mandatory."

Max sometimes wished his mother and father weren't so secretive and aloof, discussing dull subjects like the weather or the rising cost of food. It dismayed him, the way they always avoided unpleasant subjects.

If only he could confide in his parents about the nightmares. What would they say about the hissing creatures that flapped beside him in his dreams, demented things with sunken eyes? Lately he suspected they weren't birds at all, but something much more sinister. Maybe, he thought, these creatures really did exist, in some treacherous swamp or some hidden jungle.

"How's work these days, Dad?" he asked, knowing exactly what the answer would be.

"Excellent." Max watched his father loosen his tie. Workers at Cavernstone Hall were required to wear formal attire. "No complaints there." It was the same response he always gave.

"Mrs. Crumlin is a real pain," said Max. "She's always sticking her nose into other people's business."

"Now, Max." His mother's pale eyes swam behind her bifocals. She looked even more tired than usual, he thought. "Mrs. Crumlin has your best interests at heart, and that's what counts. What would we do without her?" She threw Max a wavering smile. "The old dear made a lovely lava cake for dessert. I'll bring it out, shall I?"

Max had so many questions—about the Great Destruction and the rise of the High Echelon, the book burnings, the new edict against the Sages—but he never managed to ask any of them. He knew those kinds of topics would be too upsetting for his parents.

The Great Destruction of 2066 had happened when Nora and Ewan Unger were his age, both growing up in Cavernstone Grey. They never mentioned it to Max. Once his father remarked that the High Echelon expected people to soldier on, work hard and forget all that had happened before. Max had gotten a lump in his throat, hearing him talk that way. How could they forget when the High Echelon had totally wrecked their lives, crushing their hopes and cheating them out of their youth?

Max turned to his mother. He could see she'd forgotten about the cake. Fork in hand, she was drawing invisible patterns on the tablecloth, as if working out a complex equation that required every ounce of her attention.

Max took a deep breath. "What exactly do you *do* at Cavernstone Hall, Mom? I mean, what's your job title and all?"

She looked up, startled. "Job title? Well—"

"Nora," interrupted Max's father, "you were about to go get us some cake."

"Oh. I was, wasn't I?" Mrs. Unger rose to her feet and walked unsteadily toward the kitchen. Max wondered what kind of medicine Dr. Tredegar was prescribing for *her*.

"Now, Max, haven't I explained all this a hundred times?" His father gave an irritable sigh. "It's quite simple. They ship us the unrefined cocoa from the landholders' factories by train. Once here, the cocoa goes through phases—the combining of sugar and preservatives, the packaging and so forth—and the final product is shipped all over the country. Cavernstone Grey Hot Cocoa is hugely popular, as are our Premium Gold-Foil Truffles. 'The finest chocolates in the country,' as they say, heh heh."

"But what do you do *specifically*?" Max persisted, secretly wishing his father were a spy instead of a factory worker. "You have an important job, right?"

Mr. Unger fiddled with his tie. "Of course it's important. Last year I never missed a day's work." He nodded toward the framed certificate on the wall—a watercolor sketch of Cavernstone Hall—his award for perfect attendance.

"I know, Dad," said Max. "It looks like an awesome place. When do I get to see it?" His father had long ago promised him a tour of the factory, but so far it hadn't happened.

"As soon as I can arrange it, Max," came the reply. It was the answer his father always gave.

Max's mother returned with the lava cake. "Enjoy, you two," she said, setting it down in front of Max. One whole side had caved in completely. Seeing it made his stomach roil.

"I'm going up to bed now. It's been a long day and I'm feeling rather fragile." Nora Unger kissed her husband on his forehead.

"Good night, dear Max, I'll see you tomorrow." Her lips grazed Max's head, soft as moth wings. The gesture nearly broke his heart.

As she drifted out of the room, a memory came back to him. He was five or six, running with his mother and Gran through a field of poppies and tiny blue flowers, sunlight streaming down, leaves tumbling around them, all three laughing uproariously. He struggled to hold on to the memory, to savor it. But moments later the colors blurred and the details slipped away, leaving him with a blank space inside his head.

When Gran was alive, his mother didn't wear bifocals or take antianxiety tablets. Those memories, he knew, were true. She never fell asleep at the dinner table either, the way she did now.

He watched the middle section of the cake ooze out as his father sliced into it with a butter knife. Ewan Unger had a toothbrush mustache and hair parted down the middle. His wife called him an old-fashioned gentleman, reserved and polite. He was also, Max observed, somewhat austere and high-strung. When Max was little his father used to make up goofy jokes, but he hadn't kidded around with Max in a long time.

"Gran loved silver owls more than anything, right, Dad?" Max asked.

Mr. Unger cleared his throat. "She loved *you* more than anything." He handed Max a wedge of cake. "Owls were second. Of course, the owls are extinct now. Pity."

"What did Gran die of, Dad? Nobody ever said."

Mr. Unger cut a smaller slice for himself. "It all happened very fast. She was healthy one day and gravely ill the next. I don't remember the details."

Max frowned, sensing his father was holding something back. Couldn't he just answer the question? "Okay, but I need to know one thing. Why didn't I go to the funeral?"

"Funerals are not for children." His father's voice went flat and dead, like Max's old robot when the batteries ran down. "Your grandmother died of complications and we were sad to see her go." Setting his fork next to his uneaten cake, he stood up. "Let's leave it at that, shall we? She's gone, Max, she's not coming back. Nothing we do can ever change that."

"I know, Dad." Seeing the pain on his father's face, Max knew he should drop the subject. But stubbornly he went on: "Where's Gran buried? In Cavernstone Grey?"

"We'll discuss the matter another time, shall we? I'm off to bed now, it's been a difficult day. Good night, Max, enjoy the cake." He gave Max's shoulder a brisk tap and strode out of the room.

Max stifled a sob. "Good night," he whispered.

But he knew there was nothing good about it at all.

CHAPTER EIGHT

"I'm going to be an explorer one day, because explorers dig up ancient bones and buried cities," said Rose that night as she reached for a low-hanging branch. "My dad says it's a highly elevated profession."

Max knelt beneath the owl tree, trying not to think about his parents. He pictured a black curtain falling across his mind, blocking out the scene earlier that evening at the dinner table. Using Mrs. Crumlin's paring knife, he absentmindedly scraped at the moss, careful not to get dirt on his mittens.

High above sat the silver owl, mute and elegant, watching.

"You've got to be dead smart to be an explorer, and tough as nails, because of the tremors," Rose went on, swinging upside down. "I mean, if you're not careful a long-lost city could fall on top of you." She shook her head, as if to emphasize her point, and a dryad beetle fell from her hair and landed next to Max. "Anyway, it won't be a problem for me."

He looked at the squashed beetle in disgust. At least it wasn't a deathwatch beetle—though he was starting to have a sneaking suspicion that Mrs. Crumlin had made them up.

"My dad knows stories about olden-day explorers. He told me stuff that would curl your nose hairs." Rose swung up to a sitting position. Her matted hair glistened with cobwebs. Max wondered if she ever washed it. "They lead rough-and-tumble lives."

"You ought to brush your hair once in a while," he told her. "It's got knots and bugs in it." His owl drifted down and greeted him, nuzzling his cheek, then she hopped onto a low branch.

"Huh, shows how much you know." Rose gripped the tree and started to climb. "Explorers are too busy fighting grave robbers and digging up gold and artifacts to worry about how their hair looks."

As Rose talked, Max thought. There was something that was bothering him. If Einstein didn't know about Rose, that meant she wasn't enrolled in school. But what did she do all day? Where did she go? He had so many questions, but he was too timid to ask, for fear of Rose losing her temper or, worse, making fun of him. She was so unpredictable.

"Hey, Max," Rose called down. "Do you know about a place called The Ruins?"

Max looked up. She had climbed far higher than he ever dared go. "Sure I do. The Ruins are near Cavernstone Hall, where my parents work."

"My dad scouted them out. He thinks they're downright eerie. He says something peculiar is going on in there."

"Your dad's wrong. The Ruins are derelict." Max wiped the knife on his jeans. He was a bit envious of Rose's having a spy for a father. His dad, he knew, would never be caught dead near The Ruins. "Mrs. Crumlin says they're empty as eggshells."

"Hey, Max, time to pop that bubble you're in!" Rose clambered down the tree, swinging monkey-style off a branch. "Crumlin's lying again." She shook her head, throwing off twigs and leaves. "You can't trust her, she's part of the machine. She's dangerous!"

"*Dangerous?* My parents hired her to be my guardian!" Max could hear the owl's talons, clicking against the bark, and the low thrumming of her voice.

Rose threw Max a sideways glance.

"Okay, I admit she's nosy and snoops around my room, and she's a terrible cook. But that doesn't make her a bad person." Max had no intention of defending Mrs. Crumlin, but Rose's know-it-all attitude was getting to him.

"Fine, Max, have it your way, let's just say your guardian is a cog in the wheel. Let's just say she's misinformed. Misinformation is something secret agents deal with all the time." Rose stood peeling a slug off the tree. "Everyone knows guardians are paid by the High Echelon."

Max stared at the black dirt caked under Rose's raggedy fingernails. It looked permanent. What did she mean by *a cog in the wheel*? What machine was she talking about? He wondered where she picked up her quirky expressions.

Max saw the owl lean toward him, nearly falling from the branch, blinking her golden eyes. He blinked back at her. If he could speak owl language he would tell his owl how fierce and storm-tossed she looked.

Rose thumped around the tree, whacking a stick against the trunk. Max was about to say something about the stolen boots when she interrupted him.

"My dad has got Cavernstone Hall on his radar too," she said darkly. "He says it looks suspicious."

"That's not true!" cried Max, exasperated with her outlandish accusations. "My parents work there and it's a top-quality chocolate factory!" Feeling anxious, he reached for his owl. When she folded up her wings, she was small enough to hold in his hands. Pressing her to his chest, he leaned over and kissed the top of her head. She was so beautiful.

Swinging her stick, Rose clumped off into the high grass. "You are so out of touch, Max Unger!" she yelled. "I hope you know the High Echelon plans to raze the forests and bulldoze the riverbanks. They'll mow down the fields and dredge the rivers and marshes! They'll shut down the towns and concrete everything over! You won't recognize this place anymore!" She spun in circles, knocking the tops off the cattails. "Then they'll build their ridiculous domes and take control of everyone's minds."

Max paled. He set the owl on a branch. It was disturbing, that word *raze;* it sounded extreme. He pulled down his earflaps. It made him nervous, hearing about mind control and bulldozing. Why did Rose make everything sound so *radical*?

"They can't knock down every single tree!" he shouted back. "My owl won't have anywhere to live!"

Rose whirled around, brandishing her stick. "Max, wake up,

the High Echelon doesn't care about some mangy bird!" She stomped over to him. Her eyes were so fiery, he imagined sparks flying out of them. "They want all the silver owls dead!"

Max looked at his owl, sitting perfectly still on the branch. Beneath the sparkling feathers, her golden eyes darkened. He reached over to comfort her, gently stroking her throat.

"Stop saying that, will you?" He felt his stomach coil into knots.

"My dad told me the *real* story." Rose leaned toward him. Her breath had a tart, fruity smell—like apples. "The government made up all that stuff about the silver owls being wiped out in the Great Destruction. The Destruction didn't kill them off—the High Echelon did! It issued a secret edict and hunted them down and killed every one! Maybe a few silver owls got away, but they won't survive, because the government's going after them!"

Max felt a cold dread slice through him, sharp as a knife blade. He could tell that for once Rose wasn't making things up. But what did these actions by the High Echelon mean? Sages hunted down, silver owls murdered. Hearing about these things chilled him to the core. Was this what Gran had meant by Absolute Dark?

Feeling overheated, he unwound his scarf and pulled off his cap, pushing his limp brown hair off his neck. His scalp felt prickly, the way it often did when he was agitated.

"Hey, Max, can I see that tattoo on your neck?" asked Rose. "What kind did they give you?"

"Nobody gave me a tattoo," said Max irritably. "It's a birthmark." He jammed his cap back on before she could get a better look. Secretly, though, he felt special having it. Mrs. Crumlin called it a sun mark and said it made up for all those weak genes he had.

Before he knew what was happening, Rose leapt up, snatching his cap. "Give that hat back to me!" he yelled. "I'll get an ear infection! Give it back or you'll be sorry!"

She danced around, waving the cap. "Show me your tattoo and you can have it."

Max threw her a toxic look. He hated being teased. On the playground, years ago, he remembered kids pushing him down and calling him "shrimp." They had all been bigger than him and ten times tougher.

Rose stuck the cap on the end of her stick and twirled it around.

"You are so annoying," said Max. Knowing she was too quick for him to catch, he sat cross-legged on the ground. "Okay, I give up. But be quick, okay?" He leaned forward. "My head's getting chilled."

Rose knelt beside him and examined his neck closely, her expression changing from curious to confused as she traced the mark's outline with a bony finger. "Your tattoo's shaped like the sun! That's the High Echelon's official logo, you see it on everything. Guess they have something really special planned for you, Max."

"That's not true! I was born with this," he growled. He'd had enough of Rose and her talk about the High Echelon. "Mrs. Crumlin says my sun mark is lucky."

"I don't know about that, Max. How can it be lucky if you're allergic to sun particles?" She tossed him the cap. "I hate to give you the bad news, but you're branded."

"What are you talking about?" Max jammed his cap on his head. Why did Rose talk in riddles all the time?

"Where have you been, Max Unger, on another planet? You weren't born with that sun tattoo! The High Echelon gave it to you because you're a Night Seer, so they can keep track of you and send you to some far-off place underground for your apprenticeship. They hate Night Seers!"

"I'm *not* a Night Seer." Max whipped his scarf back on, knotting it tightly around his neck. "You've got it wrong, Rose. Gran told me all about Night Seers. They were magical beings who spoke the language of owls and they lived in olden times, but not anymore. Night Seers are a thing of the past."

Had Night Seers been real? he wondered, suddenly unsure. Or was he remembering characters in a fairy tale?

"Shows how much you know," Rose shot back, her voice brimming with self-assurance. "Remember how weird vapors and parasites were released after the Great Destruction, and all of a sudden people had night blindness and phobias—like fear of the dark?"

"I know about that stuff," bristled Max, not admitting that he'd forgotten the details.

"After the government threw the Misshapens into the forests, *nobody* went out at night!" Rose held his gaze with her green eyes. "But some people weren't afraid of the dark, like you and me, and your gran. Didn't you ever wonder why the night doesn't faze us? We love the dark because we're Night Seers!"

Max stared at her, marveling at this unexpected information. He thought of all the nights he'd spent with Gran hiking through the countryside, searching for plants and animals, remembering how the darkness always gave him a feeling of peace. These were memories he hadn't lost—not yet, anyway.

"Night Seers are born with a tiny birthmark on the back of their necks," said Rose quietly. "The government goes to the hospitals and checks all the newborns and that's how they find us."

"What kind of birthmark?" he asked. This was beginning to sound a bit far-fetched.

"It's an owl," she replied. In a dramatic voice she added, "They call it the Mark of the Owl."

The owl stirred, giving off a low hoot. Max felt a shiver go down his back. It made sense, he thought, because Night Seers and owls were connected. And the Mark of the Owl sounded like an olden-time expression.

"But I don't have an owl birthmark," he said.

"Yes you do! They tattooed over your owl, just like they tattooed over mine! They want you to forget you ever had an owl birthmark!" cried Rose. "Night Seers are bottom-feeders in this society. We get all the miserable apprenticeships, like working underground in the mines."

"Not me," said Max huffily. "I'm going to be an owl tracker." He knew the moment he said it how ridiculous it sounded.

"An owl tracker?" shrilled Rose. Max winced at her smug, high-pitched laugh. "You crack me up!"

"I'll never work for the High Echelon!" Max blustered. "Besides, I have to find the Owl Keeper." Why had he said that? He struggled to remember. "There's an ancient tower and I—I have to go there! I have to go soon, before it's too late!" He took a deep breath, startled by the intensity of his words.

"*You're* going to go into the forest, looking for some broken-down old tower?" said Rose, sounding skeptical. "You'd be scared out of your wits."

Max closed his eyes, trying hard to call up the past. What was it Gran had told him? Something about the Frozen Zone and the Owl Keeper, something about Absolute Dark.

"Fine, Max. After all, you can't hang around the owl tree forever, seeing as the High Echelon's going to chop it down. So go ahead," Rose sneered, "do something gutsy!"

A drop fell from the tip of his nose. "You don't think I have it in me, do you?" He wiped his nose on his jacket sleeve. "You think I'm a wimp."

In Gran's eyes he'd been a bright, fearless boy, curious about nature, who tramped through bogs and collected wild eggs. What had gone wrong? Why wasn't he brave anymore?

But Rose's answer surprised him. "I think you're brave. Anybody who comes out here after midnight and has a terrible ailment like yours plus a weird tattoo has to be a little bit brave. But if you're scared of going into the forest, you'll never find the Owl Keeper or the silver owls, or find special plants like the deadly purple sphinx. Your life will be wrecked, Maxwell Unger, because you lacked courage!"

Max looked at his silver owl and thought of all the terrible things she'd suffered, most of which he could only guess at. When he first saw her, she'd had a damaged eye and broken wing, and her frail body was covered in snow. She had been so courageous and long-suffering, allowing him to feed her and comfort her and put drops in her bad eye. He admired her beyond words.

"You're wrong," he said, in a burst of defiance. "I don't lack courage, I'm as brave as the silver owl. I'll prove it to you!"

Rose broke into a wide grin. "Okay, Max Unger," she said. "It's a deal."

CHAPTER NINE

Max stumped beside Rose through a field of dry stalks, pale russet in the mist. He looked for the two moons, but they were hidden behind fast-moving clouds. On a distant plateau, the Frozen Zone gave off a wintry light, chilling him to the bone.

The town clock struck midnight. Rain drizzled down as they crossed the railway line, careful not to slip on the ice-coated tracks. Everything looked spookily unreal, thought Max, drained of color, like the photos in his family albums. He hadn't been this far from home since his owl-tracking nights with Gran.

He couldn't stop shivering, despite his many layers of flannel and wool. If only he'd thought to bring his silver owl along. She would have enjoyed riding inside his pocket, and Max always felt braver when she was around.

At the edge of the field, empty factories and warehouses huddled together like a comic-book Wild West town. Max studied the old-fashioned signs: LLOYD BROTHERS CEMENT & MIX, DOCTOR ORLIK'S MEDICINAL LOZENGES, GREY MOP WRINGER, TINTERN COFFIN MAKERS, WORMWOOD'S WATER TREATMENT PLANT. He knew that, over the years, these businesses had been seized by the High Echelon and shut down.

"Afraid, Max?" whispered Rose.

He could see her teeth, shining in the dark. Her round eyes floated through the darkness. Fine drops of mist sparkled in her coppery hair, like star glitter. She might have been a ghost.

"Nope," he said, keeping his voice steady. "I'm a Night Seer, remember? I love the night."

It was true: he felt surprisingly at ease in this alien midnight world. He swaggered through the tall grass, trying to exude confidence. Rose didn't seem to notice.

Tonight he and Rose were going to carry out a daring plan. Using his mother's smart card, they would sneak inside the mysterious Cavernstone Hall. Max knew it was a totally reckless idea—Rose's, obviously—but it gave him the chance to prove his courage.

Of course, he had other reasons for wanting to go there. Curiosity, for one: finding out what sort of jobs his parents really had and seeing the place where they worked. Then there was the darker side of Cavernstone Hall: the not-quite-real secluded building he flew over in his nightmares. Why was he always dreaming about it?

Sometimes he worried that, in some inexplicable way, his nightmares predicted the future. If so, did it mean his future was connected to Cavernstone Hall? He hoped not, seeing how his parents had been beaten down by their jobs. He told himself that going into Cavernstone Hall and seeing how ordinary it was might put a stop to his dreams.

A train whistled in the distance. Hair knotted from the wind, Rose charged headlong across the field, oblivious to danger. Max raced after her.

The streets of Cavernstone Grey twisted and turned. The two children clumped through the poorer section first, where decrepit streetlamps cast their feeble light on narrow, cramped houses with roofs of corrugated iron. Max felt a cold uneasiness building inside him. What if someone saw them through a window and called the Dark Brigade?

They entered a tree-lined avenue where the wealthy residents lived. Max's boots echoed along the paved streets. Here stood three- and four-story timbered houses, with peaked roofs of orange tiles and filigree balconies. Their wood frames were painted bright shades of yellow and red, the official colors of the High Echelon.

Which one was Einstein's house? Max wondered. There were numerous Tredegars in Cavernstone Grey, and they were known as a clan of tightly buttoned, square-toothed grinners. All of them held high government positions.

"Hey, Rose, where's your house?" he asked.

Rose shrugged. "Other side of town. I'll show you next time."

"Does the bus take you to school?"

"I don't take any bus. My dad teaches me everything I need to know."

"Then you have lessons at home, like me?" Max persisted, wishing she would tell him more about herself.

"Something like that." Rose gave an irritable sigh. "Can we cut the small talk? I have to concentrate on not getting lost."

Max went quiet. He supposed Rose had a point: after all, they were on an important mission and needed to pay attention.

They headed up Blackbone Street, past boarded storefronts and sandwich eateries, bookshops with smashed windows, abandoned shopping arcades, a theater with CLOSED FOR THE SEASON scrawled across the double doors. Max was astounded to see how neglected and run-down everything was. He had no idea that the town had fallen into such a state of decay.

"I hope nobody's watching," he said, looking around at the shuttered windows and closed doors.

"Don't be such a worrywart!" Rose snapped. "Everybody's asleep, even the guard dogs! Besides, nobody can see us. We're as good as invisible."

Rose was right, he thought; the mist and darkness were like a cloak thrown over them. Anyone looking out of a window would see shadows and nothing more.

GOVERNMENT SUPPLIES, Max read on a shop door. EZRA DEAK'S JUNK SHOP, said another sign. Carved over a marble entryway were the words BANK OF THE HIGH ECHELON, LTD.— EST. 2066, and on a cement wall someone had spray-painted DEATH TO SILVER OWLS! The slogan made Max's blood run cold.

A banner hung from the pillars of the library, bold letters proclaiming: CITIZENS' DOME CONSTRUCTION SCHEME (CDCS): YOUR BENEFICENT GOVERNMENT, WORKING FOR THE PEOPLE, and in smaller letters: THIS BUILDING HOUSES DOME CONSTRUCTION MATERIALS. LOOTERS WILL BE PROSECUTED.

What a terrible loss, thought Max, reflecting how in Gran's time the libraries had been filled to overflowing with books of every size, shape and topic. It was devastating to think they had all been confiscated and burned.

Rose paused beneath a tattered awning, ceremoniously unfolding a scrap of paper. "My dad drew this." She pulled a mini-flashlight from her pocket. "We're here. See?" She waved the tiny beam over a map. "We keep going till we reach Rye Corner, then we turn left onto Gravesend Road. That'll take us all the way to Cavernstone Hall."

Max studied the lines and symbols, sketched with painstaking care. "Your dad's a good artist," he commented. He wondered if spies had to take courses in map drawing.

"That's just one of his many talents."

Max frowned. "I think you have a problem."

Rose clicked off the light. "What do you mean?"

"I know you stole Mrs. Crumlin's boots. And that map—I bet your dad doesn't know you took it. I bet he doesn't even know you're here." The words spilled out before he could stop them. "You've got sticky fingers, Artemis Rose Eccles. You could get arrested for stealing those boots!"

"My dad knows exactly where I am!" Rose shot back. "Anyway, what about *you*, mister goody-goody? You stole your mother's smart card right out of her handbag!" She jammed the map into her pocket. "Quite a feat, owl boy." Her tone was cruel and mocking. "You could end up in Children's Prison, you know."

Max's mouth fell open. The prospect of jail had never crossed his mind.

They marched along in silence, following the road out of town. Max remembered stopping by a farm here with his mother years ago to buy eggs and pepper plants and a loaf of spelt bread. Then the memory melted away.

Rye Corner was a muddy crossroads marked by a wooden sign leaning to one side. As they turned onto Gravesend Road, Max gazed at the empty paint-peeling farmhouses spaced far apart, the derelict barn painted with a cough-drop advertisement, its words too faded to read. Warning signs were posted on barbed wire fences around the abandoned farms: KEEP OUT! they read. TRESPASSERS WILL BE SHOT.

Waves of despair rolled over him. He hadn't expected any of this: not the caved-in barns or crumbling fences, not the rotting wheat in the unplowed fields. It was as if the life had been punched right out of this place.

"I guess the tremors hit the farms really hard," said Rose. "Looks like everybody gave up and left."

Max felt a lump at the back of his throat. He'd known food was manufactured down south at the landholders' factories, but no one had told him that they no longer farmed here. Why hadn't he known that everything had fallen apart, that all the farmers had given up and moved away?

"Look," said Rose, pointing to a billboard the size of a barn.

COMING SOON: YOUR VERY OWN SOLAR-POWERED DOMED CITY, read the sign. BID FAREWELL TO RAIN AND SNOW, SAY SO LONG TO NIGHTTIME JITTERS! ARTIFICIAL LIGHT TWENTY-FOUR HOURS A DAY. PERFECT WEATHER FOR A PERFECT WORLD. CITIZENS' DOME CONSTRUCTION SCHEME (CDCS). PLANNING THE FUTURE WITH YOUR NEEDS IN MIND.

She turned to Max. "Once that ugly plastic bubble goes up, this place will be a ghost town."

"Take a look around," he said grimly. "It already is."

CHAPTER TEN

Max stepped up to the wrought iron gate with CAVERNSTONE HALL spelled out in iron script across the top. The gate was attached to a high brick wall that enclosed the entire property. Gripping the metal bars, he peered through. His first impression was a disappointing one. The building was nowhere near as grand as the framed watercolor sketch that hung in the dining room at home.

Cavernstone Hall crouched on a low moraine, a gloomy hulk of a house with pointed roofs, arched windows and leaning chimneys, constructed of somber gray stone. Around it bleak trees twisted in the wind, scattering leaves across the steep lawns.

Max was aware of its history. Once the family estate of Ezekiel H. Cavernstone, founder of Cavernstone Grey, the building had fallen into disrepair. It was auctioned off and purchased by monks, who turned it into an orphanage. According to Gran, when the High Echelon took it over, officials imprisoned the monks and put the orphans to work, turning the mansion into a government-run factory.

"Where are the Dark Brigadiers?" he asked. "It looks awfully quiet."

"Not to worry. My dad says the guards change over every hour." Rose held up a luminous watch with suns and moons and extra dials. "Ten minutes to go."

"I like your watch. Is that your dad's too?"

"He won't miss it," she called back as she plunged into the sea of ferns and cattails growing along the wall.

Max floundered after her, thorns scratching his face and wrists, branches clawing at his sleeves.

"Slow down!" he yelled. Mrs. Crumlin would blow a gasket if he tore his jacket.

"Quiet!" ordered Rose. "The wolves might hear."

"Wolves?" croaked Max, as a branch whipped across his face. He pushed it aside, his cheek smarting. "That's a joke, right?"

Rose gave him a drop-dead look. "Plague wolves guard all the government's properties. I can't believe you didn't know that."

"But wolves are extinct! It says so in the textbooks."

"Yeah, well, the textbooks say lots of things." She threw him a sardonic smile. "The government injects black wolves with a deadly virus, see, and they carry plague germs from the olden days! If a plague wolf bites you, count on dying instantly."

Max slumped against the bricks, breathing hard, trying to make sense of what Rose was saying. Why would the government allow infected wolves to patrol their properties? It had to be a scare tactic, he decided, a rumor designed to frighten people off.

The rain drizzled harder, drenching his woolen cap and soaking his hair. He felt miserable. "If plague wolves existed, Mrs. Crumlin would have told me. She'd want me to know something like that." He knew that was true—Mrs. Crumlin wouldn't keep him in the dark—but still he worried just a little.

"Crumlin tells you zilch!" hissed Rose. "Trust me, Max, plague wolves are real. They're totally crazed, too. The High Echelon starves them so they're ready to attack at a moment's notice."

Max stared at her, not knowing what to believe. Standing in the rain, cobwebby hair dripping, she seemed more like a disembodied spirit than a human being. What if he had imagined Rose after all?

"Maybe this wasn't such a good idea," he said, thinking of the numerous flaws in their plan. He'd far rather be in bed reading *Owls of the Wild*, or sitting on a branch next to his silver owl. "Let's come back some other time."

Rose glared at him. "Cut the whining."

Max sighed. Rose was real, all right. He could never have imagined anyone as bossy as her.

As they edged along the wall, he listened for wolves, but the only sound he could hear was the wind, roaring down from the north. Rose brushed her hand along the bricks, tapping each one. At last she stopped, tapping harder, prying a brick loose. More tumbled out around it and a gap appeared.

She wriggled through the gap, moving fast and expertly, not making a sound, the way Max imagined a spy would do. He followed, whacking his forehead and scraping his knee on the bricks. Because of his thick jacket and layers of flannel shirts and sweaters, it was a tight squeeze. Finally, huffing and puffing, he made it through.

On the other side Rose slouched against the wall, staring through the trees at Cavernstone Hall. Max put his hand to his forehead, feeling a bump start to rise. Whatever had possessed him to come here? Why had he let Rose talk him into it?

He followed her gaze, beyond Cavernstone Hall to a black shape on a hill, its jagged outline spiking into the sky. The Ruins! And, to his surprise, there were lights glimmering in the windows.

"Still think they're empty as eggshells?" Rose jabbed him with her skinny elbow. "No time to gawk, owl boy, we're on a mission. When the guard leaves, we'll run up the hill and around the back."

Max clutched his stomach, feeling nauseated.

"Stay close to the trees so the wolves don't see you," she added. "Lucky for us, they've got lousy night vision."

To calm himself Max pretended this was all a board game and he was a game piece, skulking from tree to tree. If Jackson Branwell Eccles's watch was correct, the changing of the guard was taking place this very minute at the factory's main entrance. This was their big chance to sneak into Cavernstone Hall.

Safely through the trees, they slipped around the back of the building, where a flight of steps led to a columned veranda. Max followed Rose up to a polished door with a window shaped like a sun. Through the frosted glass a dim light filtered in.

She nudged him. "The card, Max." Her eyes were bright with excitement.

Max dug into his pocket. The inside of his mouth felt dry and cottony. His mother's smart card was a key: contained within it were tiny computers that could open doors, scan identities, decipher coded messages. He knew that any unauthorized user would end up in deep trouble. But if he turned back now, Rose would never forgive him.

"Swipe it," she ordered, hopping from one foot to the other. "Hurry!"

Hand trembling, he ran the card through the machine. A green light blinked on and off, and the door swung open. Max peered into a cavernous hallway.

Rose pushed him aside, nearly knocking him over, and stormed into the building. Nerves wired, muscles taut, Max took a deep breath and stepped inside.

The air smelled bitter and he recognized the familiar scent of chocolate. A marbled hallway came rushing at him. Chandeliers glittered dimly overhead. The walls were papered in manic, swirling yellow suns that indicated this was a government-run business. A murky red carpet ran the length of the floor.

"Max! Come on!" Rose called.

He caught sight of her running toward a curved staircase. What was she so charged up about? he wondered, loping behind her, taking two steps at a time. The point of this reckless adventure was that he'd show Rose just how brave he was. Or did she have other reasons for coming here—reasons she wasn't telling him?

He stopped on the landing to catch his breath. Through a window of rippled glass he saw rain sweeping past The Ruins. Were those flare lamps inside, wavering off and on, or reflections of the lights at Cavernstone Hall? It was impossible to tell.

Hands on hips, Rose waited at the top of the stairs, tapping her foot impatiently. "The idea, Max," she said, "is to keep moving." She pointed to a red door embossed with the official logo, a yellow sun. "Let's go in here first."

Max stared at the skull and crossbones painted beneath the sun and felt his guts shrivel. A sign above the door warned NO ENTRY and depicted a snarling black wolf.

Max was stunned. What if Rose was telling the truth and the government really used plague wolves to attack intruders?

"Skull and bones means only one thing," said Rose, oblivious to the wolf warning. "Poison. That card of yours opens all the doors here, right? Hand it over, Max."

"Are you crazy?" said Max, recoiling in fear. "Look at the picture on the door! What if there are wolves in there?"

"We see a wolf, we run." She snatched the card from his hand and swiped it with a flick of the wrist. "Fast." The door jolted open.

With mounting horror Max watched Rose enter a vast room

with high ceilings and panels of dark wood, its painted floorboards littered with junk. He sidled in after her, bracing himself for a wolf attack.

Computers hummed, machines pulsated, dust seethed. Overhead, Max could hear rain drumming against the skylights. There was a strange energy here that he found unsettling. The room seemed at odds with the rest of the building, which was elegant and old-fashioned. These surroundings were more industrious, more *serious* than a quality chocolate factory.

To Max's relief there were no signs of wolves on the premises. Still, he wasn't taking any chances. He inched forward, looking this way and that, poised to run. But nothing jumped out.

He was certain his parents didn't work in this room. They held top-level positions, not drone jobs. The workers here spent their time flicking switches on machines and staring at numbers on computer screens.

All at once Rose went into high gear, moving through the room like a whirlwind, overturning waste bins, throwing open cupboards, rummaging through drawers, dumping file folders on the floor.

"What are you doing?" cried Max, startled by her frantic behavior. "Are you looking for something?"

Her muffled voice drifted out from under a desk. "I'll let you know when I find it."

Trying to keep calm, Max inspected the various charts and diagrams that were pinned to the walls with thumbtacks. They were written in codes and symbols that made no sense to him. Were they recipes? Train schedules? He didn't have a clue. Yet by the look of things, nothing in this room was remotely connected to the shipping or production of chocolate.

He edged slowly toward the other end of the room, surprised to see it had been converted into a greenhouse, crammed with flowers and plants and fitted with floor-to-ceiling windows. More puzzled than ever, Max tramped over for a closer look, noting a hose coiled on the wall and sprinklers in the ceiling.

Amid the chaos of vegetation, one plant springing out of a clay pot caught his eye: lush, velvety, with dark purple leaves.

"I don't believe it!" he gasped, staring at the deadly purple sphinx. It was identical to the one Rose had found by the owl tree.

"What did you find?" cried Rose, rushing over. "Deadly nightshade!" she breathed, leaning across his shoulder.

"Its cousin, you mean," Max corrected her. "Deadly purple sphinx." The sickly sweet scent caught in his throat and he started to cough.

"My dad suspected the government was smuggling poisonous plants into the country and growing them to use as biological weapons. This is proof, Max!"

"My mom and dad would never work in a poison factory," said Max, insulted.

What sort of place would be guarded by wolves, which were supposedly extinct? he wondered. Unless the sign on the door was a lie, a trick to keep people out. Plague wolves couldn't be real, he told himself, they were just an empty threat. He gave a sigh of relief.

"This room must be a side business," he said. "I bet they send all the drones and nerds here."

Rose gave a cynical snort. "Just to clue you in, this is more than a chocolate factory. Max, there's something I should tell you. My father has a PhD in toxicology, so he knows all about poisons."

"Hold on," said Max. "You told me he had a PhD in undercover surveillance."

"That too. I told you he's an egghead." She threw Max a wide smile. "Anyway, when the High Echelon took over, they sent him to work in a factory like this where he carried out secret experiments."

Max gulped. "What kind of experiments?"

"Gene splicing, toxic germs, all sorts of gruesome stuff. Sorry I lied, Max," she added, eyebrows quirked. "I wasn't sure I could trust you—not at first, anyway."

Max didn't think Rose sounded sorry at all. And there was something in her expression that made him suspect she wasn't telling him everything.

"You mean your father isn't a secret agent for the High Echelon? He doesn't exterminate people?" Max suddenly felt small and idiotic. "You lied to me about your father going to spy school?"

Rose shook her head. "He doesn't work for the High Echelon, he's against it! The government never sent him to spy school! My dad works for the Tarian!"

"The Tarian? What's that?"

"They're a resistance group! My dad and I are on the run; the Tarian are hiding us in a barn on the other side of town." She focused her huge green eyes on Max. "My dad has night blindness, so I offered to come here and check things out."

Too furious to say a word, Max stood, hands in his pockets,

scowling. Did Rose expect him to believe her father had let her go to Cavernstone Hall in the middle of the night and risk being captured by the Dark Brigade?

Unperturbed, she pointed to a row of glass jars. "See that purple-colored powder? Chances are that's ground-up deadly purple sphinx—in other words, *poison*. The government adds tiny amounts to the hot cocoa mix. That way nobody dies when they drink it, 'cause it's only a little bit."

"Why would they mess around with their bestselling hot chocolate?" sputtered Max, fed up with her nonsensical stories. "Why would the High Echelon want to poison everyone?"

"My dad says they make two kinds," she went on, ignoring his outburst. "The first is ordinary cocoa, but the second cocoa has trace amounts of poison. If you drink it day after day you become weak, your mind goes murky, you feel drowsy and blah. You get fevers and sore throats and your eyes are always itching."

Max shifted nervously from one foot to the other. Rose had just described every one of his symptoms. "Why would the High Echelon allow people to drink poison?" he asked, trying not to let his voice quaver. "Tell me that, huh?"

"It's all about the big picture, Max, don't you see? Mind control!" She slipped a bottle of powdered deadly purple sphinx into her coat pocket. "It's one more way the High Echelon is trying to take control of our thoughts."

CHAPTER ELEVEN

The next door Rose selected was painted high-gloss red and embossed with a pattern of yellow suns. By now Max was getting a little tired of seeing the High Echelon's logo everywhere. She stood scrutinizing it, tapping the smart card against her front teeth, as if contemplating what might be on the other side. Unlike the first door, there were no warning signs or pictures of wolves.

Even so, Max was a nervous wreck. He kept thinking about what Rose had said about mind control. It worried him, the way his memories kept disappearing, as if a giant eraser were rubbing them out. Was he somehow a victim of mind control?

Sliding the card, Rose entered first. Max followed, anxiously gnawing his fingernails. The room was long and narrow, a laboratory that reeked of strong chemicals and cleaning fluids. Max wrinkled his nose and sneezed.

Heaped up on long benches were glass beakers and flasks, and multiknobbed microscopes that looked, to Max, extremely complicated. Machines buzzed at the edges of the room and the glassware vibrated. He inched down the aisle, running his hand over glass and metal objects, feeling queasier by the minute.

Something about this room felt wrong. Max's heart thumped against his chest. He sensed something here that didn't belong, something unhealthy. *Diseased.*

"Can we go home now?" he called to Rose.

Rose didn't answer. She was zipping around in full-throttle mode, inspecting everything she could get her hands on. She dismissed a Bunsen burner with a wave of the hand. A collector's item. Totally useless.

"This thing's vintage," she muttered, peering into a microscope with dozens of dials and knobs.

Max wandered over to a workbench, trying to imagine his mom and dad working here. Somehow the image wouldn't compute. Along the bench delicate instruments were arranged in tidy rows; he stared at them with wonder and suspicion. Small and sharp and shiny, they looked like tools that elves might use. Lined up next to them were spools of thick brown thread and sewing needles stuck into pincushions. Was this some kind of repair shop?

A kind of fizziness started up behind his eyes, which he recognized as the start of a headache. He found the tiny suns on the pincushions somehow repugnant. What in the world were all those things for?

"Surgical instruments," Rose said matter-of-factly, reaching past him to touch what looked like a miniature bed. It was upholstered in red vinyl with small yellow straps attached to the sides. "Look at this tiny operating table! My dad said there were secret experiments going on!"

Feeling squeamish, Max turned away. He didn't want to imagine what type of animal would fit onto that operating table. A small dog? A raven? An *owl*?

From behind him came a gurgling noise and he felt the hairs go up on the back of his neck. Turning, he saw a maze of thin glass tubes branching out in all directions. Inside the tubes bubbled a thick frothy liquid, dark purple in color, with flecks of red glitter. He breathed in a harsh, metallic smell. Something lurched in the pit of his stomach.

There was no mistaking what was in the tubes: it was the medicine Dr. Tredegar injected Max with every week. He had no idea what it was called—the doctor always brushed off his questions with a joke—yet he knew beyond any doubt that this was it.

"Ugh! What's that goopy-looking stuff?" asked Rose, flitting over. "It looks vile! Must be for one of their genetic experiments."

"It's medicine," said Max. One thing he knew for sure was that Dr. Tredegar would never dream of giving kids poison shots. "I get injections for my condition and this is what they give me."

Rose's eyebrows shot up, but she didn't say a word.

They hurried down the red-carpeted staircase to the first floor, where Max noted with satisfaction that everything looked completely normal. He mentally checked off the offices, the mail room, coat hooks, mirrors, an umbrella stand, a punch clock. Even the employee bulletin board looked drab and ordinary.

They followed the burnt chocolate smell to a door at the end of the hall. Ignoring the sign marked AUTHORIZED PERSONNEL ONLY, Rose pushed open the door and strode inside.

Max followed her into a vast kitchen of marble counters, gleaming sinks and sparkling chrome fixtures. The windows were covered with louvered shutters painted in creamy reds and yellows. A kitchen like this, he thought, might be featured on the cover of his mother's *Homes and Domes* magazine.

Rose skidded across the tile floor and disappeared through an archway. Wandering around, Max felt relieved to see how old-fashioned everything looked. Pots and pans hung from suspended steel racks, the floor was waxed to a high gloss, a refrigerator rumbled in the corner. He clambered onto the counter and opened a cupboard. Inside he found dozens of familiar yellow boxes.

Rose skidded back in. "There's a pantry in there, stuffed to the gills with hot cocoa."

"See, Rose, the real thing." Max held up a box. "I call this lady on the box Wavy Gray." He tapped the illustration. "I bet my mom and dad take all their breaks here and fix themselves hot cocoa."

"You better hope not. That box is yellow."

"So what?"

"Food shops sell red boxes—that's the ordinary cocoa," she said. "The yellow ones are laced with poison."

Max teetered at the edge of the countertop. "That's not funny, Rose." Feeling a bit unsteady, he sat down and slid onto the floor.

"My dad's a pharmacologist, he should know." Rose tugged open the refrigerator door. "That cocoa makes you feel woozy, right? And you can't remember things sometimes?"

"It's a bedtime drink, it's supposed to make you sleepy." Tired of arguing, Max suddenly felt ravenous. "Do you see anything to eat?"

He peered over Rose's shoulder. The refrigerator shelves were empty, except for one. On the middle shelf thin corked bottles, filled with a viscous liquid, were organized in tidy rows.

Rose picked up a bottle and inspected it. "Definitely not drinkable." She gave it a shake.

Max watched as tiny yellow bubbles floated up to the surface, corkscrewing up and down, each with a black dot at the center. Mystified, he leaned closer—and his stomach caved in.

They weren't bubbles. They were eyes. Panic shot through him, like an electric jolt.

"Rose?" he whispered.

He saw her swallow, unable to look away from the floating eyes. "I'm out of here," she rasped, thrusting the bottle back onto the shelf.

She slammed the refrigerator door. Without warning, lights flashed overhead. A siren began to wail.

Max's heart fell to his knees.

"Run!" cried Rose, sprinting across the room.

Clamping his hands over his ears, Max took off. Sirens blared and lights flashed as he raced down the hall. He hated the way loud noises always clanged and echoed inside his head.

Rose screeched to a halt. "A guard!"

Through the sun-shaped window, Max saw a blurred figure. His heart racketed against his ribs.

"Head for the pantry!" shouted Rose, and they charged back down the hall. In the kitchen she flew across the tile floor, Max skidding behind her.

The kitchen door banged open and he froze. A tall skeletal figure rushed in: a woman in frightening night goggles and a crepe mouth mask, blue-dyed hair streaming down her back. She wore lizard-skin boots and a high-collared cape the color of blood.

Slinking beside her was a huge animal with red eyes and black spiky fur. Dirty white foam dripped from its mouth. Max's stomach did a double flip. Plague wolves were real!

The creature snarled. Terror surged through Max. Paralyzed with fear, he gazed at the wolf's sharp curved teeth. Then, out of nowhere, Rose appeared; she pulled him behind her into the pantry and they tumbled through a door.

With a bang, it slammed shut behind them and they clattered down a ladder, into a vast cellar lit by flare lamps. Once they'd reached the bottom, Rose pushed the ladder and sent it crashing down. Max blundered ahead, disoriented by the shadows, knocking over a stack of wooden crates. Heart thudding, he pushed aside old machinery as he and Rose stumbled over broken desks and filing cabinets, dented freezers, smashed computers heaped in piles. Overhead he could hear the woman running.

The wolf howled.

Rose clutched his hand and they ran wildly down a stone passage, into complete and utter darkness. Terror gripped Max's chest, squeezing his lungs so he could hardly breathe. His only hope was that the guard wouldn't follow. The ladder was gone and night goggles, he'd been told, only worked properly out-of-doors.

The passage twisted and stretched, winding deeper into the earth. Max raced on, gripping Rose's hand, boots pounding over wet stone. The tunnel narrowed, its dripping walls closing in around them. He could see a faint light ahead. Huffing and wheezing, he lurched toward it.

Moments later they stood before a wooden door. There was no handle, no smart-card machine, just a door of ancient pitted wood that Max guessed hadn't been opened in at least a century. He scratched his head, trying to think what to do next.

Rose didn't hesitate. She swung her leg back and kicked. To Max's surprise, the bottom half of the door fell in. "Dry rot," she said, and kicked again.

The door splintered and collapsed. A dreamy light flooded over them.

Max gazed up a flight of stone steps that wound upward, vanishing into the light, and a million scary thoughts crowded into his mind. What if the Dark Brigadier knew a shortcut and was up there with the wolf, waiting to attack?

Rose scrabbled up the steps, coat swirling around her. "I don't believe this!" she shouted down to Max. "Come here, quick!"

Heart banging, Max scrambled after her, wishing he had his owl with him, to give him a boost of courage. At the top of the steps stood Rose, framed beneath an elaborate curved doorway. He looked about, bewildered, at the endless arching spaces around him.

"What is this place?" he whispered.

"Don't you know?" Rose's eyes glowed with feverish excitement. "We're in The Ruins!"

CHAPTER TWELVE

The grainy air trembled. Pillars arched above them, and Max stared at the worn carvings, the high stone walls, the thick candles that dripped from suspended iron wheels. His skin went cold and clammy.

Rain wept against the stained glass windows. The space around him was vast and terrifying; thick gnarled columns trailed off into the gloom. In the hushed silence nothing moved.

"This is a cathedral!" said Rose, her voice filled with awe. "That tunnel we were running in? That was a crypt, Max, it had to be!"

Max looked around in wonder. Gran had told him about cathedrals, and how many of them dated back to medieval times. She'd been furious with the government for pulling them down.

"My dad said the High Echelon turned some of the cathedrals into prisons," murmured Rose, "but this doesn't look like a prison to me." She wandered off, looking strangely enchanted by everything. "Who lit all these candles, do you think? Monks?"

Max knew very little about monks. The High Echelon had branded them superstitious outcasts, but Gran said many monks supported the Silver Prophecies. He wondered if there were monks living here now.

But all he could think was, whoever was here—monks, prisoners, wolves—he didn't want to meet any of them. What he really wanted was to go home.

"I've got a bad feeling," he said, catching up with Rose. "Listen to me!" He grabbed her arm. "Something's not right here. This place is even creepier than Cavernstone Hall!"

"Hey, Max, this is an opportunity with a capital *O*." Shaking him off, she strode away. "If I can tell my father any little thing about The Ruins, he'll be so grateful and happy."

Max frowned. He somehow doubted her father would be pleased to know she was inside The Ruins.

She glanced back over her shoulder. "You're not scared, are you?"

"Of course not," he muttered. But naturally he was. He was petrified. "Okay, five minutes."

Max knew she wasn't listening. Rose never listened. Growing more anxious by the minute, he trailed behind her, noticing how everything in the cathedral was covered in dust and cobwebs, and coated with layers of grime. They should call in Mrs. Crumlin, he thought wryly, she can clean this place up with her extra-large feather duster.

Candles sputtered, shadows crouched and leapt. From high overhead, strange serpentine creatures stared down. Along the walls, he could see coffins tucked into marble niches, engraved with skulls and angels, their inscriptions so faded they were impossible to read. A statue of a winged lady gazed at him with a mournful expression, its paint flaking away.

"They're hiding something here, don't you think?" said Rose, checking under a bench of rotted wood. "My dad says the government's experimenting with exotic bugs. They've created germs that can wipe out entire cities."

Max hoped she was exaggerating, but he had a feeling she wasn't. He wished he could remember what Gran had said about the High Echelon's secret experiments.

Boldly, Rose drew back a curtain of tattered brocade. Dust billowed around them. Max caught a whiff of mold and something else that set his teeth on edge. He peered into a deep alcove, its concave ceiling painted in shades of gold and cornflower blue.

Without warning his sun mark went cold, pressing like an ice shard into his neck. Startled, he jumped. This had never happened before.

"What do you think is in those boxes?" Oblivious to Max, Rose was pointing at the stacks of metal boxes, arranged in rows along the wall.

There were at least a hundred, guessed Max. He stepped forward bravely and lifted off the top box. It looked eerily familiar, like something he'd once seen in a dream. Etched into the lid were the words SKRÆK #176.

"What does that mean?" he wondered aloud. "It must be imported from some foreign country."

"Maybe it's a new brand of minicomputer," suggested Rose, "or a machine that scans fingerprints. Hey, I bet they're smuggling stuff across the border! Or what if—" Her voice fell to a tremulous whisper. "What if it's a box of exotic bugs? Or something even weirder?" She nodded at the box. "Open it."

As Max started to open the latch, he heard a faint scratching sound. Alarmed, he almost dropped the box. Then he saw the tiny holes punched into its sides. His legs wobbled and his heart beat fast. Whatever was in there, he thought, needed air.

"Give me that." Rose snatched the box away, fingers scrabbling at the latch.

Before Max could stop her, the lid to the box sprang open. An acrid odor filled the air. A wire mesh screen stretched across the box's top, attached to the edges with tiny copper nails, forming a cage. Beneath it stirred a pale indeterminate shape.

Max moved closer. A claw shot up, talons raking the screen. "It's alive!" he shrieked.

"Yech, it smells disgusting!" Rose shoved the box at him. "Hold on, let me get my flashlight."

Trembling, he held the box as she shined her beam into it.

"Whatever's in there can't get out," she said. "It's inside that wire cage."

"I don't know, Rose, look how sharp its claws are—" Max saw the creature twitch, startled by the light. It had no hair and its slimy skin was nearly transparent, with a tangle of pulsing veins underneath. His breath caught in his chest. It was the creature from his nightmares!

His first impulse was to drop the box and run, or else be sick.

He felt his arms and knees go weak. So he hadn't invented the creature after all. Somehow it was real!

"Holy cow!" said Rose, taking the box from Max and setting it on a stone shelf. "It looks like a huge worm." She turned the box around, studying its contents from different angles. "A giant grub, maybe?"

Max was too terrified to speak. How could Rose be so casual? Why wasn't she frightened? He heard the creature's wings crackle as they opened. It was a sound he remembered clearly from his dreams.

"Looks like somebody hacked those with a scissors," said Rose.

Max stared at the creature in horror and disbelief. Its face looked pliable and half-formed, like one of Mrs. Crumlin's griddle cakes. The eyes were sunk deep into its head, so deep he couldn't see them. It was all he could do to not throw up.

"It can't be a worm or a grub, can it?" Rose went on. "Because it's got those tacky-looking wings." Her eyes grew bigger. "Hey, it could be a genetically spliced mutant! My dad would know for sure. You can bet it was made in a laboratory."

"You don't know that," said Max, his voice shaky. "It could be some animal we never saw before, something from a swamp or a jungle—"

Nostrils quivering, the creature flicked its stringy tongue.

"Yeeks, black licorice!" Rose glanced up at Max. "See how its tongue forks at the end? These mutants are lethal, you know, they can slice you to ribbons in minutes flat."

Max nodded. She didn't have to tell him—he already knew.

The creature snarled at them, showing two rows of tiny serrated teeth.

"Nice choppers," quipped Rose, as if she wasn't in the least bit scared. "That's how it rips things apart."

Max was repulsed, horrified. His heart hammered so loud he was sure Rose could hear it. How could she be joking at a time like this? His stomach churned wildly.

He looked over at Rose. Her green eyes were gigantic, like they belonged to some extraterrestrial being. Rose is frightened too, he told himself, she's just good at hiding it.

The creature pressed its face to the screen and hissed. Max jumped. "It's got no eyes!" he screamed.

"Those little operating tables, the teeny-tiny instruments," Rose whispered. "The eyeballs in the fridge, Max! They were going to give it eyes!"

"Don't say any more, Rose, I don't want to know." Max backed away, sickened to the core. The creature writhed and squirmed, clawing at the sides of the box.

He had to get away from here; his nerves were shot and his sun mark throbbed painfully. Worst of all, the creature's shrieks were getting inside his head.

"I'm going, Rose," he said. At this point he didn't care what she thought of him. "Are you coming?"

"Look, it's bleeding, Max! It cut itself on the wire."

Max peered into the box, trying not to gag. He could see a trail of purple-black liquid, flecked with bits of red, oozing from its leg.

He looked up in horror at Rose.

"Those glass tubes," she murmured, leaning closer to the box, "that bubbly purple stuff with red bits in it . . ." He watched the color drain out of her face. "Oh, Max—"

Thoroughly rattled, he shook his head vehemently. "No, Rose, that would never happen." He knew Dr. Tredegar would never inject him with blood from a gene-spliced creature. "Only mad scientists in comic books do things like that."

And yet, he thought, only a mad scientist would create a genetically altered mutant like this one.

"Forget your stupid comic books!" shouted Rose. "Mad scientists work for the High Echelon! The government funded all this!"

Max felt a roaring inside his head. Sickened and overwhelmed, he slumped against the wall, the harsh reality sinking in at last. It was time to stop kidding himself and admit that Rose was right. Gran had always said the High Echelon was evil, but he'd never realized how truly malevolent it was. How could he deny the secret experiments, he asked himself, when he was staring one in the face?

Rose grabbed his hand, squeezing it so tightly his bones felt crushed. "Do you know what this means? They're giving you this mutant's *blood*! Why, Max?"

The creature flung its grublike body against the mesh, whipping its head back and forth. As it twisted and turned, Max saw a yellow shape on the side of its head and beside it the number *176*.

"A tattoo!" gasped Rose. "It's got a sun tattoo, like the one on your neck!"

Max was stunned. What was a mutant doing with a tattoo that matched his birthmark? He swallowed hard. It was too much of a coincidence.

Before he could think any further, a shout rang out from below, followed by a low, prolonged howl. The hair on his head stood straight up.

Rose slammed the lid and latched it. "Run!" she ordered, and raced off.

Max scooped the box under his arm. "I'm taking this with me!" he called out. With the box shut and the creature hidden from view, he felt almost brave.

Rose stopped in midflight. "Are you insane? That thing's a cold-blooded killer!"

"I'm not leaving it here," he said stubbornly, then started running.

It was a total act of lunacy, he knew, and Rose would never understand. For that matter, *he* didn't understand. What was this sudden compulsion to save this bizarre creature? He didn't have an answer. It was as if the impulse to rescue it had been programmed inside his head.

"It's your funeral, Max!" shouted Rose, sprinting ahead of him. "I'm sure Mrs. Crumlin would love a cuddly new pet!"

They raced from door to door—twisting the glass knobs, pulling the wrought iron handles, kicking the dark heavy wood—but all the doors remained firmly locked.

The metal boxes inside the alcove began rattling and banging. Each box, Max realized, contained one of these gruesome creatures. His pulse started to race.

"If those mutants get loose they'll tear us to shreds!" cried Rose. Then, wrenching the box from Max, she said, "I need this."

"Hey!" he yelled in alarm as she sprinted away. "Where are you going with that?"

He raced after her, but in his haste Max tripped over a broken plaster statue and fell headlong onto the floor, bashing his knee.

Sprawled across the marble tiles, he watched Rose clamber onto a bench, her eyes fixed on a stained glass window.

"Sorry, maggot-breath," he heard her say. She raised the box over her head and threw it.

The box containing Skræk #176 sailed through the air, smashing a stained-glass angel and a circle of doves. The window shattered; rain gusted in. Max blinked and Rose was over the sill.

"Hurry, Max!" she hollered from outside. "Jump!"

Rising shakily to his feet, Max limped over to the bench and stepped onto it. His knee ached painfully and his head was pounding so loud he couldn't think. From the alcove, he could hear high-pitched shrieks coming from inside the metal boxes.

Gripping the windowsill, he looked out into the rain and his head began to spin. With his sleeve he brushed away bits of broken glass. He felt nauseated and light-headed—not surprising, since vertigo was part of his condition.

The plague wolf howled again. Terrified, Max scrabbled up onto the sill. Rain soaked his face as he took a deep trembling breath. Then he jumped.

He landed in the high wet grass, rolled a few times and came to a stop. Sitting up, he squinted through the rain and darkness, searching for Rose.

Beside him he saw the metal box upended in the grass. He crawled over, dragging his wounded leg. Setting the box upright, he unlatched the lid with shaking fingers. With fear and apprehension, he bravely peered inside.

A putrid smell wafted up, turning his stomach. Blind and shivering, the creature crouched in a corner, making no sound at all.

Its teeth glinted like tiny needles. Max stared down at the slippery, rancid-smelling creature with a kind of wordless terror. He could feel the skræk's utter coldness, its ferocity and brutality. Yet despite his feelings of repugnance, he also felt pity for so desolate and lonely a creature.

He noticed the top of the cage had gotten twisted in the fall. If he pulled the wire mesh out, Skræk #176 could escape. Max chewed his lip, deliberating. Should he set it free? After all, it was a living, breathing creature—sort of.

"Max!" he heard Rose shout. "Where are you?"

Impulsively he gripped the torn wire and wrenched it back. His stomach roiled in fear and revulsion. What he was doing was dangerous, he told himself. Yet the urge to save the skræk seemed to be hardwired into his brain.

"Fly away," whispered Max, shaking the box. He heard the crackle of two thin wings as they unfolded, reminding him once again of his dreams. "Go!" he ordered. "You're free!"

The creature shot out of the cage and into the air. One wing—scratchy, smelly and jagged at the edges—brushed Max's forehead. The skræk flapped, then sank into the wet grass.

Heart pounding, Max jumped back, watching it try again, only to be knocked down by the rain.

"Max!" cried Rose, running toward him.

He grinned as the creature finally sailed into the air, buffeted by the wind. Soaring skyward, Skræk #176 flew off, rustling and squeaking—a farewell of sorts, Max supposed—into the rain-soaked night, leaving him to wonder what on earth he had just done.

CHAPTER THIRTEEN

Max opened the back door and staggered into the kitchen, dripping water over the linoleum. He had limped home through the torrential rain and was soaking wet. Worried his father might be up eating a late-night snack, he froze in midstep. But the room was empty and silent.

He crept over to his mother's handbag, hanging on a peg by the door, and slipped the smart card back into her wallet. Then, with one of Mrs. Crumlin's burnt dish towels, he tried to mop up the mess, but his knee hurt so badly he couldn't bend down.

Back in his room he peeled off his drenched clothes and

stuffed them under the bed. He was so weary he was seeing double. Heaving a sigh of relief to be at home at last, he crawled under the quilt and fell into a deep sleep.

He slept through most of the following day. If he had dreams, he didn't remember them when he awoke late that afternoon. His knee felt stiff and sore. Mrs. Crumlin arrived with a bowl of crushed millet chowder and his medicine. If she knew about him sneaking out last night, she didn't let on.

"Mrs. Crumlin?" he said, slurping the cough syrup. "Have you ever heard stories about plague wolves?" He choked as the syrup stuck halfway down his throat, remembering the terrifying creature in Cavernstone Hall.

Risky talk, he knew, but he had to know whose side she was on. Was her loyalty to him—or was the government paying her to report back to it?

Mrs. Crumlin narrowed her black eyes. Max felt the air crackle between them. "Plague was wiped out decades ago," she said curtly. "The High Echelon's brilliant technology put an end to that."

He handed her the spoon, wiping his sticky fingers on the quilt. "So there's no such thing as black wolves infected with plague virus?" he asked, trying to sound casual. "They're a myth, right?"

She threw him a brittle smile. "Of course they're a myth, you silly boy. Wolves went the way of the trout and the polar bears, and those animals have been extinct for ages. Where in the world did you hear such an absurd story?"

"Nowhere. I made it up." Max closed his eyes and sank into the pillows, heart racketing inside his chest.

That's it, he thought. Mrs. Crumlin lied to me about The Ruins and now she's lying about the plague wolves. She's totally untrustworthy. On the other hand, was the High Echelon feeding her half-truths, keeping her in the dark like everyone else about its secret experiments? Did she, he wondered, know about the skræks?

"Maxwell Unger!" shrilled Mrs. Crumlin.

His eyes flew open. Lips pursed, she stood before him, feet planted on the rug, holding up his dripping jacket. One of the pockets hung by a thread. "Whatever happened to this? How could you be so careless?"

Max shrank under her beady gaze, realizing that he'd done a poor job of hiding his clothes under the bed.

Mrs. Crumlin brushed clumps of matted grass and mud off the jacket. "Where on earth have you been?" She stumped over to him and, reaching down with her large hand, pushed the hair off his forehead. "How did you get that goose egg?" she demanded. "And those scratches on your face? Hmmm?"

"I had an accident," he said, recoiling from her touch. "It was raining and I fell down the back steps." She would never believe him, but he didn't care—not anymore.

"I am aware that you wander outside in the night, Maxwell. Your father says I have eyes in the back of my head, even when I'm not here, and I daresay he's right." She hung the sodden jacket over a chair. Max watched the water drip off, forming tiny puddles on the floorboards.

"Am I correct in assuming that you keep within the boundaries of your parents' property, Maxwell?" She set the bowl of soup on his nightstand. "You wouldn't be hiding anything from me, would you?"

"I'd never do that, Mrs. Crumlin." Max reached for the soup.

A cog in the wheel. That was how Rose had described Mrs. Crumlin, which Max took to mean a drone who worked for the authorities. Was Mrs. Crumlin reporting things he said to the High Echelon? That would explain why she was always peppering him with questions.

Her expression turned cold and distant. "Keep in mind, Maxwell, should you encounter any lurkers, lurchers or runaways on these midnight excursions of yours, you are to inform me at once. Understood?"

"Yes, Mrs. Crumlin." He stirred his soup, not daring to look up. Her suspicious tone made him uneasy. Could she know about Rose, or was she just guessing?

What would happen if he told her the truth? He was sure Mrs. Crumlin would act out of blind loyalty; she'd have no qualms about reporting Rose to the authorities. He realized he knew deep in his bones that Mrs. Crumlin was on *their* side, not his.

She bustled about the bedroom, moving things around on his bureau, plumping pillows, dragging his wet sweaters and long underwear out from under the bed. Now he was seeing Mrs. Crumlin in a new light. Was her wise, kindly guardian routine just a facade? He wondered if behind the flour-stained dresses and graying hair tucked into a hairnet there was a devious, calculating, much scarier Mrs. Crumlin. He had a sinking feeling that the answer was yes.

"Shall I set up a game of Dark Hearts and Winding Shrouds in the parlor?" she suggested. "That might cheer you up."

"No thanks," said Max. "My throat's scratchy. I just want to sleep." He dipped his spoon into the broth, vowing never to believe another thing Mrs. Crumlin told him. And he would never, ever say anything that might give Rose away.

"Suit yourself." With a hurt look, she whisked away his wet clothes and stomped out.

Max set the broth aside and jumped out of bed, his thoughts turning to the skræk. He wondered where it was now. Had it found anything to eat? He pictured the creature flying through the forest, or hanging upside down in a bat cave, resting after its traumatic ordeal.

He didn't know why he had felt compelled to set it free. It had been an irrational act, utterly insane. Rose had been furious last night when she saw Skræk #176 flapping away. And what, he wondered, was going to happen to all the skræks locked up in those boxes?

He stood before his bureau mirror, looking at a thin boy in pajamas with mousy brown hair falling into his eyes. He held up a small hand mirror, examining the dull yellow sun at the back of his neck. Rose was right: it was the same symbol he'd seen on the doors and walls of Cavernstone Hall. But how did the sun tattoo connect him to the skræk? He was mystified.

If he squinted a certain way, he could see remnants of something else beneath it: the Mark of the Owl! Ancient and profound, this mark, he realized, was his true birthmark.

How could he have been so gullible, believing Mrs. Crumlin when she said the sun mark was lucky? She'd lied about that, too.

• • •

"My father says skræks are the High Echelon's new top-secret weapon because they have no-fear genes," said Rose that night, sitting with Max under the owl tree. "The government's setting them loose the day everyone moves to the domes." The air was crisp and cold, and puffs of breath floated out of her mouth.

Max wriggled uncomfortably inside his duffle coat, which was far too small. He had worn it because Mrs. Crumlin was mending his winter jacket. "But won't they go after people and kill them?" he asked.

"That's the point! Those skræks are out of control and nobody will be able to leave the domes—it'll be too dangerous!"

"But if the government made the skræks, it must be able to control them," mused Max, trying not to wake the silver owl, who was asleep on his lap. With her feathers glistening in the moonlight, she looked so peaceful. "What's a no-fear gene, anyway?"

"No-fear genes mean you're not afraid of anything," said Rose, waving her arms around. "Nothing in the whole world scares you! And here's the zinger: no-fear genes are selling on the black market!"

What an amazing invention, thought Max. He wondered if he could save up enough pocket money to buy a no-fear gene. If he had one, he'd never have to worry about being nervous or scared, or kids teasing him, or being afraid to climb to the top of the owl tree. His life would change in a hundred different ways.

"He says they're selling skræk eyes, too!" said Rose excitedly. "Remember those weird eyes we saw? They tried to transplant them into skræks, but it failed. And, oh yeah, my dad says our detective work last night was par excellence. That means first-rate."

Max looked at her in surprise. "You told your father about *me*?"

"Why not? We're a team, aren't we?" She wiped her nose on her sleeve.

"I guess so." He felt a sudden warm glow spreading inside him. It was the same expansive feeling he had each time he looked at his silver owl.

"I wish you could've seen our old brick house in Tattersall Heath," murmured Rose dreamily. "My bedroom looked out over cornfields and orchards and red-gold wheat and junked tractors, and in the distance was a shut-down theme park. I loved that place."

"It sounds special," said Max. How could the government plow over places like Cavernstone Grey and Tattersall Heath? he asked himself. How could their homes just disappear?

"My dad said Tattersall Heath was one of those places where heaven and earth meet," said Rose softly.

"Like the owl tree?" Max felt a tickling at the back of his throat. Tears pricked his eyes and he blinked hard, trying to fight off the sadness. The owl tree, he knew, was doomed too.

Rose nodded. "Yes, the owl tree." She gave Max a sad, quirky smile. "By the way, Max, I told my father about those disgusting injections you get."

Max pulled down his earflaps. He didn't want to hear her father's opinions regarding his medication. "It stabilizes my condition," he muttered.

"Max, the High Echelon's notorious for that sort of thing, like poisoning hot cocoa!" she said in her smart-alecky voice. "What about side effects? Ever ask yourself what that mutant blood is doing to you?"

Max said nothing, but his mind was racing. What exactly *were* the injections doing to him? He thought about his disjointed memories and the problems he had remembering things.

The owl rustled in his lap, giving low hoots to let him know she was upset. Max smoothed her ruffled feathers, wishing he had solutions to all the problems that were piling up. Never again would he trust Mrs. Crumlin, and ditto for Dr. Tredegar.

"I'm tired of everybody lying to me." His voice sounded sullen. "Dr. Tredegar, Mrs. Crumlin. And *you*! You told me your father spied for the High Echelon, and now you say he's against the government. What am I supposed to believe?"

"I had to be sure, Max, I had to know your silver owl wasn't a trick." Rose reached over and patted the owl. "Lots of kids around here come from High Echelon families, and they're all loyal to the Alazarin Oro."

"The Alazarin Oro?" said Max, puzzled. "They haven't been around for centuries!"

"Better check your facts, owl boy. My dad says the people who run this government all belong to the Alazarin Oro. It's an olden-time secret society."

Max felt her words like a punch to the stomach. "But the Alazarin Oro turned the silver owls to stone!" This was one myth he knew by heart and would never forget. "They fought the Sages and silver owls in a huge, bloody battle at Silvern that went on for days! The Alazarin Oro are pure evil!"

"I know that, Max." Rose plucked a squashed bug off her sleeve. "That's why they want to take over everybody's minds."

"The Alazarin Oro vowed death to all silver owls!" croaked Max, his thoughts and emotions in turmoil. "Gran always said it was about revenge, but I never understood. Now I do—the High Echelon's going after the Sages to get revenge!"

"We need to find that Owl Keeper you told me about," said Rose, grabbing his arm. "Fast."

The owl flitted to Max's shoulder, making low, anxious noises in her throat.

"You're right, we've got to warn him," said Max, feeling galvanized. "The Prophecy says the Owl Keeper will bring together Sages and silver owls to fight the dark forces. It's obviously talking about the High Echelon."

"My dad says we have to keep fighting," said Rose determinedly. "We can't give up, ever."

Max gave a deep sigh. He and Rose were just two kids. How could they defeat the government and its deadly creatures?

Where, he wondered, was the Owl Keeper? How were they going to find him? He had always imagined the Owl Keeper appearing one moonlit night, walking stick in hand, striding along the river path, calling out to the silver owls. Falling like flames from the sky, they would streak down to him, swifter than shooting stars. That was where his daydream always ended.

In real life, terrible things were happening all around him, but he hadn't even noticed—not until Rose had pointed them out and he'd seen the skræk for himself. Max thought back to The Ruins and the secret experiments, the prisons and sealed borders and people disappearing, the government tracking down Sages and killing owls.

That was when it hit him. His world, and everything in it he believed to be true, had just disappeared. The realization shook him to the core. He could no longer ignore the insidious things that were happening, or deny the far-reaching powers of the High Echelon, which were spreading across the country like a cancerous blight.

Absolute Dark, he realized, was here.

CHAPTER FOURTEEN

Slouched in the Ungers' hallway, Einstein handed a stack of assignments to Max. Today his jacket was festooned with more buttons than ever: YOUR RELIABLE GOVERNMENT: BUILDING A SHINING WORLD; COMING SOON: A PERFECT CITY; TAKE BACK THE DARK and DOWN WITH FORESTS, UP WITH DOMES.

"Who's that guy?" Max pointed to the comic-book character stitched on Einstein's jacket pocket.

"You've never heard of Oliver Owl Slayer?" said Einstein, grinning. "He rescues kids from the evil silver owls!"

Max nearly choked. He wanted to ask Einstein who was filling his head full of lies, but he didn't have a chance to open his mouth. Einstein was all worked up about something.

"Hey, Max, the High Echelon sent the Dark Brigade to our school today!" he crowed. "They came into our class unexpected like, looking for a girl: a runaway!"

Max gulped as panic rolled over him. Was Einstein talking about *Rose*?

"They've issued an all points bulletin for a girl on the run: tall skinny kid, red hair, black coat. She's been taking stuff off clotheslines and stealing vegetables from the outdoor stand on Blackbone Street! They already caught the father—found him in some barn two weeks ago."

Max stifled a gasp. The Dark Brigade had Rose's *father*? Why hadn't she told him? Did that mean she'd been on her own for the past two weeks, pretending her father was still around?

He noticed Einstein's pale eyes fixed on him. "Hey, Max, didn't you mention some girl a while ago? You said she was tall with red hair that stuck out funny."

Max leaned against the wall, afraid he might topple over. "There wasn't any girl," he wheezed. "It was a dream, remember? I always have weird dreams when I get a fever."

Einstein shrugged his bony shoulders. "The Dark Brigade is interrogating all sorts and sundry. They want to know if anyone saw this girl. And know what? They can tell if you're lying because they have these newfangled lie detector machines. They hooked Cheever Oaks up to one of them!"

"I don't have anything to hide," said Max, hardly daring to

breathe. "So what if I dreamed about a girl with messy hair? It was a coincidence."

"Coincidence, eh?" Einstein rubbed his stubbly skull. "If you say so, Max."

"Is there a fugitive loose in Cavernstone Grey?" Mrs. Crumlin shouted down the hall. Max could see her in the kitchen doorway drying a saucepan.

"That's right, Mrs. Crumlin, a young girl," answered Einstein. "The Dark Brigade captured the father and they're tracking the girl as we speak."

Max could feel himself sweating profusely under his flannel pajamas. They'll never catch Rose, he told himself, she's fast and clever and she'll outwit them every time. But he still worried.

Einstein grinned. "Nobody defies the High Echelon and gets away with it, eh, Max?"

Max nodded, wishing he could sink into the floor. If only he were more like Rose, whip smart and always with a quick answer.

"I've got to run—tomorrow's the deadline for the jingle contest!" said Einstein, reaching for the door. "I'll keep you posted!"

"Mind the draft!" squawked Mrs. Crumlin and Max jumped back. Einstein hurried out, slamming the door shut.

"What do you know about this runaway girl?" Mrs. Crumlin stomped down the hall, gazing at Max with flinty eyes. "Is there something you need to tell me?"

"I don't know about any runaways," he mumbled, feeling his cheeks flush.

"It would be unwise to hide any secrets from the High Echelon,

Maxwell. Surely you are aware that the consequences would be severe." She pressed her lips into a tight line. "*Extremely* severe."

Max winced. The thought struck him that Mrs. Crumlin might actually *enjoy* reporting him to the authorities and seeing him hauled off to jail.

"Absolutely nothing gets past the High Echelon," she went on. "They've installed cameras everywhere. Any wrongdoings will be quickly discovered. As you know, Children's Prison is filled with young people who thought they were smarter than the authorities."

"I told you," said Max, staring down at his slippers, "I don't know anything." Mrs. Crumlin had made them and the fabric was bright red with tiny yellow suns—suns that matched the ugly tattoo on the back of his neck.

He found it hard to swallow. Had the authorities filmed him and Rose racing around Cavernstone Hall, he wondered, with Rose making messes everywhere she went? Were there pictures of them wandering through The Ruins? He shuddered, sick with fear. He could feel his life closing in on him like a folding spyglass.

"You haven't been yourself lately, Maxwell. I confess I'm a bit worried. Care to talk about it?"

The suns on his slippers danced in circles. He felt queasy looking at them. "I think I'll go to bed, Mrs. Crumlin. I can feel one of my headaches coming on."

"You're hiding something from me," she said, brushing her dress with the flat of her hand. Flour drifted to the floor in a powdery shower. "I know you are."

Max felt his ears burn. He hated how she niggled her way into his brain, trying to pick it apart. But she could ask all she wanted—he'd never give Rose away.

From the kitchen came the blast of the radio announcer: "Citizens can now breathe a sigh of relief when it comes to protecting our borders and guarding our new domes! Authorities announced today the development of a highly intelligent, expertly trained attack animal capable of flight and charged with restoring order in the country. Designed by government scientists in the most advanced laboratories in the world, these new weapons will be released into the wild on the seventh of July, the same day citizens move into the domes."

Max froze, trying to suppress a hysterical fear rising inside him. The announcer was talking about *skræks*! He dug his palms into his forehead, trying to ward off the headache.

Mrs. Crumlin gave him a push toward the stairs. "Go up to your room and have a little think," she said. "Try to remember if there isn't something you've forgotten to tell me, Maxwell. Later on we'll have a friendly chat, all right?"

But Max didn't answer.

As he flopped back on the pillows, Max heard the doorbell chime. It must be Einstein, he thought, probably he's left a book behind. Then a scarier thought struck him: what if the Dark Brigade was here with their lie detector machines? He leapt out of bed and tore out of the room.

Heart pounding, he leaned over the stair rail, peering down into the hall. Then, remembering last time, he stepped back into the shadows so he wouldn't be seen.

"Do come in, Doctor," he heard Mrs. Crumlin say in a jolly voice. "I trust that unkempt beast is tied up on the porch?"

What was Dr. Tredegar doing here? Max wondered. His usual day was Tuesday.

"Did you hear the news?" the doctor asked Mrs. Crumlin. "They're releasing the skræks as planned."

"Oh yes, they've just announced it on the radio!" she said excitedly.

"How are things with the boy? Giving him plenty of desserts and hot cocoa, I presume," Dr. Tredegar said in a furtive voice. "Notice any changes: memory lapses, headaches, that sort of thing?"

"Headaches, yes. Such a strange, distant child, locks himself in his room for hours at a time." Mrs. Crumlin reached into her apron pocket. "I did find this, however, inside his jacket." Max watched her hand over a crumpled piece of paper and his heart sank. His owl's secret message! How could he have been so careless, leaving it in his pocket?

"Probably encrypted," muttered the doctor, holding the paper up to the light. "I'll take it to the lab, see what they can do."

"And the twelve?" Her voice was so low Max had to strain to hear. "How are things coming along with them?"

"The chosen twelve are progressing nicely. We've moved them to a facility in Sengeneth for extra training."

"Ah, the hills of Sengeneth. Lovely."

"The facility head jokingly refers to them as the 'Twelve Henchmen of Sengeneth.'" Max could almost see the doctor's dark, sardonic smile. "Has a poetic ring to it, wouldn't you say?"

"Indeed it does," replied Mrs. Crumlin, her voice filled with admiration. "Maxwell!" she trilled. "Come out of your room, you have a visitor!"

Max waited a few moments, then yelled down, "I don't need a doctor! I'm not sick!"

"Just a moment of your time, Maxwell." Dr. Tredegar materialized at the bottom of the stairs, his red and white blazer glimmering in the dark. "Hurry!"

Max shuffled down, mulling over the conversation he'd just heard, and joined them in the parlor. Sliding into the rocking chair, he barely glanced at Mrs. Crumlin, planted in her favorite doily-covered armchair. The doctor, slender as an insect, was perched on a wicker footstool.

Judging by their serious expressions, this was a meeting of some significance. Maybe at last, he thought, they were going to level with him about his injections. It was about time.

From the porch came a desperate bark. Through the window Max could see the shaggy black dog straining at its leash.

"Perhaps you should put that animal out of its misery, Dr. Tredegar," said Mrs. Crumlin.

The doctor flashed a sharklike smile. Max noticed that his square yellow teeth needed a good brushing. "Excellent hunter, that hound. Very quick at catching owls."

Picturing his silver owl, Max felt the words stab at his heart.

"The reason I've come today," began the doctor, clicking open his medicine bag, "is because you need an extra boost, Maxwell. Your twelfth birthday is approaching, as is your apprenticeship. Since you are growing older, you'll require higher doses of medicine to stabilize your condition." His eyes darted back and forth behind his tinted lenses. "I'm stepping up your injections to twice a week."

Higher doses of *what*? Max clenched his hands to stop them from shaking. "I want to know about side effects," he said. "What are they?" He had never before questioned anything the doctor told him.

Dr. Tredegar lifted an eyebrow at this. "None at all."

"What's the medicine you're giving me?" demanded Max boldly. "I want to know the name!"

The doctor riffled through his bag. "The serum combines various medications," he said in a testy voice. "The name is of no importance." He waved his hand dismissively and busied himself with the InjectaPort.

Mrs. Crumlin threw Max a warning look. "We haven't time for silly questions."

Max knew Dr. Tredegar was hiding the truth from him and he was sick of it. "Why are you giving me so many injections? I want to know!" Angry, he leapt out of the rocker. "Why don't you tell me the truth?"

Mrs. Crumlin clucked her tongue. "Let's not get hyperfrenetic, Maxwell, it won't do to get agitated." She sat him back down, a little too roughly. "He's been poorly lately, Doctor, not at all himself."

"Perhaps a sedative?" murmured Dr. Tredegar, his lips twitching.

Alarms buzzed inside Max's head. Why had the doctor asked Mrs. Crumlin about desserts and cocoa drinks? He thought back to all the mugs of hot cocoa, the bitter cakes and muffins he'd eaten over the years. The tablets for headaches and fevers, the home remedies for upset stomachs. Was Rose right? Were they slowly poisoning him, killing off his memories? He just couldn't figure out *why*.

"Arm at the ready," ordered Mrs. Crumlin.

Out of habit, Max obediently thrust out his arm.

Dr. Tredegar held up the InjectaPort. "Rick rack ruin—"

Mrs. Crumlin joined in: "Over before—"

The doctor crept forward on tiptoes. "You can say—" His sour breath reminded Max of Mrs. Crumlin's pickled slugs.

The InjectaPort was inches away from Max's arm. He stared at the bubbling liquid and, remembering the bleeding skræk, felt sick.

"Crimson—"

"No!" shouted Max, leaping up, knocking into the floor lamp. "I don't want you jabbing me, you needle-happy old man!" He kicked the lamp. "You're lying, both of you, you're trying to control my brain!" Losing his temper was something he'd never done before. With spiteful glee, he kicked again.

The lamp swayed precariously and fell, crashing onto the card table. The table collapsed, sending Mrs. Crumlin's jigsaw puzzle into the air. With a kind of perverse satisfaction, Max watched 1,001 puzzle pieces go flying all over the room.

"Maxwell!" shrieked Mrs. Crumlin, red blotches creeping up to her chin.

Whenever Mrs. Crumlin became agitated, she always broke out in hives. Serves her right, thought Max, the ridiculous old bat.

"What have you done, you little fool!" snarled Dr. Tredegar, not at all his usual pleasant self. "Mrs. Crumlin spent hours on that dome puzzle!"

"I know what you're giving me!" yelled Max. "It's genetically engineered blood!"

The adults froze, staring at him with open mouths.

"And this!" He pointed to his neck. "You said my sun mark was a birthmark! That's a lie! It's a tattoo and the High Echelon put it there!"

Mrs. Crumlin and the doctor exchanged glances that he couldn't quite understand.

"Someone is feeding you misinformation," said Dr. Tredegar, eyeing Max warily. "Whom have you been talking to?"

Blood rushed to Max's head. "You think I don't know anything!" he shouted, voice cracking. "Well, I know plenty!" Of course, he only had his suspicions. Sorting this out was like trying to piece together one of Mrs. Crumlin's giant jigsaws.

The doctor made a grab for his arm. "You're not going anywhere," he snarled, steering Max into the nearest chair. "Sit!" His insectile fingers dug into Max's shoulders as he pushed him down.

Max looked up in surprise. Today he was seeing a new and startling Dr. Tredegar, not the mild-mannered gentleman he had known for years. He struggled to get away, but the doctor held him in a rock-solid grip.

Mrs. Crumlin sat down across from Max, clasping her pudgy hands. "The sun mark means you have been selected by the High Echelon for a most important job. That is why they sent me to be your guardian."

I knew it, he thought, glowering at her. Mrs. Crumlin was a puppet hired by the High Echelon. Still, he was confused. If the government hated Night Seers like Rose said it did, why had a guardian been sent to protect him? Even more mystifying was why the High Echelon would care about some kid whose granny was a rebel and kept banned books in her house.

"Why is there a creature with the same tattoo as me?" he blurted out.

There was a stunned silence from the adults.

"Don't say skræks aren't real!" he cried. "I heard you talking about them just now!"

Unruffled, Mrs. Crumlin turned to the doctor. "I think I know what this is about, Dr. Tredegar. You see, there is a runaway child in town and I daresay our Maxwell has made a new friend." Her eyes narrowed to thin slits. "I knew you were keeping something from me, Maxwell Unger."

"I wasn't!" he yelled. "I don't know any runaways!"

"Lying will get you nowhere fast." Mrs. Crumlin heaved a great sigh. "Very well, Phineas, let the boy go." She smoothed her dress and the apron over it. "The authorities have granted me permission to discuss Maxwell's future."

Max felt Dr. Tredegar relax his ironclad grip.

"Until this week I had orders to keep silent," she began. "Now I can talk about your apprenticeship, which is linked to the government's exciting new defense strategy."

Max went rigid. Were they going to make him a Dark Brigadier? The thought of wearing a mask, goggles and the High Echelon's standard-issue cape, and marching in lines and shooting rifles at owls revolted him.

"I won't join the military!" he shouted. "I hate uniforms! I'll go AWOL!" He wasn't sure what AWOL meant, but he knew it wasn't good.

"Let me finish!" she snapped. "You will be training a special attack animal to defend our domes and keep the borders safe."

Max flashed back on the plague wolf with its spiky fur, sharp teeth and foaming mouth. "Train *wolves*?" he asked shakily, going cold all over.

"What nonsense! Wolves have been extinct for decades," replied the doctor, his voice tense.

Liar, thought Max, but he said nothing.

Face flushed, Mrs. Crumlin leaned forward. "Foolish child, I'm talking about a creature with superior fighting talent, designed by the smartest scientists in the world. It attacks, destroys and always wins because it has *no fear*."

Her last two words were like a blow to the head. "*Skræks!*" whispered Max. A deep and profound terror flooded his body, and his stomach turned. "I—I—" he stuttered. "I won't do it, those things are disgusting! It's not in my nature!"

"Oh, but we have medicine to alleviate your fears," said Dr. Tredegar reassuringly. "And we have ways of changing *your* nature as well," he added darkly.

Max could hardly breathe. He had no doubt that at last they were telling him the truth, but he didn't want to hear it.

"What works in your favor, Maxwell," said Mrs. Crumlin, "is that these creatures have no eyes." She smiled uncertainly. Her pale, doughy face reminded Max of an underbaked cookie.

"Attempts were made to graft eyes onto the skræks," explained Dr. Tredegar. "But the transplants failed. Unfortunate, that."

Max felt his stomach twist at the memory of the squirming body, the torn wings, the *missing eyes*. "No!" he screamed. "I won't do it!"

With a fierce cry of despair, he doubled over. How could this possibly be his destiny, training gene-spliced mutants to kill?

"The High Echelon selected you years ago, Maxwell, when Project Skræk was in its infancy. You were considered perfect for the role," twittered Mrs. Crumlin. "They were looking for a smooth stone amid the broken ones, a tabula rasa, as it were, untainted by civilization, a child of the Prophecy, plucked from a state of naïveté." Her eyes shone feverishly. "That would be *you*, Maxwell. For the High Echelon decrees there can only be one Skræk Master."

"You're out of your mind!" he cried, his voice at once disgusted and incredulous. What was all this talk about stones and prophecies? Mrs. Crumlin was obviously delusional. Maybe she'd listened to too many episodes of *Flamingo Valley*.

"When everyone from Cavernstone Grey moves into the domes, you will move in with the skræks." Mrs. Crumlin clasped her hands to her bosom. "You'll need to familiarize yourself with them, of course, learn their ways and so forth. I've no doubt you'll adjust in time. And of course you will be given hardworking assistants."

"The word *skræk* comes from old Danish," said the doctor with a wink. "Translated, it means *fear*."

Max stared at him, appalled.

"Skræks are rather unpleasant creatures, I'll grant you that," chimed in Mrs. Crumlin. "Still, they are a marvelous experiment, genetically designed to protect us from radicals, traitors, runaways and the like. They will hunt our enemies down and, if necessary, exterminate them."

Max's stomach did a double flip. He didn't need anyone to explain the meaning of *exterminate*.

"Of course, their main objective will be to seek out and destroy any remaining silver owls." Her voice struck a gleeful note. "No one will be safe in this country until each and every one is eradicated."

Max stiffened. They wanted him to kill the things he loved most? Was this their plan, to twist his love of silver owls into something hateful and repulsive?

"The High Echelon thinks of everything—including the no-fear gene." Mrs. Crumlin's tone was falsely soothing. "These injections will make your Transmutation much easier. No fear, Maxwell, think of it. And your conscience will be crystal clear. No feelings of guilt at all."

Max looked at her, stunned. He would be no better than a robot, without thought or emotion. And the no-fear gene—that was the one Rose had told him about, the gene they were selling on the black market!

"I won't!" he shouted. "You can't make me!"

Ignoring his outburst, Mrs. Crumlin continued: "The Transmutation takes place the day before your twelfth birthday, just before midnight. The timing could not be more perfect."

"No!" bellowed Max.

"Let's get on with this, shall we?" growled the doctor. "Steady the boy's arm, Mrs. Crumlin."

Max looked up to see Dr. Tredegar skulking toward him with the InjectaPort. No way, he told himself, I'm not letting that lunatic near me anymore.

The doctor took another step and Max leapt out of the chair. "Get away!" he screamed, and raced out of the room. Before they could nab him, he bolted upstairs.

CHAPTER FIFTEEN

Max turned the key in the lock and dragged a chair against his bedroom door. Tears streaming down his face, he dove beneath the quilt.

Okay, so Mrs. Crumlin and the doctor had finally come clean and told him the truth. But what good was truth when they were sneaking no-fear genes into him and gearing him up for a life of killing things and living with mutant monsters? They were planning to change him, perhaps in some irreversible way—and the thought terrified him.

It was clear that they had been plotting behind his back for years.

What an idiot he'd been, listening to their stupid lies. Didn't they realize that he was Max Unger, the boy who loved owls? He was the kid who waited under the owl tree every night for the Owl Keeper to come. He would rather die than kill anything—especially an owl.

Downstairs he could hear Mrs. Crumlin and the doctor having a long, drawn-out conversation. Who were the mysterious twelve they had talked about, he wondered, who were being trained in a facility in Sengeneth? And what were they being trained to do?

Their muffled voices drifted up, filling Max with anguish and rage. He burrowed deeper under the quilt, trying to shut them out, while disquieting thoughts filled his head. Did his parents know anything about his apprenticeship? Were they part of the High Echelon's plot—or had they been deceived too?

Sobbing, he fell into a dreamless sleep.

He was startled awake by a knock at the door. Outside his window he could see the two moons, rising against a cold black sky.

"Are you awake, Max?" his father called in a weary voice. "Aren't you coming down for dinner?"

"Go away!" shouted Max, choking back a sob. He wasn't ready to face his parents. "Leave me alone!"

His gaze traveled around the room, resting on his collection of odd-shaped stones, his jar of found objects, an empty lizard bowl, a model wind-borne vessel tied to a strand of wire. All these things were going to disappear soon, when his parents moved to the dome and Cavernstone Grey was demolished.

His father gave another timid knock. "Max?"

"I hate you! I hate all of you!"

"Let me know when you're ready to talk," mumbled his father, sounding dejected. But Max didn't care; all he wanted was to be left alone.

The world around him seemed utterly black. His chest ached every time he thought about Rose. Where was she? Had she found a safe place to hide? He knew what would happen if they caught her: she'd be sent to Children's Prison and he'd never see her again.

He envisioned her knotted hair, smelling of leaves and tree sap, her green eyes flecked with gold. The way she swung so expertly from the branches of trees, spiders falling from her long coat. Her silly high laugh, her lopsided smile. He even missed her bossy voice.

He had never had a true friend before—not a human friend, anyway, not someone like Rose. She was gutsy, unique, like the deadly purple sphinx. And once, beneath the owl tree, she had kissed the top of his ear, making his heart racket inside his chest.

Max was so distraught that he realized he was coming down with a fever. Chilled and semi-delirious, shivering all over, he stayed in bed, sweat rolling off his forehead, the quilt hiked up to his chin, thumbing through *Owls of the Wild*. But the words jumped around on the pages too much, so he returned the book to its hiding place under the closet floorboards.

The next morning Mrs. Crumlin left a bowl of turnip soup outside his door. Max ignored it, vowing never to eat her poisoned food again. All through the morning and early afternoon he stayed in bed, drifting in and out of sleep until late afternoon, when a knock at the front door woke him.

He jumped out of bed, rushed to the top of the stairs and leaned over the railing. Down in the hallway he saw Einstein handing Mrs. Crumlin a sheaf of papers. "Sorry to hear Max is sick," Einstein said. "Hope he gets better soon."

"Just between you and me, I think it's all in his head," Mrs. Crumlin replied. "Never mind about him, tell me the latest news."

Max gripped the wooden rail until his knuckles turned white. "Not Rose," he whispered to himself. "Please don't let it be Rose—"

"The Dark Brigade's identified the runaway they caught two weeks ago," Einstein announced. "A man named Eccles, ex-ecology professor from Scattersea, next town over. Fancies himself an intellectual revolutionary, dead set against the High Echelon's policies. A traitor!" he added with a sneer.

It saddened Max to hear Einstein talk that way, knowing his friend's attitude was fueled by the High Echelon's lies. But hadn't Rose said she came from Tattersall Heath? It was hard to know what to believe from her anymore.

"This Eccles fellow will get his comeuppance," said Mrs. Crumlin in a self-satisfied voice. She gave a low chuckle and Einstein joined in.

Their laughter struck Max as cruel and smug. He had never noticed before just how fanatical they were.

"And that's not all, Mrs. Crumlin!" said Einstein in a voice that made Max's stomach lurch. "The Dark Brigade nearly caught the runaway girl yesterday! My uncle Phineas joined in the chase, and you'll never guess what happened!"

Holding his breath, Max listened with a growing sense of dread.

"My uncle devised this contraption, see, for shooting poison darts at wild animals—slows them down to a crawl. So he shoots this dart at the girl and it's tipped with some new experimental drug. She won't get far, because in two days or so her vision will be messed up and—bingo!—they'll nab her."

Mrs. Crumlin gave a low chuckle. "Oh my word, that's Phineas Tredegar for you, coming up with another brilliant invention! I've always said he was a genius."

The two of them started laughing again.

Horrified, Max backed away, their manic laughter ringing in his ears. *Rose! They blinded Rose!*

He fled to his room, locking the door behind him, and sat trembling on his bed, trying to calm himself. Where was Rose now? He had to save her from the Dark Brigade! But how? What about the High Echelon and its creatures? What about his allergies to sunlight?

The other option was to stand his ground and fight them all to the bitter end. Who am I kidding? he asked himself, I wouldn't stand a chance.

He ached to know where Rose was hiding and whether she was safe. Without her father, Max knew she was totally alone, running from the Dark Brigade, with no one to turn to—except him.

He had to find her.

Late that night, certain that his parents were asleep, Max slipped out the back door and raced downhill to the moonlit grassy field. The air was frigid and he wondered if Rose was warm enough in her ratty old coat and rubber boots.

He wore three sweaters, one on top of the other, knowing he might be waiting all night for Rose to turn up. She was bound to come, he told himself, she had no place else to go. But what if she couldn't see because of the poison dart? How would she find her way to the tree?

The moment he saw the owl tree, with no Rose swinging from a branch, Max got choked up. Her absence, he realized, was as if the two moons had been ripped from the sky, leaving a black hole behind.

With alarm he noticed something new: a length of tape wrapped around the tree, cordoning it off. Puzzled, he ran over. Tied to stakes hammered into the ground, the tape was bright red with yellow suns. Max's heart sank. The High Echelon was planning to cut down the owl tree!

Panic raced through him. Where was his owl? Looking up into the tree, he searched the branches for her, giving a few wild hoots. But he was so upset he sounded more like a sick frog.

He hooted again. At last he saw the silver owl, looking bedraggled, staring down reproachfully from the top of the tree. Relief washed over him. She was safe!

But he could see that her feathers drooped and her good eye wasn't as bright as usual. Suddenly he was afraid for her. Did she realize the danger she was in? If the Dark Brigade found her, she wouldn't be able to save herself because of her broken wing!

"Oh little owl, you're still here!" he cried, climbing onto a low branch. "I wanted to come last night, but I was sick with a fever."

The owl hopped down from branch to branch and snuggled against his jacket, as if to say she forgave him. She looked a bit frightened, he thought.

"The Dark Brigade were here today, weren't they? I don't know what I'd do if anything happened to you," said Max, extracting a thistle from her wing. "Everything's in a mess: Rose is on the run, my future's a disaster, and Mrs. Crumlin found your secret message"—his eyes filled with tears—"and now you're going to lose your home!" He held his owl close, marveling at the pure silver of her wings. "I want to take you and Rose someplace safe! I want to run away but I'm too scared!"

The owl regarded him with luminous eyes. If he understood owl language, she would probably answer with comforting words. Her sadness was palpable; it tore at his heart.

"I have to find Rose," he said determinedly. He found a peach in his knapsack and offered it to his owl. "I was sure she'd be here." The owl nibbled daintily, but when she had finished she still looked sad. "It's not midnight yet. I think she'll come."

The owl regarded him with her magnificent solemn eyes. Most of the time her expression was serene. But not tonight—tonight she seemed to emanate sadness and fear.

The two sat on the branch, being sad together. From his perch in the owl tree, Max watched the dark rushing river far below. If he squinted he could see the glowing eyes of the Misshapens, bobbing through the forest on the other side. Their eyes chilled him to the bone.

Hours passed. The night grew colder. Clinging to the tree trunk, Max fell into a dreamless sleep.

The owl hooted, jolting him awake, and he nearly fell from the branch. He could hear a rustling at the base of the tree. Was it a wolf? His heart stopped. He didn't know if plague wolves could climb trees.

Boots thumped, grass crackled. It sounded like the Dark Brigade.

Max pictured them marching through the field in their outrageous capes and goggles, lie detectors strapped to their backs. He shook with fear and his heart pounded crazily. There was nowhere to hide; he was trapped in the middle of a field.

"Max?" croaked a thin voice. "Are you there?"

Max hesitated. Was this a trick to draw him out into the open? The silver owl flapped from a branch, hooting at him. He peered down through the leaves and saw a girl in a long coat and oversized boots, hair sticking out in a hundred directions. His heart leapt for joy.

"Rose!" he cried, scrambling down the trunk.

Slumped against the tree was Rose—unwashed, wild-eyed and sleepless—her coat in tatters. Dark circles beneath her eyes gave her a scary, witchlike appearance.

"Rose, it's really you!" Max threw his arms around her. "I was afraid I'd never see you again!"

Rose gave him a listless hug and he could tell her heart wasn't in it. She was exhausted—probably hungry, too. He noticed she seemed extra-thin, as if she'd snap in two if he squeezed too hard.

"You're not safe here!" he gasped. "The Dark Brigade's looking for you!"

"I know, Max, the town's crawling with them. They chased me all over the place and someone shot an arrow at me!" Rose's eyes flashed angrily. "It went through my coat and stuck right here, in my arm, but I pulled it out."

Max sucked in his breath.

"It didn't hurt much," she said, and he could tell she was trying to sound brave. "I was so angry, Max! *I'm* the one called Artemis, *I'm* the huntress—it should be me shooting arrows at them!"

"Are you okay?" asked Max, wondering nervously how the poisoned arrow had affected her vision. "Can you see me?"

Rose pulled away, staring at him with haunted eyes. It looked to Max as if the light had gone out of them.

"Course I can see you," she said, frowning. "You look like the same goofy kid as always. Got any food? I'm starving."

Max breathed a sigh of relief. Rose hadn't been blinded after all! Maybe, he told himself, the experimental medicine had been faulty, or the dose too low.

"I've got peaches," he said, searching through his knapsack.

"What's with the red tape around the tree?" she asked as he handed her a peach.

"The Dark Brigade was here! They marked the owl tree." A weary sadness fell over him. One by one, the High Echelon was taking away the things he cared about most. "I guess they'll cut it down soon."

"Told you, didn't I?"

While Rose devoured the fruit, Max noticed with alarm that her hands were raw and bleeding, and there was a nasty scrape down the side of her face.

"I forgot the thermos," he said, feeling bad. "Sorry, there's nothing to drink."

Max thought guiltily of his comfortable bed, his warm house and its well-stocked pantry. While he'd been sulking in his room, Rose had been running, hiding, scavenging for food. How could he feel sorry for himself when he lived in comfort and security?

"That's okay, owl boy." Rose huddled against the bark, gnawing on the peach. "I don't trust Crumlin's hot cocoa anyway."

Max had never seen her so shaken. He was used to Rose being bossy and confident, but now it seemed all the fight had gone out of her. Should he tell her that the arrow was a poison-tipped dart? Was this the right time to mention it? Somehow he didn't think so. What if it made her even more disheartened?

Rose gave a tired sigh as she lifted a clump of hair from her neck. Max caught a flash of yellow. "A tattoo!" he said.

"Don't you know anything, Max Unger? I'm a Night Seer, same as you. They marked me for the diamond mines."

It hadn't occurred to him that Rose must have a tattoo as well. But of course she did—he remembered her mentioning it the night she told him about the Mark of the Owl. Intrigued, he asked, "Can I see it?"

She leaned forward, pushing a strand of knotted hair off the nape of her neck. In the light of the two moons Max could see the diamond-shaped tattoo. He traced it slowly with his index finger.

"It feels kind of rough," he said, wondering how many other kids their age had similar tattoos. "If I squinch up my eyes, I can see your owl mark underneath." It was sad to think that the Night Seers had been banished to the darkness, when once they had been magical and revered, able to understand the language of silver owls.

"My dad and I ran away before the High Echelon could take me off to the mines." Rose used her sleeve to wipe her mouth. "We had this plan, see, we were going to spring my mom out of jail." She had eaten every bit of the peach and was sucking on the pit.

"Your mother's in *jail*?" said Max, caught off guard. He felt hurt and angry. This was one more secret Rose had kept from him. "Why didn't you tell me? I mean, people get arrested every day in this country—it's nothing to be embarrassed about!"

Rose got a little haughty then, but that only endeared her to Max. It was like the old Rose. "I'm not embarrassed!" she bristled. "I'm proud of her! Her name is Violet Silvertree-Eccles—it's hyphenated—and they took her to prison when I was eight. But I don't like to talk about it."

Max winced, thinking of other parents who had been taken away by the Dark Brigade. As far as he knew, none of them had returned. His own parents never mentioned the subject, but Mrs. Crumlin was always quick to condemn, saying the High Echelon never arrested anyone without good reason. He realized now that the opposite was true, that ordinary people were being arrested for speaking against the government.

"My mother used to write letters," Rose continued. "They came folded up in skinny envelopes with words crossed out in black ink. I answered every single one."

"Who would cross words out?" Max wondered why Rose had said "used to." Didn't her mother write letters anymore?

"I hate the Dark Brigade! My life got wrecked because of them! It's their fault my family got busted up." Rose punched the air with her fist. "My mom's in a high-security prison in the Low Dreadlands. I'm going to crack that jail cell wide open and spring her out! Want to come with me, Max?"

"Sure, Rose." Max smiled just a little. Maybe Rose hadn't lost her spunkiness after all. "I'll help you fight the Dark Brigade, because I hate them too." Poor kid, he thought, she's all by herself—she's like an orphan with no one to look after her.

"Anyway, it doesn't matter." Her voice grew shaky. "The letters stopped coming."

Max stared at her dirty face and scuffed knuckles and bleeding hands. He hadn't had a chance yet to tell her about his own problems and what the High Echelon had planned for him, but he knew this wasn't the time. He could see she needed to talk.

"We've been running for weeks, me and my dad, hiding in empty buildings." She flicked the peach pit into the grass. "The Tarian hid us in a barn on the other side of Cavernstone Grey." She stared at Max with sorrowful eyes. "Two days ago the Dark Brigade turned up. My dad pushed me through a trapdoor, then they stormed in and dragged him away. He didn't have time to hide!" Her face crumpled and Max's heart fell as she burst into tears. "I don't know where they took him!"

The owl fluffed her wings and gave a mournful hoot. Rose, calming down a little, reached out to stroke her feathers.

Max put a hand on Rose's shoulder. She hiccuped. He couldn't bear to see her so upset.

"It's my fault," she said, looking downcast. "My dad said it was time to move on, but I wheedled him into staying a little longer, because . . . well, because of you, Max, and the silver owl and all the adventures we were having. He didn't know I was sneaking out in the nights to see you—he thought I was asleep in the hayloft!"

Max blushed. Rose had wanted to stay because of *him*? Guilt crept over him: that meant her father's capture was Max's fault! Rose and her father should have been miles away by now, making plans to rescue her mother.

"But you told me your dad was sending you out on night missions! You said you were checking out places like Cavernstone Hall and The Ruins and reporting back to him!"

Rose hung her head. "Yeah, I know." She hiccuped again. "I made all that stuff up."

"Rose," he said, looking her square in the face. "Your dad's been gone more than two days. Einstein told me they caught him two weeks ago! You've been on your own all this time—why didn't you tell me, Rose?"

Her eyes grew wet with tears again as she began to sob.

"Please don't cry," pleaded Max, brushing away her tears with his mitten. "Listen, we can have more adventures." His mind raced. "We'll go looking for the Owl Keeper! We'll find the path from the song and follow it—"

What was he saying? He'd never leave Cavernstone Grey, no matter how much his world imploded. The town was surrounded by forests filled with plague wolves, Misshapens and skræks. The Dark Brigade was lurking everywhere. He had his allergy to sunlight to think about. He could never run away, he told himself.

Rose looked up expectantly. "The Owl Keeper has special magical powers, right?"

"Of course he does," Max replied with false confidence—as if the solution were that simple.

Rose gave a weak smile. "Well, in that case, he can help us both."

"Sure he can," mumbled Max, furious with himself for making a promise he knew he would never keep.

He glanced guiltily over at the silver owl. The owl tilted her head, as if she were considering what he'd just said.

CHAPTER SIXTEEN

Quietly they crept in through the back door, sneaking through the kitchen and hallway, up the staircase to Max's bedroom. He sat Rose down on his bed and wrapped the quilt around her. The only friend who'd ever been in his room before was Einstein. He'd helped Max with long division and an essay called "Famous Leaders of the High Echelon."

Rose was so exhausted she leaned against the wall, already half asleep. He knew he had to hide her, but where? The cellar? The attic? Under the porch? There was no place where Mrs. Crumlin didn't snoop, especially since finding the owl's secret message.

"Wait here," he told Rose, and rushed downstairs. He whizzed around the kitchen, boiling up milk and honey, returning with a full thermos and a steaming mug for Rose. It felt a little strange being responsible for someone else, since in the past he'd been the one being looked after. Still, it was a good feeling. The word, Max decided, was *chivalrous:* he felt like a knight of old.

"Here, eat something," he said, tossing a bag of cookies, a loaf of bread and a slab of cheese on the bed. "They're all from the store," he added, in case she was worried about being poisoned.

Rose took a sip of the warm drink, but before she could take a bite of something to eat she'd nodded off. Max caught the mug before it spilled on the quilt. "Wake up!" he whispered, shaking her gently. She looked so tired he was afraid she might fall asleep and not wake up again. Her face was white and her eyes were sunken, with black rings underneath that worried him. What kind of drug had Dr. Tredegar placed on the tip of that dart?

"Maybe I should go where your owl was going," she said in a groggy voice. "To the sea."

"I *think* that's where she was going. The message in her beak was about ships." He considered for a moment. "How far is the sea?"

Max knew about the sea from Gran, who had been there as a young girl. The sea, she said, was endless and beautiful, filled with glassy waves and terrifying creatures that didn't need air to breathe.

"The sea is a long way," said Rose in a hoarse whisper.

"Did I ever tell you about my shell?" he said, trying to keep her awake. Gran had given him the shell as a memento of her childhood. "It was my granny's when she was little."

Much to his relief, Rose perked up. Her eyes blinked and she sat up straighter. Max took it as a hopeful sign.

"A real seashell?" She looked impressed. "My dad says all the shells disappeared when the ice sheets melted and the cities sank! There were tons of shells before the Great Destruction, but they got churned up and crushed under the sea. The only shells left are flukes."

"Sounds like me: a fluke," said Max, trying to make a joke. Seeing Rose's puzzled expression, he added: "You know, because I'm allergic to sunlight. I wasn't always, though—when Gran was alive I spent every minute of my time outdoors."

"You are a strange one," murmured Rose. "Can I see your special seashell?"

Max was lifting the loose floorboard in the closet when the doorbell chimed, followed by strong knocks that echoed throughout the house. He stiffened, not daring to breathe. They never got very many visitors, but no one ever came to the house after dark.

"Max!" hissed Rose. "What's that noise?"

The knocking started again, louder this time. Terror raced through him. The doorbell chimed, over and over. Whoever it is, he thought, they're not giving up.

He pocketed the shell and grabbed *Owls of the Wild*. Through the closet wall he heard his parents moving around in their bedroom. Their door clicked open. "Coming, I'm coming!" called his father.

Max rushed out of the closet. He heard his parents' footsteps on the stairs. Frantic thoughts whirled through his brain. He had to hide Rose!

Panic-stricken, he turned to her. "Quick! Someone's here!"

Rose sprinted to his closet and dove inside. "I smell dirty socks!" came her muffled voice as he shut the door behind her.

He crept out into the hallway and peered down the stairs to the first floor. His parents stood in flannel robes at the front door, looking up at a freakishly tall man in octagonal night goggles, a crepe mouth mask and a dark cape that buttoned to his throat. He towered threateningly over them.

Max felt his pulse thrumming inside his ears.

"Our Maxwell?" his mother was saying in disbelief. "But he's such a timid boy!" A chill went through Max at the sound of his name. "Max has never been a troublemaker. He'd never dream of doing such a thing!"

The man muttered something that Max didn't catch.

"Our son doesn't know any runaway girls!" said his father in a shaky voice. "Maxwell has a condition: he can't go outside because of his allergies to sunlight. He never sees other children! Listen, why not come back tomorrow, we'll sort this out—"

Ignoring him, the frightening Dark Brigadier elbowed past, barreling into the hallway. Max stood frozen, staring, and his legs turned to jelly.

"You can't barge in here!" protested his mother, surprising Max with her defiant words.

He watched in horror as a second goggled man, humpbacked and burly, wearing a cloak that hung to the floor, pushed his way into the hallway. "Orders is orders," he snarled through his mask. "The boy comes with us tonight." He shoved Max's father aside, knocking him into the wall.

· 148 ·

In blind terror Max fled to his room, locking the door behind him. Rose stumbled out of the closet. "That is the vilest-smelling—"

"The Dark Brigade's here!" He threw her a bobbled hat and mittens. There was no time to talk. "Let's go!"

Rose pulled on her boots and rushed to the window. Flinging it open, she stuck her head out. "This way!" she shouted to Max. "Over the roof!"

He grabbed his knapsack, stuffing in the owl book and Gran's shell, along with a moth-eaten blanket, a bulky sweater, the food and the thermos. He could hear the Dark Brigadiers downstairs, slamming doors and shouting, their leather boots thudding over the floors, shaking the house and rattling the windows.

"Max!" cried Rose.

He turned to see her thin shape framed in the window. Then he heard footsteps on the stairs. Rose hopped over the sill and disappeared.

The bedroom doorknob rattled. "Max!" shouted his father. "Unlock this door!"

Max hoisted the knapsack over one shoulder. He didn't want to leave this way, without a word of explanation, but he had no choice. His father trusted him implicitly, and Max had never disobeyed him, but there was no time to say anything.

He scrabbled through the window, out onto the porch roof, willing himself not to look down. Even one story off the ground was too high for him.

Overhead, stars burned fiercely against the black sky. He could see Rose crab-walking below him across the roof tiles. Heart thudding, he followed her and crawled to the roof's edge, hoping the treads on his boots were as sturdy as the catalog advertised.

Rose slid off the roof and down a pillar to the back porch. She stood on the porch rail, steadying Max as he reached down. The rusted gutter crumbled in his hand and he froze, staring in panic at the ground below.

"It's easy, Max!" Rose shouted up. "Pretend you're climbing down the owl tree!"

Gazing at the dead leaves blowing, he emptied his mind of thoughts. Just go, he told himself. He swallowed a deep breath and gripped the wooden post.

His parents' bedroom window shot open. "Max, are you out there?" came his mother's frightened voice. There was no time to think. He leaned over, wrapping his arms around the post, and, without answering, shimmied down.

Tiny snowflakes struck his face. The soles of his boots touched the porch rail. Shivering wildly, he hugged the post, afraid if he jumped he'd break an arm or a leg. His mother called to him again.

Max let go, and the weight of his knapsack pulled him backward. Teetering on the rail, he held his breath and jumped. He landed on his feet, surprising himself, then fell sideways, rolling through the leaves. There was a thump as Rose landed beside him.

"Maxwell!" shouted his father. "Where are you?"

Max grimaced at the sound of his father's voice. Feeling sad and guilty all at once, he scrambled to his feet. Rose grabbed his hand and they raced across the lawn, ducking beneath the blankets and flannel shirts that Mrs. Crumlin had pegged to the line.

Could his parents see them running off? Max wondered. Were they stalling for time, letting him escape while the Dark Brigadiers ransacked the house? Far behind, he heard them calling, their voices tinged with desperation. Max had never heard a sadder sound.

But still he kept running.

The two children sped through the high grasses and didn't stop until they reached the owl tree. Panicked, Max searched for his owl, shouting and hooting for her until she flitted down.

"The Dark Brigade is after us!" he cried as the owl landed on his arm. "You're not safe! If they find you they'll—" He couldn't bring himself to say the word *kill*. "Quick, come with us!"

He studied the owl's face to see if she understood. She blinked her intelligent eyes and curled herself into a ball. Max gently lowered her into his pocket.

"The river!" cried Rose, who was running around the tree tearing down the government tape. "Goodbye, owl tree!" she shouted, pulling Max with her as they raced away. "We'll miss you!"

The owl tree, thought Max. They were going to cut it down and he'd never see it again! A deep sadness swept through him. Teary-eyed, he thrashed amid weeds and brambles, slogging through clumps of slushy snow. For a short moment he glimpsed the deadly purple sphinx, struggling through the moss. Then it was gone.

Max could no longer hear his parents' anguished cries. He felt as if he'd swallowed a lump of stone. When would he see them again? Maybe never. Despondent, he stumbled, but Rose caught him before he fell.

At the river they stopped to catch their breath. Gulping in the night air, Max watched the mist swirl up from the water. On the other side rose tall trees, black and sinister, some knobbled and bent, others dark and hooded. In the darkness behind them he could see small glowing eyes. A prickling sensation started at the base of his spine.

The Misshapens were watching.

Teeth chattering, Rose stamped on the frozen earth. "Here's the plan," she said in a take-charge voice. "I've got it all figured out."

Max frowned. Rose was sounding more like her bossy old self. Shouldn't he be the one making the decisions? He stared at chunks of ice floating on the water, an old, fog-haunted river that he imagined going on forever into the darkness. He had no clue where it ended.

"We take this path," instructed Rose, "then, first chance we get, we cross over the river. They won't dare follow us into the forest."

"They won't have to," said Max miserably, "because we'll be *dead*. The forest is too dangerous, Rose, the Misshapens live there!"

"Misshapens only come out at night, remember? We'll travel by day. Don't be such a scaredy-cat!"

His heart sank. "But I can't go out in the sun, remember?"

"Oh yeah. I forgot." She bunched the strings of her bobbled hat into a knot. "Don't worry, I'll think of something." She raised a clenched fist into the air. "The die is cast! Onward and upward, brave warriors!"

What sort of silly talk was that? Max wondered if Rose wasn't slightly unhinged. "What about plague wolves?" He could feel his heart slamming against his chest. "And skræks? We'll never make it out of the forest alive!"

"I suppose you've got a better idea?" Rose threw back her shoulders, fixing her dark gaze on Max. Her sunken, shadowy eyes worried him. "In case you haven't noticed, there's no other way out."

Max chewed his lip. He longed to be brave like Rose, as brave as his silver owl. If only he had the courage to be fearless and take the lead. But, if anything, he'd only succeed in dragging them down. Doomed by his allergies, hindered by his fears, Max knew he could all too easily bungle their escape.

CHAPTER SEVENTEEN

Max had no idea how long he had been running. His sides ached, his head was full of fears and his woolen underwear itched like crazy.

As they made their way through the darkness, long shadows fell across the path. In the distance he could see a line of jagged towers, lit by the crimson moon. His heart clenched into a knot. The sight of The Ruins, bleak and mystical, filled him with dread.

At last they stopped for a rest—a quick break, Rose said—and huddled together beside the river. The black water churned, hurling pieces of ice into the air.

What if Rose was mistaken and this path went nowhere? worried Max. Each time he took a breath, his lungs hurt. He wondered what was happening back home, whether the Dark Brigadiers were still turning his house upside down. Were his mom and dad safe—or had they been arrested and taken to prison?

The silver owl poked her head out of his pocket and looked around, feathers bristling with fear. Max took Gran's shell and held it to the moonlight, trying to draw strength from it. If Gran were alive right now, what advice would she give? Would she say to turn back, or would she tell him to keep going?

"That's quite a fancy shell, Max." Rose whipped off a mitten and ran her fingers over the shell's uneven edge. "This is what's called a talisman. It has special powers."

"It's a scallop shell," said Max, annoyed. Why did Rose think everything was magic?

He remembered Gran's startling blue eyes, dark and solemn, her long white hair rippling in the wind. He could almost, but not quite, hear her voice, strong and clear. His owl emitted soft, silvery hoots and those pure, sweet sounds eased the aching in his heart.

"Can I hold your shell?" asked Rose, her voice subdued. "Just for one minute?"

Max closed his hand over the shell. It was the one thing Gran had given him that he treasured above all else.

"I don't think that's a good idea," he said.

With a shrug, Rose shoved her hand back into her mitten. Max could see he had hurt her feelings a little.

"It's nothing against you," he said quickly. "This seashell belonged to my granny. It's the most important thing I own."

"I just want to hold it." Her eyes looked huge and forlorn. "I'll give it back. Promise."

Max opened his hand; the shell glimmered faintly. He knew what it was that drew him to Rose, why he liked her so much. It was that trusting look of hers, that fierce energy and passion. He loved the way she talked with such startling intensity. Rose gave off a dazzling light that made everything around her seem drab and colorless.

He didn't own much, but he had the seashell and the owl book. Rose had nothing except the raggedy clothes she wore and the ugly boots she'd stolen from Mrs. Crumlin. The least he could do was let her hold his shell.

"All right," he said. "But don't drop it or anything."

"It's very elegant," Rose said softly as he set it in the palm of her hand. She held the shell right up to her eyes, touching it the way a blind person would. Then she threw down her hat and pressed the shell delicately to her ear. "I can almost hear the sea."

"I don't think so," said Max, his heart heavy as he studied her eyes. They looked less focused. Were they going dimmer? he wondered. "Gran told me it wasn't that kind of shell."

"I said *almost*. You need to listen better, Max."

Max sighed. He could always count on Rose to be prickly and rude. The owl rummaged around nervously in his pocket. She's hungry, he thought, or sick from bouncing around in there. He fished her out and set her on a gooseberry bush, where she gave several hoots.

Max stopped in his tracks: those were warning hoots.

"What's wrong with that owl?" said Rose, still holding the shell to her ear. "Why is she making that racket?"

With growing unease, Max looked around. In the night sky, an enormous black shadow was sweeping ominously toward them. His gut went numb. It was the shadow from his nightmares! He watched it break apart into hundreds of ragged creatures, eerily silent, swooping down through the velvety dark.

A cold terror slid through his veins. "Skræks!" he yelled, scooping up the owl. "Run!"

Rose jammed on her hat and they sprinted down the path. "This way!" she cried, pulling him into a grove of trees. Terrified, Max looked back. The skræks were gaining on them. Please no, keep away, he thought, knowing they'd tear him and Rose apart if they caught them.

Tall and creaking, the old-growth trees crowded around the two children, blotting out the stars. The ground was dense with ferns and nettles, thickets, thorns and twisted roots. They ran through the dark grove until, unable to run another step, they collapsed against a leaning stone.

"Did we lose them?" whispered Rose, looking around. "Where are we? Things look kind of blurry."

Max struggled to catch his breath, too exhausted to respond. He couldn't hear the skræks flapping anymore, but that didn't mean they were gone.

"Hey, guess what?" said Rose. "We're in a cemetery. See all the gravestones?"

Startled, Max gazed at the flat, brittle stones overgrown with moss, leaning at angles around them, gleaming in the moonlight. What a creepy place, he thought. He noticed how the headstones had worn-down inscriptions and deep cracks running through them. Many had fallen, probably knocked down by the tremors. Staring at the headstones with trepidation, he half expected to see a flock of papery old souls float up from the ground.

"Hey, Max," said Rose in a hushed voice. "Is your granny buried here?"

He wished now his father had told him where his grandmother was buried. "I don't know," he replied, adding gloomily: "I hope she's not, it's too sad and spooky here. I don't think Gran would like it."

Mist coiled around them, rising up from the black earth. Max shivered, feeling the damp, raw air seep into his bones. The owl rustled in his pocket, making anxious twittering sounds. What if there were Misshapens here? A fresh wave of panic surged though him.

Suddenly he heard another sound: the frantic beating of wings. Terror seized him by the throat.

"They're back!" he screamed.

Rose leapt up and grabbed Max, pulling him to the ground beside a headstone. "Shhh!" She clamped her hand over his mouth. "They don't have eyes, remember? They can't see us, they can only hear! Don't make a sound!"

Pushing her hand away, Max huddled beside her. "What if they're here for revenge?" he whispered. "You know, because the High Echelon made them in a laboratory and didn't give them eyes?"

"It wasn't us who did it!" Rose shot back. "Now will you shut up?"

Max sat perfectly still, ignoring a cramp in his big toe. Although he'd set Skræk #176 free, he was terrified of the rest of them. He realized that Rose had no idea the High Echelon was planning to make him a Skræk Master—there hadn't been time to tell her about his confrontation with Mrs. Crumlin and the doctor. The thought of those pale wormy faces and stringy black tongues turned his stomach to mush. And those *teeth,* those sharp, yellow *teeth* . . .

A handful of the creatures circled overhead. Max felt his sun tattoo turn icy cold, pressing into the back of his neck. The last time that had happened he'd been in The Ruins. He tensed as two skræks glided down, snuffling and wheezing, their wings snagging on branches. They reeked of garbage. Gritting his teeth, he tried to stay calm. The creatures didn't seem to notice him and Rose, huddled motionless beside the gravestone.

The cramp in his toe was killing him. Yet Max knew if he moved, those razor-sharp claws would dice him up in seconds. Another skræk wheeled by, knocking clumsily into a branch, giving out a cry of pain. Repulsed by the smell, Max held his breath. It seemed, oddly enough, that the creature was looking at him through the indentations where its eyes were supposed to be.

Was it able to see him or detect him in any way? But before Max could ponder further, his vision began to blur. A familiar dark thrill rushed through him. He was vaguely aware of his body sagging against the stone.

Moments later he was airborne, winging toward a dark quivering mass that hung over the forest. He felt no fear, no vertigo, only a ravenous hunger as he spiraled above the trees. At last he reached the pulsing horde of skræks, their shrieks rising to a fever pitch. The stench was overwhelming.

Exhilarated, he soared higher into the night, his wings crackling. Hot blood coursed through his veins and a red glow filled his eyes: light streaming down from the crimson moon.

Two wiry hands grabbed his shoulders, shaking him savagely. Max forced his eyes open. The crimson moonlight vanished and the raucous shrieks melted away.

"Are you okay?" Rose had her face up to his, her eyelashes so close they were tickling his cheek. "You look out of focus." She smelled like resin from a tree, clean and alive like the forest he used to visit with his gran. "I think you fainted or something, Max. Your eyes went weird and you were, like, miles away."

"I was," he murmured, trying to gather his scattered thoughts. "I was flying—"

Rose leapt to her feet, scanning the sky. "The skræks are gone! They flew away!" She gave a cheer.

But Max shuddered. He was far from happy. What had just happened to him? It hadn't been a dream, he was sure of that. Something much more sinister had taken place—something beyond his control.

"It's okay to talk now, Max." Rose was leaning against a headstone, shaking out her boots. "They're gone."

"You won't believe this, but—" Max caught himself in time. How could he explain that he'd been flying with the skræks? Rose would think there was something seriously wrong with him. Knowing her, she'd laugh and say he was delusional.

He decided to keep quiet. After all, Rose had plenty of secrets herself.

Rose wasn't listening anyway. She was busy turning her mittens and coat pockets inside out.

"Don't be mad, I'll find it," she said, removing her hat and peering inside. "It's here somewhere."

"What? What did you lose?"

"Your shell, Max. I lost your granny's lucky shell."

CHAPTER EIGHTEEN

Max felt as if the breath was knocked out of him, as if he'd been punched in the stomach. "You lost Gran's *shell*?"

"Don't get your hackles up! It was an accident." Rose checked her pockets. "These things happen when you're on the run." She threw him a sheepish glance. "I'll find it, Max, I promise. I'm real good at finding things. It's a special talent I have."

Max chewed his lip, biting back tears, too angry to speak. How could she be so careless? Gran had entrusted the shell to him! Didn't Rose realize how rare and precious it was? Didn't she know it could never be replaced?

Furious, he stomped through the graveyard, thinking what a mistake he'd made, trusting Rose with Gran's shell. He kicked at the dead leaves, desperately hoping it would appear.

"Hey, Max, I forgot all about this!"

He looked over to see Rose waving a piece of paper.

"Look, I found this in your closet!"

He ignored her and kept walking away. Big deal, he thought, that old closet was overflowing with junk. He was so upset he didn't care when the owl wiggled out of his pocket and darted into the air.

Why did Rose always get so distracted? he wondered, jumping from one topic to the next? She never stuck with one thing for more than a minute. Her flightiness was maddening. Why wasn't she helping him find Gran's shell? Obviously she didn't care about it, he thought angrily. The shell meant nothing to her.

Max heard the silver owl hooting again. She teetered on top of a gravestone, flapping her good wing, more animated than he'd seen her in a long time.

Rose ran over, waving the paper in his face. "Here, take a look, Max. I was going to read it, but I suppose you should be first. After all, it was in your closet."

Annoyed, he snatched the paper from her hand.

She clicked on her miniflashlight, shining it over a crumpled page filled with handwritten words. "What are you waiting for? Read it!"

Max smoothed out the paper. When he saw the elaborate script he blinked in surprise. "You found this in my *closet*?" The paper was covered with faded looping letters in blue and silver ink. It was in the same old-fashioned handwriting as the owl's secret message. Why hadn't Mrs. Crumlin discovered this? he wondered, remembering all the times she'd barged into his room and snooped through his closet.

"I found it behind the wallpaper," explained Rose. "I was waving my flashlight around, see, and I saw all these places where the wallpaper was coming unstuck."

Max scowled, forgetting for a moment what he held in his hands. Sticky-fingers Rose, he thought irritably, she can never leave things alone. "You ripped the *wallpaper* off my closet wall?"

"That wallpaper was so decrepit, it fell right off! Anyway, it was boring in there, so I had to do something. A row of ships fell down and I found this paper, stuck to the wall. Sorry, I wrinkled it a bit."

Hooting, the owl fluttered in a crooked line to Max's shoulder. Gripping the paper, Max thought back to the message. Something Rose had just said tugged at his memory. "The owl's message talked about a ship."

"I'm talking *wallpaper* ships, Max." Rose tapped the paper. "Read it."

"Maybe the owl's message doesn't mean a real-life ship? *'Tear down the sails of the eastbound ship,'*" he recited from memory, "*'steering into the darkest port.'*" He glanced sideways at his owl, who sat on his shoulder listening intently, her golden eyes fixed on him. "The ship sails into the dark, right? My closet's dark— there's no light in there."

"Yeah, and it smells like dirty socks. I almost threw up."

Max dismissed her silly remark with a wave of his hand. Inside his head, he felt the click-click of gears, whirling and turning. "*'The eastbound ship'*—that side of the house faces east." Had the owl's message been meant for *him*? He skimmed the words on the crumpled paper. "This is from the Silver Prophecies, Rose! It's the song of silver and ice, the one Gran used to sing to me!"

The owl gave a triumphant silvery hoot. Max could feel her small body trembling with excitement.

"Let me see!" Rose reached greedily for the paper.

Max whisked it behind his back, the lost shell fresh in his mind. "Do you know how rare this is? This might be the only copy of the poem left in the world!"

"Maybe your gran knew she was dying," Rose said in a melancholy tone. "Maybe she hid it for you to find."

Max could feel the old, familiar sorrow. "I think you're right, she left it for me," he said slowly. "Look at the letters. Nobody writes like this anymore, except people from my granny's generation—and Gran's the only older person I know. *Knew*, I mean." His throat tightened. "Rose, I'm almost positive she wrote this."

"Good thing I found it, right, Max?" said Rose, sounding like her old self again. "Otherwise that witchy old housekeeper would've thrown it in the trash."

"You're right," he agreed. He looked at Rose. "The owl's message talks about finding the Silver Treasure. This is it: 'Silver and Ice'! This poem is the treasure!"

"It could be," she mused, "but your owl is silver too."

Max hadn't thought of that. The silver owl hopped off his shoulder onto a gravestone.

"I wonder who sent your owl to you?" Rose went on. "I mean, somebody must've put the message in her beak and sent her off with it."

Max thought a moment, mentally running down the short list of people he knew. He could exclude the untrustworthy ones like Mrs. Crumlin, Dr. Tredegar and Einstein right off the bat. And it was doubtful his mom and dad or Professor LaMothe knew anything about the poem.

"My gran had lots of friends who were Sages, so maybe it was one of them," he suggested, knowing it was only a guess.

Rose frowned. "Then that means your owl belongs to somebody else. What if they're waiting for it to come back?"

Alarmed, Max glanced over at his silver owl, flitting from one gravestone to the next. It had never occurred to him she might be someone's pet. "She's *mine*," he said fiercely, feeling a deep anger rising inside him. "And nobody's going to take my owl away from me." He would fight to the death, he knew, to keep his silver owl.

"Read the message!" urged Rose, waving her flashlight. "Hurry up before this thing runs out of batteries."

Max threw her an annoyed look. He was tired of being ordered around.

He turned his attention back to the poem. In the beam of Rose's flashlight, the words glimmered strangely—as if they weren't words at all, he thought, but tiny galaxies of light spinning on the page.

He cleared his throat. "The Way to the Owl Keeper," he began, trying to deepen his voice, "from the Silver Prophecies:

> "OWL IN THE DARKNESS,
> SILVER IN THE LEAVES,
> BLIND CHILD COMES LEADING

THROUGH THE FOG AND TREES.
THROUGH THE HAUNTED FOREST,
BEYOND THE ACHING HILLS,
DARKER GROWS THE EVENTIDE,
DEEPER GROWS THE CHILL.

ANCIENT DARK IS RISING
ON THE HIGHEST BRIDGE,
RED-EYED WOLVES ARE RUNNING
ON THE DISTANT RIDGE.
BEWARE THE EYELESS CREATURES
THAT WOULD HAVE YOUR SOUL,
CHOOSE THE BURNING SUNLIGHT,
CHOOSE THE PATH OF GOLD.

JOURNEY TO THE MOUNTAIN,
FLEE THE FORTRESS OLD,
SILVER WINGS WILL SAVE YOU
FROM THE KILLING COLD.
TWO WILL MAKE THE JOURNEY,
OLD ONE GONE BEFORE,
TO THE ICEBOUND TOWER,
THROUGH THE CRUMBLING DOOR."

He stopped reading. There was an extra verse at the end, one he'd never heard before. While the first three verses were written in blue, the last verse was penned in thick, broad strokes of silvery ink—as if Gran had meant to draw his attention to it. He continued:

"OWL KEEPER IS SUMMONED
ATOP THE FROZEN PLAIN,
OWLS AND SAGES GATHER
TO FIGHT THE DARK AGAIN.
TWO WILL MAKE THE JOURNEY,
SILVER OWL IN HAND,
SEEK THE MOONLIT TOWER
AS DARKNESS SWEEPS THE LAND.

SILVER AND ICE, SILVER AND ICE,
SILVER OWL WILL GUIDE YOU,
WITH ITS GOLDEN EYES."

Rose leaned over and patted the owl, perched on a gravestone nearby. "It gives me the shivers."

"The haunted forest makes sense," said Max, mulling over the phrases. "We're in it right now! And the red-eyed wolves are plague wolves."

"The eyeless creatures are skræks," said Rose darkly. "I really hate those things."

"Me too." Max shuddered. How could he ever tell Rose that the High Echelon had planned to make him a Skræk Master?

Rose tugged on a string of matted hair. "What does the last verse mean?"

"It's about the Owl Keeper bringing together Sages and silver owls."

"Yeah, but what about the two making a journey with a silver owl?" Rose's voice fell to a melodramatic whisper. "That's *us*,

Max! We're supposed to take your silver owl to a moonlit tower! It says so right there!"

Max sifted through his memories, trying to recall what Gran had told him. Sounds and images tumbled through his head: a tower, a silver treasure, unearthly songs rising up through the moonlight. He tilted his head toward the silver owl. Looking into her golden eyes, scattered with flecks of amber, he could almost read her thoughts. *Heed the poem,* she seemed to say to him. *Follow the path.*

Max let out a slow, measured breath. "Gran always talked about a tower on a high plateau. I think that's where we'll find the Owl Keeper, Rose!"

"Okay. The poem talks about an icebound tower and a frozen plain," she said, craning her neck and looking off in the distance. "Does that mean—"

"Yep," said Max, following her gaze. "The Frozen Zone." Just above the trees he could see its cold, jagged edges, jutting up against the sky.

Rose sucked in her breath. "Wow, Max, this is a real adventure! And the Owl Keeper lives up there in a tower, right? Hey, maybe we can stay with him! I bet he has servants and a maître d' and a television with a rotary antenna—"

"Don't count on it," Max cut in dryly, wondering what a maître d' was. "Televisions haven't been around for generations." He slipped the paper inside his jacket.

The owl gave a delicate sneeze. Max picked her up and held her a moment, stroking her feathers, then he opened his pocket and she squeezed inside.

"Max!" cried Rose.

He looked up to see a pinkish yellow light, filtering through the tangled branches. "The sun!" he gasped. Panic and fear took hold of him.

"Run!" yelled Rose.

Wheeling around, they streaked through the graveyard, dodging headstones, leaping over stone walls, sprinting through the trees. The sky was growing lighter by the minute. Soon they were running along the river, slipping and sliding on the muddy banks.

This is worse than plague wolves or skræks, thought Max, this is instant death.

"Over here!" cried Rose, pulling him toward a narrow wooden bridge.

There was no time to worry about crossing the river into a forest where wolves and Misshapens roamed at night. It was the only place to hide. All Max could do was clamber across the bridge and into the shadows, dodging the lethal rays of the sun.

Looking wildly around, Max glimpsed a cluster of shapes, half hidden in the mist, and galloped toward them. To his amazement he could see a clump of blasted walls, with stone steps winding upward—and a doorway leading into a crumbling stone structure.

Crashing through the forest, he jumped over twisted roots and ducked beneath branches. Arms pumping, he hurtled through the open doorway and into the ruined building. Rolling across the earthen floor, he landed in a cold, pitch-black space, relief spiraling through him.

Rose came flying in, her rubber boots skidding in the dirt. "Max, are you okay?"

Out of breath, he looked up at her with a weary smile, his eyes already adjusting to the darkness.

"Whew, that was a close call," she said. With a concerned expression, she pulled him to his feet, looking him up and down, checking for damage. "I was so scared for you, Max! I was afraid your skin would start bubbling up and your eyes would pop out and your hair would catch fire and—" She stopped abruptly, leaving the rest to their imaginations.

Seeing her worried expression, Max felt his cheeks go red. Rose really *does* care about me, he thought. Now that the scare was over, he brushed leaves and dirt from his clothes, gazing with curiosity at the scarred walls and beams of rotting wood. They were in a great hall of some sort. It was built of enormous stones that were covered with carvings so weathered, they were fading back into the stone.

It must have been magnificent here once, he thought. Who had lived in this place? Had they been royalty or wise people of some sort? He guessed the castle had been built centuries ago, maybe as far back as the first Sages.

Then he was struck by an awful thought and his heart sank. "My owl!" he cried. "What if I squashed her?"

But when he opened his pocket, the owl fluttered out and flew straight up to a beam in the ceiling, ruffling her feathers. She had a look of faded elegance, sitting high above, gazing at them with quizzical eyes, making soft triumphant noises.

"Did you see her fly up there?" Max stared at his owl, feeling incredibly happy and relieved. "Her wing is working again, Rose! And look at her bad eye—doesn't it seem brighter to you?" His owl was whole again! Her broken wing was healed!

"She's kind of far away to see, but yeah, I think she's beautiful!" Rose hugged him. "Your owl's going to be all right!"

Max hugged her back. "She's the most special owl in the world, and she's the toughest, too! Listen, Rose, she's singing!" He tilted his head, marveling at the mysterious sounds coming from his owl.

"I like her song, Max. It's got hope in it." Rose gave a loud sniff and spun away from him. "This place smells like the barn in Cavernstone Grey." Then her face fell. "Max, I don't know where my father is. They could've taken him anywhere!"

"Oh, Rose," said Max, feeling sad and helpless and sorry for her. Rose had such a fiery nature and most of the time she was fearless and unshakable. But seeing the anger in her eyes, and the sadness deeper down, he realized for the first time that a part of her was damaged. She carried a hidden sorrow that made his heart ache for her.

Maybe that was what drew them to each other, he reflected. They both suffered: Rose from her buried anger and sadness, Max from his illness and isolation.

"I want my dad and mom," whispered Rose. "I miss them so much, Max!"

Max's heart melted. His high spirits fell as he remembered his own parents. And he knew what it meant to lose someone you loved: after all these years, he still missed Gran terribly.

He put his arms around Rose, breathing in the tree-sap smell of her hair. What else could he do? He had no idea whether her parents were safe or not, and no comforting words came into his head, so he stayed quiet.

He thought of his parents at the dinner table, cutlery clinking, pretending to enjoy Mrs. Crumlin's scalded beet casserole. After a few days would they even notice he was gone? Would they ask each other, "Whatever happened to Max?" and shake their heads in bewilderment? A deep sadness tugged at his heart, and he wondered if they missed him.

He let go of Rose. Unscrewing the thermos, he poured the last of the milk and honey, which was lukewarm, into its lid and offered it to her. He felt compelled to say something, to give Rose a reason not to lose hope.

"Everything seems black right now, Max," she said in a quiet voice. "I feel so alone without my dad."

"But you've got me, Rose, I'll look after you," he said, trying to sound confident. "So what we do is, we keep going. We find the icebound tower and we bring the owl—"

But as he said the words, Max wasn't so sure he believed them. Away from the safety of his home and all the familiar things he'd left behind, Max felt uprooted, insecure. The world out here was so frightening and unpredictable. Still, he told himself, it was important to put on a brave face for Rose.

"It should be easy to find the Owl Keeper." Rose wiped her eyes with her sleeve and sipped the milk. "We just take your granny's poem and break it down line by line, like when my dad cracks a code." She smiled unevenly.

Max grinned, thinking how Rose could tell the most believable lies. Right then it didn't bother him—he actually sort of understood it. "But your dad's not really a spy, is he? I heard Einstein say he's a professor at a university. You made that spy stuff up, didn't you? It's not really true."

"Yeah, I did, sort of." Rose giggled through her tears. "Sometimes I get carried away. I wanted to impress you, that's all. And it worked, right, Max?"

She giggled harder and he joined in, relieved to let go of his pent-up worries and fears. Soon they were falling all over the place, laughing hysterically. It felt good to be laughing, to forget the sadness that had come before.

Max rolled over and lay flat on his back, staring up at the rafters. Something slowly drifted down. A bundle of twigs landed in the dust beside him. "Look, my owl dropped a pellet!" Excited he reached over and picked it up. His owl had never made a real pellet before. That was something *he'd* told Rose to impress *her*.

Rose looked on, curious. For once she didn't make any inane comments.

"Here's a skull," he said, gently tearing the pellet apart. "It could be a mouse, or a vole, maybe." He pulled out twigs and leaves and tiny bones, a glob of feathers, a cluster of seeds, setting them on the floor for Rose to see. She knelt down, inspecting each item, though he noticed she held everything very close to her eyes.

"Hey, Max, what's that shiny thing over there?" Rose pointed.

Max stared, incredulous, marveling at a small, gleaming object on the earthen floor. Tears of joy sprang to his eyes. His hand closed around the familiar shape, rare and delicate, with fluted edges and—by some quirk of fate—still in one piece.

Gran's shell.

CHAPTER NINETEEN

Max was drifting in and out of sleep when he heard the formidable voice of Mrs. Crumlin. At first he thought he was dreaming.

"A wonder he's survived. Such a pathetic, hyperfrenetic child." Hearing her words, Max felt a sudden creeping fear. "Well, it won't be long now—things are about to change rather quickly."

Max opened his eyes halfway and his heart sank. It wasn't a dream. Mrs. Crumlin stood inside the doorway watching him. Small and squat, she looked like an evil dwarf in a fairy tale. The person she was talking to, he realized, was outside the door, out of earshot and hidden from view. Immediately he closed his eyes again and, pretending to be asleep, listened intently.

"See that wretched urchin in black, over in the corner?" Mrs. Crumlin continued. "That's the one causing all the trouble! The boy has fallen under her influence."

A deep voice answered, the words muffled.

"I have no idea whether or not the girl can see! All I know is, she must be gotten rid of," said Mrs. Crumlin in a low, sinister tone. "Without delay. Wait here—"

But Max didn't hear the rest. Get rid of *Rose*? His heart began to race. How were they planning to do that? Through half-shut eyelids, he saw Mrs. Crumlin trundling toward him, swinging a large woven basket.

"Wake up, sleepyhead!" she chirped sweetly.

Max opened his eyes. It was no good pretending to be asleep. She stood looming over him, her smile bleak and dangerous. He heartily disliked Mrs. Crumlin, but he'd never been afraid of her before—not until now.

Sickened by the smells of bleach and pickles, and confused by Mrs. Crumlin's sudden appearance, he shrank against the wall. He was stiff and cold in this cavernous room with stone walls. Was this a prison? Then he saw the sagging beams and battered carvings and remembered: he was in a ruined castle in the forest. He'd run from the sunrise and taken shelter there with Rose.

He rubbed his eyes. But what was Mrs. Crumlin doing here? How had she tracked them down?

"It took us a while to find you, but here we are, none the worse for wear." Mrs. Crumlin looked so ordinary and out of place, with her shiny quilted raincoat and a plastic rain hat tied in a crisp bow beneath her chin. Max realized with relief that she was unaware he'd heard her comments about Rose.

"Who's with you?" he asked nervously.

"My bodyguard, of course. How could you be so foolhardy, Maxwell, venturing into the forest? Even in daylight it's treacherous. Dangers lurk at every corner!" With gloved fingers she massaged her temples. "We've been searching for you since early this morning. I'm absolutely shattered."

How are Rose and I going to get out of here? Max wondered, his eyes scanning the ruined structure. Except for the main doorway, there seemed to be no other way out.

"This may interest you, Maxwell: a wind-borne vessel delivered us here!" Mrs. Crumlin's tone was both lighthearted and boastful. "It awaits in a field nearby."

Her words caught Max by surprise. How did Mrs. Crumlin rate, flying in a wind-borne vessel? He knew they were few in number: most of the metallic pod-shaped flying craft had vanished during the Great Destruction. Known for their sturdy wings and tempered glass windows, wind-borne vessels were piloted by the Dark Brigade. Only top government officials traveled in them.

Mrs. Crumlin held out the basket she was holding. Max saw that it was filled with steaming hot muffins. "Take one, dearie," she urged, "you must be famished. They're made with golden-eye treacle—another radio cook-show recipe!"

Max eyed the muffins suspiciously. He didn't want to think what Mrs. Crumlin might have baked inside them. Why was she being so *nice* to him? he wondered. His stomach rumbled, reminding him that he hadn't eaten for a long time. Reaching for a muffin, Max went to take a bite, but it looked viscous and smelled oversweet. The cloying scent stayed in his nostrils as he dropped it back into the basket.

Mrs. Crumlin clucked her tongue. "Now then, Maxwell, I expect you're too overexcited to eat. Anxious to be home, is it? Ewan and Nora have been worried sick."

Max seethed inwardly. How dare she casually throw his parents' names around! Pain and guilt surged through him as he remembered his last days at home. He'd locked himself in his room, refusing to talk with his father and mother, and then he'd run away without a word of explanation. Now he found himself worrying about his parents all the time. Still, he knew he could never go back there—not when the High Echelon was planning to make him a Skræk Master.

"I've brought a blanket to throw over you and protect you from sun particles," said Mrs. Crumlin gaily, as if they were setting off on an afternoon picnic. "And you needn't worry about riding in the wind-borne vessel—it has lovely tinted windows!"

Max stared down at the floor, despising her, as bleak thoughts crowded into his head. If he returned to Cavernstone Grey, his fate was sealed. And Rose? He had no doubt that she'd be thrown into Children's Prison. Once inside the wind-borne vessel, strapped into their seats and guarded by the Dark Brigade, they'd have zero chance of escaping.

He had to act soon.

Rose tossed back and forth in the corner of the ruined hall, mumbling in her sleep. "Rose!" Max called out, moving protectively toward her. "Wake up!"

With a groan Rose sat up, shaking leaves from her hair, rubbing her fists into her dark-ringed eyes.

"Hello, Rose," said Mrs. Crumlin merrily. "At last I have the pleasure of making your acquaintance."

Max nearly gagged. He'd never heard Mrs. Crumlin so disgustingly cheerful as she was today. He suspected she'd been rehearsing.

Rose's eyes opened wide. Max watched her sleepy expression change to open hostility as she realized who was speaking to her. Hands clenched, she sprang to her feet, taking on a fighting stance.

But Mrs. Crumlin appeared unfazed. "Call me Mrs. Crumlin, dear. I'm Maxwell's guardian and I've come to fetch you. Come here, young lady," she ordered in an imperious voice. "Right now!"

Not moving an inch, Rose glared at the woman. If looks could kill, thought Max, admiring Rose's tough spirit. But he knew they had to make a run for it soon.

He figured they could get past Mrs. Crumlin—she wasn't too swift on her feet—but the big problem was the bodyguard. If they made it past the guard, Rose had a fighting chance. As for Max, the outlook wasn't so good: he'd be exposed to the sun's rays and that meant death. But what choice did they have?

"Maxwell never told me he had a new friend—though I had my suspicions, of course." Max saw Mrs. Crumlin give Rose a knowing smile. "I knew something was a teensy bit off. Maxwell hasn't been himself lately, but now I understand." Her bright smile hardened, then turned into a snarl. "You see, he's come under your influence, Artemis Rose Eccles!"

Max's mind snapped into focus. How did Mrs. Crumlin know Rose's full name? The authorities must be feeding her information! Wasn't riding in a wind-borne vessel and knowing things about Rose further proof that Mrs. Crumlin worked for the High Echelon?

Rose threw her skinny shoulders back. "You don't scare me, Crumpet."

Snickering to himself, Max threw Rose an encouraging look, impressed by her bravery and wishing some of it would rub off on him. Except for the time she'd taken his books and toy owl, he had never been bold enough to say anything even remotely insulting to Mrs. Crumlin.

"The name is Crumlin—*Mrs.* Crumlin to you. Insolent child, there is no excuse for bad manners!" Mrs. Crumlin was flustered, Max could tell, because her face was breaking out in hives. "Very well, I've wasted enough of my time." Her tone grew disdainful. "I've coddled and protected you long enough, Maxwell Unger. It's time you grew up." She tightened the strings of her rain hat. "We're going home."

Max said nothing. Gazing into Mrs. Crumlin's determined face, he felt the walls closing in around him.

"As for you"—Mrs. Crumlin shook a stubby finger at Rose— "you are coming with us."

Max could hear the blood pounding in his ears. If Rose was sent to Children's Prison, he'd never forgive himself. They had to make a run for it.

"Forget it, you daft smelly old fossil, I'll never go anywhere with *you!*" screamed Rose, running toward the muffins. Max watched, impressed by her defiance. She swung her foot and missed the basket.

Max stifled a cry. Rose's eyesight must be getting worse.

She kicked again and muffins flew up as the basket sailed into the air. First Max felt relief, then panic, realizing that Dark Brigadiers could surround the tower at any minute. He sprinted over to Rose, who had stopped kicking to put on her coat and boots.

"My boots!" Mrs. Crumlin's eyes narrowed to dark, puffy slits. "You're the thief who stole them!"

But Rose didn't answer. She stomped on the basket with the enormous green boots, crushing it to pieces.

"You'll regret that," said Mrs. Crumlin in an ominous tone. Then she turned to Max. "Gather your belongings."

Pretending to obey, Max began stuffing things into his knapsack, his mind whirling. The moment Mrs. Crumlin looked away, he whispered into Rose's ear. "Run!" Then he stopped her. Out of the corner of his eye he saw a shadow in the doorway. "Hold on," he warned. "Crumlin's bodyguard—"

Max watched a lean, cloaked figure creep into the hall, face hidden beneath a hood. The air turned dense and heavy. From the folds of the dark red cloak a skeletal hand slowly emerged. Something between the bony fingers caught Max's eye: the InjectaPort, glinting in the sunlight.

An icy fear slid down his back. Dr. Tredegar! Mrs. Crumlin's words came back to him: *She must be gotten rid of.* They were going to murder Rose by injection!

He knew that, whatever happened, he had to save Rose—he had to distract them so she'd have a chance to get away. He wouldn't survive—the sun's rays would kill him—but Rose could outrun them. They'd never be able to cage a free spirit like Artemis Rose Eccles, he told himself. It would be like trying to cage the wind or the stars.

Rose was his one true friend: she would risk everything to save him. And Max would risk everything to save her—even if it meant going up in flames.

CHAPTER TWENTY

Dr. Tredegar threw off his hood, revealing his slicked-back hair and frigid smile. He was light-years away from the folksy, wise-cracking doctor Max had known. His insectile body was all sharp angles, darting and quick, his eyes terrifying pinpoints behind the tinted lenses.

The doctor exhaled a dry, whistling breath. "Steady now, young lady, this won't hurt a bit," he crooned in an oily voice.

Watching Dr. Tredegar slink toward him and Rose, Max reeled back, clutching Rose's arm, feeling a deep repulsion. The InjectaPort looked lethal in the murky light.

"Ready?" whispered Max, waves of panic rising inside him. Rose nodded.

"Don't fight me on this one." Puffs of sour breath escaped Dr. Tredegar's mouth. "I'm a medical doctor, see, I would never hurt you—" Raising the InjectaPort, he lunged at Rose.

"No!" screamed Max, throwing himself between the two of them. The doctor spun out of control, slipping sideways in his alligator shoes, and Rose sprinted across the floor, pushing past Mrs. Crumlin in the doorway. Mrs. Crumlin gave a little shriek and Max saw her fall against the doorframe, then collapse.

He watched as Rose jumped over Mrs. Crumlin and raced outside.

"After that girl!" cried Mrs. Crumlin, lumbering to her feet.

Dr. Tredegar sprang to the doorway and collided with Mrs. Crumlin. Both went sprawling onto the floor, and Max saw his chance. He took a deep breath, rushed to the door and leapt over Mrs. Crumlin's puddinglike body, ready to meet his fate.

As he jumped, a skeletal hand shot out and gripped his upper arm, pulling him back inside.

"Where do you think you're going?" snarled Tredegar, scrabbling to his feet. He squeezed Max's arm tightly, cutting off the circulation. "You won't get two yards in that sunlight!" Max struggled to break free, but the doctor held him in a merciless grip.

Beyond the door Max saw the black dog tied to a tree a few yards away. Straining at its leash, it snapped at Rose as she fled up the stone steps. Panicked, he yelled, "Watch out, Rose, that dog's a killer!"

Face mottled with rashes, Mrs. Crumlin rose slowly to her feet. "Clumsy old fool!" she shouted at the doctor.

"Not my fault." With his free hand, Dr. Tredegar fumbled through the folds of his cape. "Oh dear, where did I put the InjectaPort for Maxwell?"

"The High Echelon will *not* be pleased, Phineas." Mrs. Crumlin gave a sniff of contempt. "You were told to take care of that runaway child and you failed—miserably, I might add."

"Ah, but you are forgetting. She was hit by one of my darts! That drug will kick in very soon. Her sight will go and the Dark Brigade will finish her off in no time."

Max began to shake all over, overcome by fury and horror as he realized the depth of their betrayal. Mrs. Crumlin and Dr. Tredegar had never intended to take Rose with them in the wind-borne vessel. They weren't even going to send her to Children's Prison. They'd been planning to kill her instead!

Enraged, he shouted, "You're paid killers, both of you! The High Echelon sent you to murder Rose!" He wasn't sure whether it was true or not, but when he saw them exchange a knowing glance, he knew he'd guessed right.

"Settle down, Maxwell," said Mrs. Crumlin with a tight smile. "You're becoming overwrought."

Tears spilled from his eyes. "That's why I have trouble remembering things! You poisoned my hot cocoa and my desserts— that's what gave me fevers and confused me about Gran and her stories and made me tired all the time!" An awful thought struck him. "You're doing the same to my parents, aren't you? You're poisoning their food, too!"

"You *are* fragile, Maxwell!" snapped Dr. Tredegar. "You need looking after right around the clock. Mrs. Crumlin has spent years guarding you from germs and fevers and wrong influences such as that ghastly child."

Max shot him a look of pure loathing. "She's not ghastly, she's my best friend!"

"Oh, but you have no friends, Maxwell," said Mrs. Crumlin in a low, threatening voice. "When push comes to shove, all you have is *me*. And when I'm gone, you'll have the skræks. Simply put, Skræk Master is your destiny."

Max's breath came in great shuddering gasps. It was, he told himself, a destiny he would fight to the death.

"Let's go, Maxwell. You have some catching up to do, to prepare for the Transmutation." Mrs. Crumlin's eyes were as cold as ice chips. "I'd venture to say that, once the Transmutation takes place, you will grow attached to these psychotic creatures."

Max threw Mrs. Crumlin a defiant look. He didn't care about his future or anything she said anymore. She no longer had power over him.

"Find somebody else, I don't want the job!"

"Sorry, Maxwell, but you are the one the High Echelon has chosen. You will be given assistants, of course, but only *you* can be Skræk Master."

He glared at her, despising her, struck by how savage and ugly she was. "I hate you! You're the one who's psychotic! You're evil and weird!"

"Hmm, perhaps you already fly with the skræks—in your dreams?" Mrs. Crumlin gave him a funny look. "Yes, I know what happens in your 'bad dreams,' Maxwell, despite your refusal to tell me. The High Echelon keeps me in the loop about that sort of thing."

His emotions in turmoil, Max watched a feather drift by and land on his sleeve. Wiping away hot, angry tears, he tried to pull himself together, determined not to wither under Mrs. Crumlin's icy glare.

But how, he asked himself, was he going to escape?

"Take the boy." Dr. Tredegar shoved Max toward Mrs. Crumlin and extracted a fresh InjectaPort from his pocket. "*Transmutation,* from *transmute:* to change from one nature, substance, form or state into another. I'll skip the boring details." He gave a gleeful snort. "Everything will come clear for you with this final dose."

Mrs. Crumlin grabbed Max's arm, wrenching it behind his back.

"Dose of what?" he yelled, trying to shake her off. "What are you giving me?"

"We've been injecting you with the no-fear gene, Maxwell," replied Mrs. Crumlin, as if it were the most normal thing in the world.

"The InjectaPort is actually a gene gun," said the doctor smugly. "We've been altering your DNA."

Max was stunned. They'd been injecting him with genetically engineered blood *and* a synthetic gene? He was *an experiment*— no better than a skræk or a Misshapen!

"Let me go!" he screamed in terror. Mrs. Crumlin gave him a rough shake in response.

"You'll assume their habits and thinking patterns," she went on, as if she was enjoying all this immensely, "and physically you'll even begin to resemble a skræk."

Max struggled against her, kicking her in the shin. "You're not turning me into a skræk!"

"We've kept you pure and innocent, isolated from the world, a perfect smooth stone," Mrs. Crumlin continued in her overbearing tone. "As planned, the Transmutation will take place on the cusp of your twelfth birthday, to ensure your capability as Skræk Master will be at its zenith."

"To quote from *The Secret Book of the Alazarin Oro*," said Dr. Tredegar in a solemn voice, fumbling with the InjectaPort, "'And his pure heart will blacken and wither, and all manner of Darkness will enter his innocent soul.'"

"That was lovely, Phineas," murmured Mrs. Crumlin.

Max felt a cold, sharp lump in his throat, as if he'd swallowed the blade of Mrs. Crumlin's paring knife. His stomach heaved.

There was a whoosh overhead. Max looked up to see a flash of silver, and hope returned. Astonished, he watched his owl swoop down, claws bared, wings straight out.

She looked, he realized, powerful and magnificent.

With a furious shriek, the silver owl tore Mrs. Crumlin's rain hat off her head. She screamed and let go of Max. Hooting wildly, the owl raked her talons down the woman's face and blood trickled onto her collar. The owl gave a warning cry and Max turned to see Dr. Tredegar running toward him, the InjectaPort in one hand.

Whipping around, he bolted for the door—his last chance to escape. Pausing in the entryway, he looked back to see his owl nip Dr. Tredegar's hand. He gave a defiant smile as he heard the doctor curse. Then, bracing himself for a fiery death, he sprang into the sunlight.

Blinking in the leafy shadows, Max saw with a start that the dog had broken free of its leash. Was it chasing after Rose? He raced up the steep flight of steps, anxious to find her. The air was unnaturally bright—a symptom, he knew, of his allergies. The light was so painful he could hardly keep his eyes open.

When he reached the top step, he saw trees all around and a path running into the forest. From somewhere below, he heard the doctor shout, "Don't be an idiot, Maxwell, come back! You won't last a minute out there!"

He flew down the path, feeling the sun's warmth through the trees, heating his wool hat and mittens. Where was his owl? he wondered. He wished she could be with him now, in his last moments, but she was nowhere in sight.

Dazzling sunshine flooded his vision and tears streamed from his eyes, brought on by the wind, the light and the fact that his life was ending. Leaves glimmered, dissolving into shards of fire: grass, moss and flowers, spinning out of control.

Soon his skin would bubble up, his eyes would sizzle and melt. Lesions would erupt on his arms and legs. Once his blood hit the boiling point, flames would shoot out of his skull, catching his hair on fire. He knew the symptoms by heart, since Dr. Tredegar had described them countless times.

Half-blinded by sunlight, he struggled on. This is it, he told himself, the end of everything. Sorrow washed over him. He'd never see his parents again, or know what it meant to grow up. He'd never find the Owl Keeper or the Sages or the silver owls. Yet in the midst of everything he had one happy thought to hold on to—at least he had Gran, and the owl, and one true friend, Artemis Rose Eccles. He wouldn't have missed them for anything.

Max raced downhill to a sunlit field where russet grasses swayed in the wind. Beyond the field he could see a vast bridge of gray-blue stone arching over the river. Eyes fixed on the bridge, he ran for all he was worth, pumping his arms and legs, fighting for breath.

With a start he saw Rose at the far side of the field, running toward the river, the doctor's black hound snarling at her heels. He wanted to call out to let her know he was there, but he was sapped of energy; it was all he could do to move his limbs. Could Rose outrun the dog? he wondered. Would she make it across the bridge to a safe place?

High overhead the clouds parted and the sky cracked open. Max plunged into the field, staring at the bright blue glorious sky and the fiery globe that was the sun. Blue sky, golden sun—he had forgotten how beautiful they were.

He charged ahead, bravely waiting for the sun's rays to finish him off. But as he ran, he grew confused. Why wasn't it happening—the smoke, the flames, the fiery explosion? Light poured down, thick as butter, warming his face. Beads of sweat rolled out from under his hat. Sunlight danced around him, yet nothing was happening.

Then he realized. Nothing was going to happen.

CHAPTER TWENTY-ONE

"I didn't burn up!" cried Max in amazement. "I'm not allergic to the sun!" Were sun particles real? he wondered, or had Dr. Tredegar made them up? Giddy with joy, he raced through the field, his pursuers momentarily forgotten. An endless blue sky stretched overhead. "Rose!" he shouted. "I'm still alive!"

He couldn't remember ever seeing such radiant colors—vivid yellows and reds and greens—all vibrating dizzily around him. Was this how the world appeared to other people every day? The sky rotated above, surprising him over and over with its blueness.

Ahead, light bounced off the gray-blue stones of the ancient bridge. He could see Rose standing at the distant end of it, looking off in the opposite direction: a slight, dark, dreamy figure with a black dog at her side.

What was Rose doing with that savage animal? Did it have her cornered on the bridge? Was it ready to attack? Worried for her safety, Max raced on, pounding over the stone floor bridge.

"Rose!" he yelled, his panic mounting. A brisk wind whipped against his face. "Rose, are you all right?"

"Max!" shouted Rose, turning.

Halfway across the bridge, Max skidded to a halt. He'd suddenly noticed that one side was missing a section of the stone rail. Someone—a maintenance worker probably—had casually leaned a two-by-four wooden plank across the empty space.

Staring at the plank, he thought how easy it would be to fall. And falling was one of Max's worst fears. Without meaning to, he peered over the side, and froze when he saw the drop. The water was hundreds, maybe thousands, of feet below—so far that his mind couldn't work out the distance. He had never been up this high in his life. Far, far beneath he saw a vortex of black water spinning madly.

His stomach lurched and he felt the cogs and wheels inside his head crunch to a halt. In an instant his joy evaporated. Panic overwhelmed him.

"Max, they're coming!" Rose yelled. "Run!"

Transfixed, he heard a sound drift over from the field—the smooth hum of a glider—and he felt a cold rush of dread and panic. The wind-borne vessel was landing!

Moments later Mrs. Crumlin's voice came calling out to him: "Stay put, Maxwell, don't you move!"

"Run, Max!" shouted Rose.

Fear and sadness subdued him as he stood there, shivering wildly, unable to escape. This was the effect extreme heights had on him: they paralyzed every inch of his body. He wanted more than anything to be brave and rescue Rose, but his feet were stuck fast. He realized he wasn't going anywhere.

Moments later, he heard Mrs. Crumlin, huffing and puffing as she clumped her way across the bridge toward him. "Don't move or you'll fall!" she shrilled.

Then her sausage fingers hooked onto his collar. Max slumped in anguish, helpless to fight back, and a dark curtain of despair fell over him.

"I have the boy, doctor!" crowed Mrs. Crumlin triumphantly. "Frightened as a rabbit, he is!"

Max could see Dr. Tredegar loping across the bridge in a yellow slicker and alligator shoes, carrying his red leather medical bag.

"Nasty little beggar!" The doctor shook a fist at his shaggy black hound. "Where have you been, you ungrateful mongrel?"

Max stared in bafflement at the scene. Instead of attacking Rose, the dog sat cowering next to her, looking frightened to death.

"Leave Helios alone!" shouted Rose. Max watched, confused, as she threw her arms around the animal's neck, looking like they'd been friends all her life.

"Correction, young lady!" shouted Dr. Tredegar, and Max saw

him flash his square teeth. "That flea-bitten beast has no name! It belongs to me!"

"He's my dog now!" she yelled back. "He's Helios, the sun god!"

Wasn't it just like Rose to name a dog after a Greek god? thought Max. Rose was a warrior girl, all right: she always stood her ground no matter who threatened her. She'd even won over that vicious hound.

Then, from behind, Mrs. Crumlin's slablike arms closed around him, squeezing the breath out of his lungs.

The doctor collected himself and turned his attention to Max. "Righty-o, son, we have some work to finish, don't we?" Twisting his mouth, he reached into his bag. "Long overdue, this injection." He gave the vial a quick shake.

This was so unfair, thought Max drearily. He had finally realized he wasn't sick or allergic to anything, only to be captured by these two maniacs.

"You poisoned me and lied about my allergy to sun particles!" he croaked. "Look, I'm alive! The sunlight didn't kill me!"

"All part of the High Echelon's plan," replied Mrs. Crumlin tartly. "We kept you out of harm's way, didn't we? Our job was to distance you from the rest of the world."

Max tuned her out. Instead, he admired the claw marks down the side of her face. Nice work, owl, he thought.

"Sunlight was never an option," added Dr. Tredegar. "It weakens the retina. Skræk Masters need excellent night vision." He glowered at Mrs. Crumlin. "Why is this boy so much more trouble than the others? These endless questions and accusations, this incessant running away! I'm fed up chasing after this child."

Max stared at the doctor in surprise. There were *other* kids like him? Were they getting injections too? The thought sent an icy tingle down his spine. Then he remembered Dr. Tredegar talking to Mrs. Crumlin about the "chosen twelve."

"You're doing this to other kids, aren't you? You're giving them injections like me!" he shouted. "The twelve, right? The Twelve Henchmen of Sengeneth?"

"Clever boy," murmured Dr. Tredegar.

"Yes, Maxwell, you will have twelve able-bodied apprentices, all the same age as you." Mrs. Crumlin pushed back Max's sleeve and wrenched out his arm. "Don't move a muscle."

"After this injection not even your little runaway friend will recognize you." Dr. Tredegar gave Max a ghoulish smile. "Cold, clammy skin, paper-thin wings, pointed teeth. And, oh yes, a distinctive odor that gets more pungent with time."

Max stared at him in wide-eyed horror. He felt faint, disgusted, dizzy with shock. "Get off me!" he yelled, flailing against Mrs. Crumlin, wild with terror. "You're not making me a Skræk Master, you're turning me into a skræk!" he screamed, punching, scratching, spitting and kicking.

"You are mistaken, Maxwell." Mrs. Crumlin kept her arms locked firmly around him as he tried to claw his way out of her grasp. "A Skræk Master must instill fear in the enemy, his every command must be obeyed by the skræks. The High Echelon's grand scheme is to infuse your human features with those of a skræk. With your changed appearance and no-fear genes, you will be truly terrifying."

"Keep the boy still!" growled Dr. Tredegar.

Gripping Max's shoulders, Mrs. Crumlin shook him so hard he thought the bones in his neck would snap.

"Rick, rack, ruin—" sang the doctor.

"Run, Max!" yelled Rose. He could see her on the far end of the bridge, waving her arms. "Run for your life!"

He couldn't run, he was being held too tightly, but he realized there was one thing that he could do. Shaking off his mitten, Max slipped his free hand into his pocket.

Dr. Tredegar slunk toward him, the InjectaPort winking in the sunlight.

Mrs. Crumlin chimed in: "Over before you can say—"

Max closed his fist over Gran's shell.

"Crimson—"

With fierce resolve Max tore away from his captor and slashed the shell across the back of the doctor's hand. Dr. Tredegar shrieked and the InjectaPort clattered to the ground.

"You little fool!" snarled the doctor, holding up his hand. "Look what you've done!"

Max noted with grim satisfaction the blood streaming from the man's fingers. "You come anywhere near me or Rose and I'll kill you!" he screamed.

A snarl still on his lips, Dr. Tredegar took a step back, nursing his wounded hand. Max could see he was only inches away from the broken section of the bridge.

Then, as if out of nowhere, the silver owl swooped down, hooting and flapping bravely, one wing a bit stiff. At the sight of her, Max's hopes soared. His owl was coming to rescue them!

"A silver owl!" yelled Mrs. Crumlin. "Kill it!"

"Don't you touch her!" cried Max, enraged that anyone would harm his beautiful owl. He brandished the shell at Mrs. Crumlin, blood dripping from its edges.

"How dare you threaten me!" huffed Mrs. Crumlin as she started toward Max. But before she could take a step, the shaggy black hound sprang to its feet.

"No!" shouted Max, terrified that the dog would tear his owl apart.

"Attack!" ordered Dr. Tredegar. "Destroy the owl!"

With a shrill cry, the owl landed on Helios's shoulder and the dog growled. Max's heart lurched. He's going to kill her! he thought, watching openmouthed as the owl clung to the dog's fur. But instead of going for the owl, Helios raced toward the doctor, the owl crouched on its back, blinking her eyes fiercely.

Max was terrified. Why wasn't his owl flying to safety? Had she damaged her wing again? He felt faint and sick, thinking that his silver owl might die.

"Rose, call off Helios!" he shouted.

"Attack, you stupid beast!" ordered Dr. Tredegar.

Max watched the dog jump up, its paws thumping against the doctor's chest. Arms flailing, Dr. Tredegar staggered back, his alligator shoes striking the plank, sending it flying off the bridge. The doctor's bloody hand reached for a railing that was no longer there.

After that, everything seemed fast and wild and not quite real to Max. Eyes bulging, Dr. Tredegar clutched at the air, his tinted glasses sliding down his nose. Mrs. Crumlin barreled forward, pushing Max aside, and the doctor grasped her pudgy hand.

For one brief moment, Max saw their eyes lock in horror and disbelief.

The doctor's gangly frame teetered backward and, with a shudder, he let go. For an instant he froze in midair—then he was gone. Stunned, Max looked over the bridge's edge and his heart leapt into his throat. This isn't happening, he thought, it can't be real.

He watched Dr. Tredegar spinning down, down through the gorge, slicker flapping, mouth opened in a silent scream. Max imagined him as a bird with yellow wings, hurtling to the river in a downward spiral. He squeezed his eyes shut.

Hearing a splash, Max sucked in his breath. Opening his eyes, he peered once again into the terrifying abyss. He could see, many hundreds of feet below, black water churning around the tiny shape of Dr. Tredegar. In disbelief, Max watched the waves close over the doctor's head, pulling him under.

Shivering uncontrollably, Max stared into the raging maelstrom; then light flooded down from the sun, so unexpectedly dazzling that he could no longer see.

Feeling his legs give way, Max sat down hard on the bridge. Next to him lay the doctor's tinted glasses, one lens smashed, and the InjectaPort bubbling with purple liquid.

He couldn't stop his teeth from chattering. "Dr. Tredegar is gone," he said to himself, "sucked into a whirlpool." It had happened in less than a minute. He'd never seen anyone die before. When he touched the InjectaPort, the cold metal sent a shiver through him; without thinking he slipped it into his jacket pocket.

He looked up and saw Mrs. Crumlin stumping toward him. "I knew you and that urchin were nothing but trouble," she seethed. "What a despicable thing you've done, Maxwell, murdering Dr. Tredegar!"

Max scuttled away from her. Why was it his fault? Did she mean that if he'd warned Tredegar about the missing rail, he'd still be alive? Or was she referring to his threat to kill the doctor?

"Shut up, you old dingbat!" yelled Rose. Max watched Rose bury her face in the dog's fur. "Max didn't kill him, Helios did!" The silver owl darted back and forth, skimming over her head.

"We have a problem, Maxwell." Mrs. Crumlin ignored Rose and stared at him with lusterless eyes. "A rather serious problem, I'm afraid. Never mind, we'll sort it out." She held out a muffin. "Here, eat this."

Max stared at it, feeling queasy.

"Don't touch that muffin, Max!" yelled Rose. "Run!"

Max was suddenly ravenous. He reached for the muffin, then quickly pulled his hand away. Even in his tired and confused state, he knew better than to eat anything Mrs. Crumlin offered him.

"Don't be a fool!" Mrs. Crumlin waved the muffin in front of his face. "You need this for strength and nourishment, Maxwell. Now, *eat it*," she ordered.

"No—" Max started to say, but before he could utter another word, Mrs. Crumlin was cramming the muffin into his mouth.

To his horror, he accidentally swallowed a chunk of it. The custard was rancid—he could taste the foulness of it right away—and it seared his mouth and throat. In a panic he spit out the rest of the muffin.

At once his head felt strange and airy as if his skull had been hollowed out. He realized that this had been no ordinary muffin, but a megastrength one. Mrs. Crumlin had added some medicinal ingredient to the muffin mix, a toxic flavoring to dull his mind.

"What did you put inside this?" he tried to say, but the words got jumbled inside his throat.

Mrs. Crumlin, smelling of bleach and bitter chocolate, loomed over him. "It will be dreadful if they send you to Children's Prison. Imagine being locked inside a cell all day long. No windows, no trees, no Mrs. Crumlin to cheer you up with goodies and mugs of hot cocoa. Solitary confinement for life will not be a fun time. And that's what under-thirteens get for murder."

Confused and angry, Max stared up at her, convinced she was trying to frighten him. Gran said the High Echelon had always used fear to control people—it was their most powerful weapon—and Mrs. Crumlin obviously took her cues from the High Echelon. She would do whatever it took, he realized, to carry out orders.

"Run, Max!" hollered Rose.

"I didn't kill the doctor, I just threatened him!" cried Max, shaking with rage. "The dog pushed him over and you know it."

"Ah, but the authorities don't know, do they?" Grabbing his arm, Mrs. Crumlin pulled him roughly to his feet. "When I file my report, whom do you think the High Echelon will believe? An underage runaway—or me?"

Max didn't answer. The gut-numbing vertigo was back and he could no longer think straight. Thoughts fell and scattered in his head like board game chips.

"Forty years I've worked for them, so I think we know the answer to that." Nudging him forward, Mrs. Crumlin steered him to the gap in the bridge. "It certainly is a long way to the bottom, isn't it? Takes one's breath away. Avert your eyes—I would."

Max gazed into the black raging river and his head began to spin. Images of Dr. Tredegar came flooding back.

"You're traumatized, Maxwell, you've had a severe shock," said Mrs. Crumlin in a condescending tone. "Come along now, time to go home."

Traumatized. Shock. Max thought the words sounded scary and ugly. *Home.* That was a good word. It made Max think of food and warmth and eiderdown quilts, silent evening meals and rounds of Dome Delirium in the parlor. Mugs of hot cocoa, Mrs. Crumlin slamming around mixing bowls, songs on the radio—

A voice cut through his thoughts. "She's lying, Max, she's deranged!" shouted Rose. "Remember the Owl Keeper!"

"Block that voice out of your head," ordered Mrs. Crumlin. As she led him off the bridge, he felt the last of his willpower slip away.

His thoughts reduced to sludge, Max stepped into the field. There was a bitter taste inside his mouth: that disgusting muffin. Never mind, he told himself, it was important to obey his guardian and he must never, ever talk back to her. She was the voice of authority.

"The wind-borne vessel!" cried Mrs. Crumlin, pointing. "They've moved it to the other side of the field. Hmmph! Seems we have a walk ahead of us."

Max tried to speak, but his mind was mixed up like batter. He knew he should be excited to be returning home, but for some reason he wasn't.

"The owls!" That voice again, as distant as the stars. Rose's voice. "We have to find the silver owls!"

Totally blank on the inside, Max waded through the tall grass. Cold tendrils of fog moved shadowlike through his head. Who was Rose? And why was she shouting about silver owls if they were extinct?

And if they weren't yet extinct, he told himself, it was going to be his job to make sure they were soon.

CHAPTER TWENTY-TWO

Hunched against the wind, Max plodded across the field, his mind as blank as a sheet of paper. In the distance a high voice was shouting his name, but he no longer knew whose voice it was. His will to fight was gone.

Dark clouds blotted out the sun and a heavy mist drifted down. The wind-borne vessel hovered wraithlike over the field. Max knew he should be brimming with excitement—he'd never ridden in a wind-borne vessel before—but he was too detached from everything around him to even care.

Only one thing was real, and he saw it each time he closed his eyes: a tiny human shape with yellow wings, spinning down and down in an endless spiral. The image terrified him.

"Did you hear me, Maxwell?" asked Mrs. Crumlin in an icy voice. "I asked you to hand over the InjectaPort."

Max threw her a quizzical look. The InjectaPort, he knew, was somehow important.

"I saw you sneak it into your pocket." Her tone was sharp. "Dig it out. Now!"

Automatically he reached into his jacket pocket, thinking how it must be true that Mrs. Crumlin had eyes in the back of her head. He pulled out a thin metal object and held it in his hand. When he shook the InjectaPort, he could see liquid sloshing inside. That sparkly stuff meant something, but he couldn't remember what. Fog thickened around him, shrouding the windborne vessel and blurring Mrs. Crumlin, giving the scene an air of unreality.

"This way to the aircraft." Mrs. Crumlin steered him to the right. "The InjectaPort, Maxwell. Hand it over."

Max held the InjectaPort at his side, unwilling to let go of it. He stole a glance at his guardian's big, billowing frame as she stomped through the grass in her quilted raincoat, its hem muddied and torn. Unlike his grandmother, who had loved the outdoors, Mrs. Crumlin seemed awkward and out of place.

A stray thought entered his head and he struggled to keep a hold on it. Something about Gran . . . Had Mrs. Crumlin, he wondered, ever known his gran? Did she know what Gran had died of or where she was buried?

"Did you know my grandmother?" he blurted out.

"I did not." Her voice was cold and dark. Around her eyes he could see the skin was crumpled.

"But you remember when she died, right?" Max persisted, eager for any crumb of information. "I wasn't allowed to go to the funeral, but I just wondered if maybe you ... ." His voice trailed off.

Mrs. Crumlin ground to a halt. She looked Max evenly in the eye and a small grin took hold of the corners of her mouth. "There was no funeral. Your grandmother isn't dead." With fussy, brisk movements, she patted down her rain-frizzled hair. "Celeste Unger was sent to prison—a life sentence."

Max opened his mouth, then shut it again, unable to utter a word. His beloved gran was in *prison*? The knowledge was like a blow to the head, jolting him out of his stupor.

"I don't believe you," he said at last, his voice thick and muffled. "My granny's dead."

"Ah, but I should know, Maxwell," came Mrs. Crumlin's steely reply, "seeing as I was the one hired to monitor your grandmother's subversive activities."

The shock of her revelation set his dulled thoughts into motion. Max realized he was thinking clearly once again. "You spied on my granny?"

"Of course I did; I work for the government and that's my job. Celeste Unger had the audacity to defy the High Echelon. She was a traitor, a betrayer of the cause!" railed Mrs. Crumlin. "Rash, impulsive, crazy as a june bug, that was your grandmother—always stirring up trouble. They had no choice but to shut her away."

Max swallowed hard, stunned by this discovery. When he thought of the years he'd spent without Gran, missing her desperately, believing she was gone forever, a deep sorrow cut through his heart. But she wasn't dead, she was *alive*! He didn't know whether to laugh or cry.

"The government put up with her antics far too long," Mrs. Crumlin added with a sniff. "Time and again she lied to the authorities. All those banned books she kept hidden inside her house. A travesty, if you ask me. Scandalous!"

Rage swept through Max as he thought of all the years Mrs. Crumlin had deceived him, feeding him one lie after another. Most of her lies hadn't amounted to much, but this one was different. This one had broken his heart.

"You knew about my gran?" He could hardly get the words out. "And you *never told me*?"

"We had our orders. Everyone, including your parents, believed Celeste Unger was dead. Only I knew her true fate—and the High Echelon, of course. That is how the government works, you silly boy," she said irritably. "Remember your school slogan: All We Do Is for the Higher Good. There it is: we are here to serve the High Echelon." She gave a slow, self-satisfied smile, beaming with pride, obviously pleased to serve such an all-powerful authority.

"Not me!" shouted Max, sickened by her pompous words and sly expression. "I'm not serving anybody!" Why had she fabricated all those stories? Why hadn't she wanted him to know his grandmother was alive? And why would the High Echelon choose a traitor's grandson to become a Skræk Master?

"Listen to me, Maxwell." Eyes glittering, Mrs. Crumlin gripped his wrists. "The no-fear gene will render you strong and fearless. You won't be a weird sickly child anymore, you'll have superhuman abilities." A shrewd look spread over her face. "Forget your grandmother. The High Echelon has chosen you, Maxwell Unger, to safeguard this country." Her voice fell to a reverential whisper. "To be a Skræk Master and fly with the skræks is an honorable destiny indeed."

Somewhere in the mist an owl hooted.

With a shudder, Max wrenched himself from her grasp. He remembered those disgusting dreams: flapping beside creatures that smelled of blood and decay, slime dripping from their half-formed faces. His stomach twisted at the memory.

"Now give me the InjectaPort, Maxwell." Mrs. Crumlin held out her hand.

"Whoo-hoo!" hooted the owl again.

The silver owl! With a start Max recognized her warning call. How could he have forgotten her? Feelings of remorse and confusion washed over him. How could he have run off and left his owl behind?

Something inside him snapped. "You can't turn me into a Skræk Master!" he shouted. "I'm Max Unger, the boy who loves owls, and that's who I'll always be!" Purple droplets sprayed from the tiny needles as he waved the InjectaPort around. "I don't care about your stupid no-fear gene! So what if I'm not strong and fearless? I have Rose, and my mom and dad! I have my silver owl! My gran, too! They're the things that matter to me!"

Mrs. Crumlin threw him a withering smile. "You have no choice, Maxwell, it is not your decision to make." She lumbered toward him, her eyes bulging with fury. "Give—the—InjectaPort—to—me."

"Get away!" he screamed, alarmed at her fanatical expression.

Mrs. Crumlin lunged forward. Terrified, Max leapt to one side; then, to his horror, he slipped in the wet grass. Falling to the ground, he landed on his back. Before he knew what was happening, the InjectaPort flew from his grasp.

Startled, he watched it soar overhead in a gleaming arc, vanishing into the fog. He waited to hear it thump to the ground. But everything was silent. This was a field, with no trees overhead to snag it—so where had it gone? he wondered. Perplexed, he struggled to his feet, staring up into the fog.

"Where did the InjectaPort go?" demanded Mrs. Crumlin, stomping in circles. Max could see red splotches flaring up on her neck and ears. "It can't stay in the air indefinitely!"

Had the fog muffled the sound of the InjectaPort when it fell to earth? Max ran through the tall grass, guessing roughly where it might have landed, but there was no sign of the InjectaPort.

From overhead came a whirring sound; he looked up and glimpsed a shape, wheeling in intricate patterns through the fog. The silver owl! Max could see the InjectaPort clasped in her beak. Her eyes were fierce and unblinking. Smart bird, he thought, grinning. She's coming to my rescue again!

"This blasted fog isn't helping any," grumbled Mrs. Crumlin. She clumped back and forth, her bloodshot eyes glued to Max. "What are you grinning at, you miserable boy?"

Before he could reply, the owl gave a triumphant hoot.

"Hear that?" cried Mrs. Crumlin. "The silver owl is back! Oooh, just wait, I'll wring its skinny neck—"

Max glanced up to see the silver owl open her beak and let go of the InjectaPort. It hurtled down, falling straight toward Mrs. Crumlin. She gave a thin cry of rage as it struck her shoulder.

"Take it out!" she screamed, thrashing around like a wounded animal. "Do something, Maxwell!"

Max reeled back, staring at the top half of the InjectaPort. He could see that the bottom part had gone right through Mrs. Crumlin's raincoat and lodged firmly in her shoulder.

"You're useless!" she shrieked, her face contorted in rage. "You always were! Do something!"

Max kept his distance, afraid of going any closer. He watched Mrs. Crumlin grip the InjectaPort and wrench it out of her shoulder. Pale with shock, she held it up. The InjectaPort was empty.

Max felt relief flood through him.

"This was meant for you!" screeched Mrs. Crumlin, swaying back and forth, eyelids fluttering. "*You* were supposed to get the no-fear gene!"

Nauseated, Max watched her shriek and sway, clawing at her shoulder.

"Ten times the normal dose!" she howled. "We needed *ten times* to start the Transmutation! This isn't fair, Maxwell! I was only doing my job!"

Max grimaced, watching the blotches on her skin turn a cadaverous shade of gray. Was she going to die? Her arms slumped to her sides and her puffy face went slack, as if all the wrinkles had been shaken out. Then she collapsed with a thud into the grass.

CHAPTER TWENTY-THREE

Max stared down at Mrs. Crumlin, sprawled in the tall grass, her eyes turned to downward-slanting slits, the side of her face raked by claw marks. Her coat was rumpled and torn, her sturdy shoes coated in layers of mud.

He knelt on one knee, struck by an icy numbness, frightened and yet relieved. She would have chased him to the ends of the earth, he knew, to carry out the High Echelon's orders. Now, at last, he was free of her.

He looked closely and could see her breath was coming fast and uneven. At least she was still alive. Eventually the pilot of the wind-borne vessel would get tired of waiting and come looking for her. Anyway, that's what Max hoped would happen. Though he also knew there was an after-dark scenario, one in which the Misshapens would come out and find her. He didn't want to think about that.

He stood up, feeling a tremendous weight slide from his shoulders. White fog, thick and silent, drifted around him, erasing Mrs. Crumlin's features and turning her into a lumpy blur. She reminded him of those dead people in Egypt called mummies, wrapped in white shrouds and buried in golden tombs. He'd seen pictures of mummies in Gran's *Wonders of Ancient Times*.

Where was his silver owl? He called for her, but there was no reply. Perhaps she'd flown back to the bridge. The bridge—why was that important? He struggled to remember. *Rose!* Rose was waiting for him at the bridge! How on earth had he forgotten her? But he already knew the answer: he had swallowed the poisoned muffin.

He pulled a sweater from his rucksack and shook out the crumbs. It would keep Mrs. Crumlin warm until help arrived. He lowered the sweater, but as he leaned nearer his insides curdled.

Her shape was recognizably human, and yet as he got closer he saw that Mrs. Crumlin was changing into something very different. He could see knotted veins pulsating beneath the slimy gray skin of her face. And on each hand her sausage-shaped fingers ended in sharp, pointed claws.

He staggered back, sickened to his core, watching two scrappy wings tear through the shoulders of her coat, shredding the fabric to pieces. Horror-struck, he dropped the sweater and raced off.

• • •

Max ran wildly, searching for the stone bridge and Rose and his silver owl, confused by the shifting fog. At one point he found himself beneath a wing of the wind-borne vessel. In a corner of his pocket he could feel Gran's shell. Was it stained with Dr. Tredegar's blood? He couldn't bring himself to look at it. The drowned doctor was one more thing he didn't want to think about.

At last, after what seemed like hours, he saw the outline of the bridge in the distance. Exhausted, almost crying, he staggered toward it, struggling for breath.

"Who is it?" shouted Rose. "Stop where you are!"

Max could hear the dog growling.

"Rose!" he shouted, racing across the bridge. "It's me!" Through the mist he saw her sitting cross-legged, the dog curled at her feet, his silver owl gliding protectively above her head. Max smiled to himself, thinking how these two animals were keeping his friend safe.

As he stumbled toward Rose, the owl floated down and fell limp on his shoulder, tucking her bad wing close to her body. "Are you all right, little owl?" Seeing how tired and bedraggled she looked, Max patted her gently. "Thanks for saving my life," he murmured. "You know, you're the most amazing owl in the world." She crawled to her sleeping spot beside his neck and settled in.

"Max!" cried Rose. "Where have you been?"

He ran to his friend, pulling her to her feet. "My owl saved my life!" he said excitedly. He noticed a smear of dried blood on Rose's cheek. "And Mrs. Crumlin is, like, a giant skræk! She got the extra big dose meant for me and—"

Then he noticed Rose's eyes. They looked muzzy and blurred, like two glazed marbles. "Your eyes!" he gasped, holding her at arm's length. "What happened?"

Her grimy fingers fluttered before his face. "It's a white fog that comes and goes," she whispered. "I see shadows and wispy images, moving real slow, like ghosts. Then after a while it goes away and I can see again. But I'm scared, Max, I don't know what's happening!"

He felt his stomach twist. "Rose, I know what it is," he said, feeling terrible that he hadn't told her earlier. "Remember when the Dark Brigade chased you with an arrow?"

"How could I forget?" said Rose hotly. "The arrow went right into my arm and stuck there and I had to pull it out!"

"The arrow was tipped with an experimental drug, Rose! Tredegar shot it at you! I heard Einstein telling Mrs. Crumlin— he said they used some vision gene—"

"An *experimental drug*?" Rose went pale. "What's going to happen to me?" she whispered. "At first I thought it was the fog, but then I realized— Oh, Max, did my eyes get wrecked? Am I going to go blind?"

"I—I don't think so," said Max, though he really had no idea. Seeing her frightened expression, he added, "But you're alive, right? You're still Artemis Rose Eccles, yeah? And we're still together: you, me and the silver owl! Don't worry, the Owl Keeper will heal your eyes. He can do stuff like that!" Rose looked a bit cheered up by his words, Max thought. But deep down he was worried.

"Don't forget Helios." She ruffled the dog's fur. "He's— *Max!*"

She turned to him, startled. "You're out in the sun! You didn't burn up!"

"I was never allergic to sun particles, Rose," said Max. "They lied to me! They made me think I was this sickly kid who was different from everybody else!" He thought wistfully of those years of anxiety and isolation, the years when he'd had no friends at all.

"I knew it!" Rose jumped up and the dog leapt up with her. "Those evil, wheezy bloaters, I hate them! Everything they said was lies! They tried to keep you from being ordinary, Max, they tried to take everything away!" She squared her shoulders and jutted out her chin. "But you stood up to them, didn't you? You were really brave!"

"Yeah," he said, feeling a rawness in his throat as the sadness returned. "I guess I was." The thought of being brave suddenly made him think of Gran.

"Rose, want to hear something amazing?" he said, a childish joy bubbling up inside him. "My granny's alive! The authorities told everyone she was dead, even my parents, but it wasn't true— Gran's in prison! Mrs. Crumlin admitted everything!"

Rose gave a joyful shout and threw her arms around him, waking the sleeping owl on his shoulder, who fluttered into the air. "I'm so happy for you!" she cried. "It's even better than not going up in flames!"

Max hugged Rose back. Through her shabby wool coat he could feel her heart pounding.

"Hey, Max, what if your gran met my mom in prison?" said Rose, looking hopeful. "Maybe they're plotting to escape this very minute!"

Max nodded, hoping that it might be true. "Maybe, Rose."

The silver owl flew into his coat pocket and a chill fell over him as he remembered the wind-borne vessel, waiting in the field for Mrs. Crumlin. They were, he knew, in terrible danger. Any minute now the Dark Brigade could show up. "Let's go, Rose," he said, clasping her hand. "We've got to get away from here!"

The two children ran from the bridge and uphill, to a path strewn with leaves of burnished gold. The black dog raced behind, sniffing the air. Bursting out of Max's pocket, the silver owl soared into the trees. Max saw with growing dread that the path ran straight and deep into the forest.

He knew they had no choice but to follow it. If they went in any other direction they risked meeting the Dark Brigade or the pilot and crew of the wind-borne vessel. He longed to go home, to find out whether his parents were safe, but he knew he'd be arrested and sent to Children's Prison. There was no going back, he realized: the way to Cavernstone Grey was closed to him forever.

The owl wheeled above their heads, leading them on, stopping every so often to rest her wing. Cattails waved, etched with frost; branches clattered in the wind. Snow crystals floated through the frozen landscape. Rose stamped by Max's side as they clambered higher through the trees, the path glistening before them.

"What do you see now?" Max asked Rose as they hurried through the woods. She seemed to be stumbling more often and veering off the path. "Can you see where we're walking?"

"Everything's turning white again. I see shadows and outlines of things that come and go and flicker out of reach, and I hear leaves crunching, but I can't see them. Are the leaves dead, Max?"

"No," huffed Max as they headed up a steep incline. "Not at all!" He wondered if there was some way to counteract the drug on the poisoned arrow. "The leaves are golden, Rose, like the poem," he said, trying to sound upbeat. "This has to be the path to the Owl Keeper!" He scooped up a leaf and gave it to Rose.

"Gold is lucky, Max," she said, twirling the leaf as they ran. "It's the color of your owl's eyes." Then she ground to a halt. "What's that noise?"

Max froze, listening to a deep droning high above the trees. It sounded like a huge whirring insect. He looked up to see the underbelly of a wind-borne vessel, then a second one close behind. "It's the Dark Brigade!"

They began running again, crouching low at the edges of the path to avoid being seen. How powerful were the Dark Brigade's binoculars? Max wondered. Mrs. Crumlin once said they'd invented computerized spyglasses that could see through buildings and trees, but he suspected she'd made that up to frighten him.

As they wound their way higher, Max scanned the forest for signs of shelter. They needed somewhere to hide; they couldn't run from the Dark Brigade forever. And he was worried what would happen once the sun went down—and the Misshapens came out.

Maybe, he thought, we'll find one of the old makeshift villages Gran used to talk about. Cloistered in the forests, the villages had been built by resisters and outcasts and hard-thinking visionaries. Moving from one settlement to the next, the resisters had eluded the High Echelon for years, never staying in one place long. Max always liked to think they'd made it across the border.

The path grew agonizingly steep and a freezing wind stung their faces. He could see the silver owl hopping from branch to branch and the dog shaking icicles from its fur. His nerves jangled, Max could hardly think straight. To calm himself, he began singing softly:

> "OWL IN THE DARKNESS,
> SILVER IN THE LEAVES,
> BLIND CHILD COMES LEADING
> THROUGH THE FOG AND TREES.
> THROUGH THE HAUNTED FOREST,
> BEYOND THE ACHING HILLS,
> DARKER GROWS THE EVENTIDE,
> DEEPER GROWS THE CHILL."

He swallowed hard. He hadn't given much thought to the "blind child" part before. Was the Prophecy talking about Rose?

"We need a plan," he said, steering Rose around an upturned root. A plan, he thought, would make him feel less anxious, more in control. "Too bad we don't have a map like the one your dad drew. That was so cool."

Rose went quiet and he knew she was thinking sad thoughts about her father. "My dad never has plans," she said at last. "He makes things up as he goes along. That's because my dad likes to be open-minded and flexible. He likes to be surprised."

Max sighed inwardly. He hated surprises.

Black branches towered overhead, rising against a pewter sky. Sleek and insidious, the wind-borne vessels glided just above the trees, buffeted by the wind. Each time the droning grew louder, Max and Rose dove off the path and into the forest.

Snow lashed at their faces as the path curved, and Max glimpsed a roof shrouded in icy mist. "Rose, there's a house ahead!" he said excitedly.

"Hurray!" cheered Rose. But Max could tell by the way she squinted her eyes that she was having trouble seeing.

As they neared the structure, he saw snow-laden branches straggling out through broken windows. The building stood solid and round, glistening with ice, its battered doorway facing them. Over a shuttered window hung a sign with faded letters. It reminded Max of the ticket booth at Cavernstone Grey's train station, where he'd once gone with Gran.

"'North Forest Railway—northbound from Tigris to Port Sunlight and environs,'" he read aloud. "This town must be Tigris." He frowned, thinking how the railway station in Cavernstone Grey would one day be deserted like this one.

Rose took off her hat and shook it out. Her long red hair was powdered with snow. "I always wanted to ride on a train," she said in a dreamy voice. Her eyes went wide. "Hey, my dad talked about Port Sunlight! I think he was headed there next!"

Max blinked at her in surprise. If this train went north, that meant Port Sunlight was in the Frozen Zone. "Why would he go to the Frozen Zone?"

"Search me," she said, brushing ice off Helios. "My dad doesn't tell me everything, you know."

Max stroked his owl, who had flitted from a branch and clung tightly to his arm. She appeared wary and alert, her golden eyes studying the landscape.

"Let's go," he said, feeling anxious again.

The path took them past the ticket booth and through a gateway of rough-hewn wood. Max could see remnants of a high fence that had once barricaded the settlement, and beyond it a crooked line of rooftops. Apprehension and relief swept through him. The town was still standing!

Keeping close to each other, Max and Rose stepped through the gateway, into the silent town. Heavy snow sifted down, muffling their footsteps as they trudged past empty shops, houses sealed with ice, a clapboard inn with shuttered windows. Thick strands of ivy, coated in frost, choked gutters and chimneys, and spilled down the sides of buildings. Max could see where trees had pushed through walls and roofs.

"I can't see," whispered Rose. "Everything's white again."

"Not much to see anyway," said Max, worried that these episodes of Rose's were happening more frequently. "Looks like the town was wrecked by tremors or something."

Snow fell in waves and gusted down off rooftops. Max realized with growing alarm that all the buildings were frozen shut. His mind raced. Where were they going to sleep?

The dog, glued to Rose's side, began to growl. The silver owl hooted nervously, then dove into Max's pocket.

Max turned a corner, half-blinded by snow, growing more fearful by the minute. Without warning a high-pitched howl broke the silence.

"A wolf!" gasped Rose. "I can see the outline of it, Max! That thing's huge!"

Max froze, panic engulfing him. Snow swirled and he glimpsed two impossibly tall shapes garbed in red, faces covered with masks and goggles, and beside them a large creature with spiky black fur. Dark Brigradiers—and a plague wolf!

Clutching Rose's hand, he sprinted toward an ice-covered house, hurling himself against the front door. It was frozen solid. He kicked frantically, shattering the layers of ice, while Rose bore down on the handle. At last the door gave way, creaking on rusted hinges as it swung inward. They tumbled into a dark, glacial room.

Max slammed the door and bolted it. "The snow will cover our tracks," he said, trying to sound confident. "The wolves will lose our scent, don't worry."

Rose looked uncertain. "I hope you're right, Max."

Max brushed snow off Rose's coat, while Helios sniffed around, toenails clicking on the icy floor. Max spread his jacket for Rose to sit on, then dumped the bread and cheese out of his rucksack. While she ate, he walked around inspecting the rooms, disheartened by what he saw: overturned furniture, smashed pottery, a stone hearth rimed with frost. What sort of family had lived here? Had there been a boy like him? A grandmother? A dog?

The owl squirmed out of his pocket and climbed onto his shoulder, rubbing her beak against his face. Max felt a bit warmer with his owl so close.

"Helios hates it here," grumbled Rose. "So do I." Max saw her crouched next to the dog, running her hands over his fur and pulling out thistles one at a time. "He's a sun dog and he hates the cold."

"Yeah, but it's almost dark, Rose, and—" Max bit down on his lip. He didn't want her to know how frightened he was. Outside the light was fading and he hoped the Dark Brigadiers would give up and go home. But with night coming he felt a creeping dread.

What they needed was a fire, but it would be too risky to light one, even if he could. He dragged a table across the room and pushed it against the door, then blocked the two windows with bookshelves and a sideboard. In the kitchen he heaved one broken cupboard against the back door and another against the window.

By now it was totally dark outside. Exhausted, Max crawled into the corner next to Rose and started emptying out his rucksack, piling coats, sweaters and a thin blanket on top of them.

"They'll never find us here," he reassured Rose. "Besides, there's a snowstorm going on—they won't stick around much longer."

"Yeah," she whispered, "those goggles are rubbish when it comes to snowstorms." Before he could ask if that was really true, Rose said, "Mrs. Crumlin is a *giant skræk*?"

Max felt a wave of nausea, remembering. He wished he could forget, but he knew Mrs. Crumlin's hideous face was stamped on his memory forever.

And so he explained to Rose what had happened. When he'd finished, she snickered—somewhat cruelly, he thought.

"You don't understand," he said, "she's not Mrs. Crumlin anymore!"

"How can she not be Mrs. Crumlin?"

"Because she's a skræk!" Max shuddered, remembering the wings tearing through her raincoat. "Her shape is still human, but her features sort of fused with, um, skræk features." What would the authorities do? he wondered. Would they be able to restore Mrs. Crumlin to her old self? Somehow he doubted it.

"Ugh, that is totally revolting!"

"It could have been me, Rose!" he said, repulsed by the thought. "Or *you*! They were planning to get us both!"

"Your silver owl saved you," said Rose, smiling drowsily. "She's the real superhero! I mean, super*heroine*."

Max gave a sleepy chuckle, thinking how he was the luckiest kid in the world to have Rose for a friend—and a silver owl, too.

Huddled together, the two children, the dog and the owl sank into a weary sleep.

"Wake up, Max!" whispered Rose, shaking him.

He sat up, muscles tensed, startled to find himself in what felt like a dark, frozen cave. Then he remembered that they'd found shelter in an empty house.

"I looked out the window!" Rose shook him again. "Something's outside, Max! Something's coming!"

Wired with fear, Max listened, watching his breath on the air. Blinking sleepily, the owl peered out of his pocket. The frigid house was silent.

"Come look, quick!" Rose pulled him to his feet, her voice shaking with terror. In the darkness her face looked like a floating mask. "I can see weird shadows!"

Max leaned toward her, alarmed by the strange light in her eyes. He had a sudden hollow feeling. The owl let out a sharp hoot. Growling, Helios leapt to his feet and tore around the room in frenzied circles.

Gripped by a cold terror, Max raced to the window, where Rose had somehow heaved the shelves to one side.

Peering through the filthy cracked glass, he saw snow whirling around a mass of dark shapes hobbling down the road. His heart clanged inside his chest. *Misshapens!* Covered with ice and snow, they moved erratically in awkward clumps, eyes pulsing, their crooked outlines illuminated against the icy background.

They seemed to be moving toward the house with alarming speed. He felt the hairs on the back of his neck lift up. How many were there? he wondered. Had they seen him and Rose break into the house? For a nanosecond his heart stopped. Did they *live* here?

"Hurry, Max!" cried Rose, pulling him from the window. He saw his rucksack slung over her shoulder, stuffed to overflowing. When it came to quick escapes, he thought, he could always count on Rose.

Something thumped against the front door. Terrified, Max whirled around. He heard claws scraping against the wood, then a snap, a splinter, hoarse guttural screams. Helios barked at a high, frenzied pitch.

With an earsplitting crack, the door crashed inward.

"Run!" screamed Rose.

Heart pounding, Max seized Rose's hand and they fled to the kitchen, Helios yelping at their heels. The two hauled the cupboard aside and kicked wildly at the back door, cracking and shattering the ice. "Hurry!" urged Max. In the next room he could hear the shrieks of the Misshapens, high and mad and shrill.

The back door flew open, and he and Rose stumbled onto the porch, gasping and breathless, staring at each other in terror. They leapt down the steps, the dog close behind, speeding away over the ice. Sprinting between houses and trees and garden walls, they zigzagged down a maze of alleys, stumbling through snowdrifts, running headlong into darkness, leaving the village behind.

Max had no idea how to find the path again: the blowing snow and tangled trees confused him. All he could do was run in the direction of the Frozen Zone, his owl in his pocket, Rose clutching his hand, pulling him forward as if somehow she knew the way, into the blackest of nights.

CHAPTER TWENTY-FOUR

Max clutched Rose's hand as they raced deeper into the ice and mist and luminous blue snow. On all sides rose glacial walls and ice-clad trees, and whitethorn bushes hoary with frost.

Unlike Max, who was racked with anxiety and self-doubt, Rose charged confidently ahead, pulling him toward the pale cliffs of the Frozen Zone. The silver owl flew out of Max's pocket, spiraling upward. He watched her skimming and darting ahead of them, growing more lively and spirited the higher they climbed.

As they stumbled along, Max took deep breaths, yet all the while dread gnawed at the pit of his stomach. Where were the

Dark Brigadiers and their plague wolf now? he wondered, glancing around. And what about the Misshapens?

The farther up they climbed, the more difficult it was getting to breathe. "Can we stop, Rose?" he asked, puffing hard as the path grew steeper. "Just for a minute?"

"Sure," she said. "But not for long."

Max loosened his scarf. His eyes were smarting from the cold. "I thought by now we'd find the Owl Keeper and be somewhere safe and warm. Maybe I hoped too hard," he said, doubts crowding into his head. "What if Gran was just remembering some childhood story? What if the Owl Keeper is just some character in a book?"

"Don't you dare say that! That's what Crumlin and Tredegar wanted you to believe!" Rose grabbed his wrist and squeezed, crushing the bones with her wiry fingers. "Of course the Owl Keeper's real!" she cried fiercely. "And it's up to us to deliver the silver owl! It says so in the Prophecy—and that poem's the truest thing I ever heard!"

"Okay, okay," said Max, prying her fingers off his wrist. Her tenacity could be frightening.

"We can't give up now, Max, that poem's all we've got!"

He stood looking at her, the wind howling in his ears. Her hair hung in strings around her face and her lips were cracked from the cold. There was a chunk missing from her boot where snow was getting in and she was only wearing one mitten.

"What happened to your mitten?" he asked.

Rose shrugged. "Lost it."

She stamped off determinedly, Helios trailing behind. Max

noticed that the bobble on her hat was gone, too. Poor Rose, he thought. She was so brave—she didn't care about cold or hunger, she just kept going.

Despair rolled over him. He wanted to believe in the Silver Prophecies and in their mission to deliver the silver owl to the ancient tower. He wanted the Owl Keeper to be real. He'd never wanted anything so much.

But, deep inside, he could feel himself giving up.

Rose tugged at his sleeve, urging him on through a hollowed-out tunnel of snow, as if—despite being blinded—she knew the way. On the other side of the snow tunnel, they emerged onto a narrow ridge and Max could see the path once again. On his right loomed a sheer cliff, impossible to climb, and on his left a snow-filled ravine plunged into darkness. He shut his eyes, trying to block out a sudden dizziness.

When he opened his eyes, he looked across the ravine to another ridge, running parallel with the path. Above it hung the two moons, throwing their eerie light over the bleak, icebound forest below.

"Helios is breathing funny," said Rose, sounding worried. She bent down and rubbed the dog all over. "Warm up, Helios, warm up!"

Max looked at the shivering hound and noticed for the first time how cold he looked. "Yeah, he's kind of blue around the mouth," he said, sliding off his knapsack and digging through it. Helios looked gaunt and hollow-eyed, his paws glazed with frozen snow. Max pulled out the blanket and threw it over him, tying it around his neck. He hoped that the dog would be all right.

Rose jumped up. "Look, over there!" Her voice was high and breathless.

Terrified, Max peered through the trees, studying the hills, trying to make sense of the landscape. All he could see were leafless branches and barren cliffs. Where would they go if someone came after them now?

The silver owl flapped overhead. Helios shook his body out and started to whine. Too bad he wasn't one of those snarling guard dogs advertised in *Homes and Domes,* thought Max, feeling more anxious than ever.

"I see shapes, running on the snow!" Rose pointed to the other ridge.

This time Max saw them: three black wolves, running fast, dark blurs against the sky. He felt his throat close up in terror.

"Plague wolves, right?" Rose whispered.

Max's heart shriveled. He felt all hope leaching out of him. How could they outrun three hungry wolves?

"If anything bad happens," he said, swallowing hard, "will you remember we were friends?"

"I'll remember." Eyes closed, she leaned into him, kissing his cheek. Her breath smelled of peaches and her hair had a sharp, spicy odor. "Star-crossed friends, that's what we are," she said softly, "like the gods and goddesses of old."

It was just as well she couldn't see him blushing.

A freezing mist swept down, and the path, crusted with snow, grew narrower and more treacherous as they ran. Max became more fearful with each step, staring at the wizened trees wrapped in ice, the black rocks crouched along the path. Even the sky looked frozen.

Sleet began falling like frozen knives. Cold and miserable, Max looked uncertainly around. His owl, her feathers soaked with ice and snow, fluttered ahead of them, urging them on. Without warning the path widened, opening out onto a vast, frozen plain. It struck him as the kind of place where battles had been won and lost centuries ago, a place where ancient ghosts might walk.

Through the ice and sleet he could make out a line of jagged shapes ahead, looming against the sky. Fear pressed against his chest.

"I see shapes!" shouted Rose. "It's a castle!"

Max let out a sigh of relief. Maybe their luck was turning. He could see a high stone wall that curved for miles into the distance, its watchtowers jutting up at intervals: sturdy stone turrets with narrow windows cut into the sides.

His owl gave a joyful hoot.

"It's a medieval fortress, Rose! It has to be!" Max said, his excitement mounting. He envisioned a castle bristling with weapons and soldiers. "They built them around cities for protection, with towers and parapets and windows for shooting arrows out of! I saw pictures in Gran's books, but I didn't think there were any still standing. This is unbelievable!"

"That's in the poem!" said Rose, her eyes growing wide. " '*The fortress old*'!"

Max hadn't even thought of that. Could this be the place they'd been searching for? he wondered. Light spilled down from the crimson moon, infusing the snow with a reddish glow. As they rushed over the icy ground, his heart filled with hope. Soon they stood before a turret built of flat, square stones. Three enormous stone steps led to a huge door, which stood slightly ajar, almost as if someone were expecting them.

"Is this the Owl Keeper's house?" asked Rose.

Before Max could answer, a howl shattered the night. He felt the blood drain from his skull. The silver owl dove down and into his pocket.

Hardly daring to breathe, he turned to see, a few yards away, three black wolves crouched on their haunches. His gut went numb as he realized that the crimson light wasn't coming from the moon—it was coming from their eyes.

He pulled Rose protectively against him.

"Get in the turret!" he ordered, pushing her up the steps. "Quick!"

Rose flew up the icy steps, Helios clambering after her. The wolves sprang to their feet, shaking ice from their fur. Their bodies were gaunt and abnormally thin, and their eyes had a ravenous gleam. Max could see white foam dripping from their mouths.

"Max!" screamed Rose from the turret entrance. "Max, come inside!" She started back down the steps.

Eyes burning, the largest wolf began to make low, guttural, menacing sounds deep inside its throat. Max had never heard such terrifying growls.

Emboldened, he stood on the bottom step, eyeing the wolves defiantly. For once in his life, he was determined to be brave. He'd fight the wolves to the death if he had to. He would do anything to protect Rose and his silver owl.

Then his eyes widened in horror as they began running toward him.

CHAPTER TWENTY-FIVE

Paralyzed, Max watched the wolves streak toward him. Flecks of dirty foam flew from their mouths. He was beyond panic, beyond fear. This is how it ends, he thought, astonished that his life could be over so quickly.

"Max!" screamed Rose, clattering down the steps behind him.

Max felt her mitten touch his head, dispelling all thoughts of death, and whirling around, he caught hold of her hand. They raced up the steps and into the turret, slamming the door behind them.

Gasping for breath, Max lay on the cold stone floor, astonished to be alive, Rose sprawled next to him. The owl struggled out of his pocket and into the air.

"Rose—" he said, rising to his knees. "Rose, can you see?"

A snarling plague wolf thudded against the door, knocking it open. Helios reared up, barking. Too frightened to scream, Max scrabbled to his feet, hauling Rose off the floor.

The wolf crouched down, hackles raised, its eyes the color of burning blood, ready to spring.

"Max, watch out!" screamed Rose, pointing to a second wolf. Smaller than the first, it looked wilder. The wolf stood poised in the doorway, its eyes consumed with rage. Max threw his arms protectively around Rose.

Then, emitting a harsh shriek, the silver owl swooped down. Max clung to Rose in terror, thinking how his owl was so brave—but she could never fight off such a powerful creature. The owl dove at the larger wolf, sinking her claws into its fur. The wolf shook her off with a startled yelp. Jaws snapping, the smaller wolf leapt up, but the owl was too swift. Max watched in breathless admiration as she somersaulted in the air, then flew at the wolf, raking her claws down its snout.

With a surprised cry it sprang back, colliding with the other wolf, and both went flying down the icy steps. Rose kicked at the door just as the third wolf lunged. With a sharp growl it sank its teeth into her boot and tore it off her foot. Grabbing Rose's coat, Max yanked her away before the beast could get her leg. Helios uttered a savage growl and the wolf, startled, backed away.

"My boot!" cried Rose, holding up her bare foot.

Max grabbed his rucksack and slammed it against the wolf, knocking the animal off its legs and down the steps.

Heart thumping, he tried to close the door, but it kept springing open. "I can't shut it!" he shouted to Rose in a panic. "The hinges are broken!"

"Think of something!" she wailed. "They'll be back!"

If only he could devise a brilliant rescue plan. But Max's thoughts were in disarray and his heart was pounding so loud he couldn't think straight. Through the half-open door he saw the wolves leaping at the owl as she circled above them, shrieking and beating her wings.

Terrified for his owl, Max whistled to her, but she kept on circling, distracting the wolves. What if they caught her? he worried. She might be clever, but she'd have no chance against them one-on-one. The thought of losing his owl was too much to bear.

"The window!" cried Rose, launching herself across the turret. "We can fit through it, right?" Standing on her toes, she peered out the narrow window.

Max rushed over and squeezed in next to her, then leaned out. His stomach dropped to his feet. He was astounded to see a steep descent into darkness, endless and terrifying. The fortress, he realized, had been built at the edge of a massive cliff.

"Bad idea," muttered Rose, her face crestfallen. "Sorry."

With a jolt Max realized that at the bottom of the cliff was what appeared to be a city, its buildings dark and frozen and jumbled together, locked inside layers of permafrost. It looked ancient—as if no one had been there for hundreds of years.

"Rose," he cried, hope rising in his chest. "That could be Silvern! That's where we have to go!"

"Yeah, well," she muttered, "we'll need parachutes to get down there."

But Max hardly heard her. Helios was barking again and outside the turret the wolves were growling. The two children ran to the door, throwing their weight against it. Through the gap Max watched in fascinated terror as the wolves snapped at the owl in frenzied leaps, blood streaming from their snouts. Shrieking, the owl swooped down, talons outstretched.

To Max's puzzlement, everything suddenly went quiet. Ears pricked, the wolves paused. Helios whined softly. The silver owl hung motionless in the air.

"Hear that?" whispered Rose. "Wings! Loose, flappy, squeaky wings!"

Max strained to listen. From the depths of the forest came the familiar, gut-wrenching sound from his dreams. Moments later, the frenzied beating of wings filled the air, and he felt his sun tattoo grow cold as ice.

"Skræks!" he gasped. His silver owl couldn't fight them off too! She was just one little owl, not an army.

"Max, quick!" Rose shouted. He turned to see her kneeling on the floor, tugging on a huge rusted ring attached to a square of beaten metal. "It's a trapdoor, like the one in the barn in Cavernstone Grey." She grunted as she pulled. "It could be an escape route!"

He rushed over and clutched the ring, pulling with all his strength. But the trapdoor held fast. You've got to do this, he told himself, you've got to find a way out. He heard a disgusting *splat* outside as a skræk hit the side of the tower and fell, gibbering and squeaking.

Panicked, he jumped to his feet, kicking the door in frustration. Sweat ran down his face as he kicked again. "Come on, come on!" he yelled. "Open up!"

"It's rusted shut!" yelled Rose, whacking her boot heel against it.

Max kept kicking. Then, with a groan, the hinged square of metal shifted. Determined, he fell to his knees and pushed, flakes of rusted iron flying up into his face.

He could hear skræks slamming into the walls and a commotion outside the tower.

"Max, the skræks and wolves are fighting!" huffed Rose, pushing the trap door with her feet.

Was that possible? he wondered. Were these creatures programmed to destroy whatever crossed their paths, including each other?

He gripped the iron ring and, exerting what was left of his strength, pulled. The trapdoor flew open, and Max stared, incredulous, down a crumbling flight of steps. Weary relief washed over him.

"An escape route!" cried Rose. "That's what it is, right, Max?"

"Yeah, it must be. Go on, Rose!"

Skræks flapped at the window, clawing at the stones, clambering and clinging to the outside walls. Where was his silver owl? He had to rescue her before they tore her apart!

"You go ahead," he said to Rose. "I've got to get my owl!"

Skræks poured through the window in a whirling cloud of

teeth and claws and ragged black wings. A sickening stench filled the tower.

"Helios!" called Rose. Max saw her reach for the dog, but she was too late. Wheezing and hissing, the skræks descended, and with a frightened yip the dog took off.

"Helios!" cried Rose, dropping the trapdoor and charging after him. "Come back!"

Max heard the door clank shut. A skræk whizzed past, startling him, and swiped his cap off his head. Terrified, he looked up at the creature, which was hissing at him through yellow teeth. The silver owl streaked past, hurtling herself at the skræk and snatching the cap from its mouth. Blind and confused, the creature gurgled and swerved away, bumping into another skræk.

Shrieks rang through the tower. Sick with fear, Max staggered off, hands over his ears, shouting for Rose. A talon shot out, slicing his forehead. Warm blood ran into his eyes. He reeled back, tripping over Helios. He heard a growl and looked down at an enormous black paw. It wasn't Helios at all. The paw belonged to a plague wolf lying on the floor, with scores of skræks attached tightly to its fur.

"Max!" howled Rose.

He looked up and ran to her. Beneath a blur of wings she stood on the closed trapdoor, arms pinwheeling, batting away skræks. Her hat was gone and her snow-soaked hair whipped around her fierce, angry face. Dodging a skræk, Helios rushed to Rose's side, barking and snapping.

Fueled by terror, Max knocked a skræk from Rose's head,

snatched her hat from the floor, then struggled to lift the trap-door. He thrust Rose's hat into her hands and pushed her inside.

"Helios!" she wailed. He grabbed the dog by the scruff, shoving him in behind Rose. The owl, Max's cap in her beak, soared down and flew through the open trapdoor.

Max lowered himself into the opening.

"Stop!" cried a harsh voice, and Max felt the bottom of his stomach drop out. Massive and alien, a hulking Dark Brigadier in a filthy cape and torn mask clambered into the turret.

"By order of the High Echelon," he shouted, his voice bouncing off the turret walls, "I demand that you give yourself up! Otherwise I will be forced to attack!"

Gripped by a heart-convulsing fear, Max pulled the hatch down over him, but not before he saw the Brigadier lift his gun and the plague wolf rise to its feet, shaking off skræks with a twitch of its back.

Rose waited on the steps below, clicking her flashlight on and off, looking more disheveled than ever. Helios shivered beside her.

"Shine your light up here!" Max shouted. "Quick!"

She flashed the light in his direction and he saw the thick iron bolt beside the trapdoor. That it had survived the centuries was pure luck, he knew. Overhead he heard a gunshot, then the sound of wolves attacking. Were they going after the Brigadier, or the skræks?

With all his strength he pushed, terrified that the Brigadier would burst through and arrest them. But to his surprise he slammed the bolt forward, securing the door, with barely any effort. He slumped against the wall in a daze. The owl flew up with his cap and settled on his shoulder. Max's heart warmed as her feathers brushed his cheek. There was no owl in the world braver or smarter than she was.

"Max?" Rose shouted up. "Are you okay, Max?"

"I'm fine," he said, rushing down the steps toward her. "But we have to go, Rose. The Dark Brigade knows we're here!"

CHAPTER TWENTY-SIX

Brushing against the frost-bound wall, Max started down the winding steps, holding tightly to Rose's hand, taking care not to slip on the ice. Down and down they went, as he tried to block out images of wolves and skræks and the terrifying Brigadier with his gun.

Max had seen diagrams of fortresses in Gran's book on the Middle Ages, so in a way the tower seemed oddly familiar. The steps had been carved centuries ago into the stonework, with long narrow windows cut into the walls at intervals. He pictured armored warriors, arrows nocked to their bowstrings, defending the walled-in city that lay below.

The tower had a faint putrid odor, and he imagined droppings from bats or mice—hopefully nothing larger than a rat. A disturbing thought flew into his head: what if there were Misshapens down here, engineered to survive the deadly cold? He forced the thought out of his mind.

"You're not scared, are you, Max?" whispered Rose.

"No," he lied, trying not to think of the massive, sprawling cliff this fortress was built upon. "Can you see where we're going?"

"Things are a bit foggy. Hold on to me, okay, Max?"

"Sure thing, Rose," he said, determined to see her safely down.

They spiraled deeper into the murky light. Max tried to move quickly, afraid the Dark Brigadier might be following them. But the ice was treacherous and many of the steps were cracked or shorn off. The wind howled, bitterly cold, shaking the tower as they descended. Rose lost her footing more than once, but Max always managed to grab her in time.

As they passed the narrow windows, he caught glimpse after glimpse of the ruined city—smashed rooftops, frozen courtyards, hulking brick structures. He stared in awe at the skeletal archways and fallen chimneys, the serpentine passageways that folded into themselves.

"Do you think he's really down there? The Owl Keeper, I mean?" whispered Rose.

"Of course he's down there," Max answered reassuringly. But really he had no idea. Was this the way to the Owl Keeper? He was so cold and exhausted he couldn't be sure of anything anymore.

Judging from the view, Max guessed they were halfway down the turret. Ice crystals floated on the air around them and the temperature dropped lower and lower. His face felt funny, like it was going numb. He hoped his owl was keeping warm inside his pocket.

He looked over at Rose and was surprised. Her eyes were glazed with frost, and ice sparkled on her hair and lashes. Her face appeared strangely luminous. She looked, he thought, like a silent, scary angel.

Then, without warning, the steps made a sharp turn and ended. All he could see was a platform, slick with ice, jutting out over the frozen city.

"Watch out!" he cried, grabbing Rose before she could go any farther. Helios bumped into them, giving a startled yelp.

Queasy with vertigo, Max inched toward the edge, his heart knocking. He realized he was looking at a parapet. There had once been a railing around it, but now it was gone—and the steps along with it.

Rose shook her head and ice flew everywhere. "Max, what is it? Why did you stop?"

"They're gone, the steps are gone!" he cried, on the verge of tears. "There's no way down, Rose! It looks like a cannonball ripped through here—or maybe it was the tremors. All that's left is this broken parapet."

The owl wriggled inside his pocket; he opened it and she pinged out.

Rose frowned. "What's a parapet?"

"It's like a balcony," he explained. "An overhang in a fortress where archers shoot their arrows."

"Oh," murmured Rose. "I'm really, really cold." She sank onto the bottom step, resting her head against Helios. The blanket Max had tied around the dog hung in tatters. "I'm so tired, Max . . ."

Worried at how drawn and dispirited she looked, Max took off his jacket and threw it over Rose and the dog.

He turned and stared bleakly into the abyss. Viewed through falling sleet, the city was a blur of hollows and shadows and yawning spaces. He stared into the darkness until somewhere amid the buildings he thought he saw a light flicker. He rubbed his eyes and looked again but saw only snow. Had he imagined it, he wondered, or could life exist in the Frozen Zone?

"I'm turning into an ice-mummy," muttered Rose, rubbing her bare foot. "I can't feel my toes."

Max saw with alarm that her toes were cracked and bleeding. Her lips had turned purple and there was frost in her hair and around her mouth. Were ice-mummies real, or had the High Echelon made them up? Max couldn't be sure about anything anymore.

He unlaced his boots and stepped out of them. "Here, put on my socks." He peeled off his wool socks and handed them to Rose. "Sorry if they're a bit wet and smelly."

She gave him a crooked smile. "That's okay."

How was he going to break it to Rose that their odds of getting out of here were less than zero? He thought about taking out his owl book and reading aloud to her, to comfort them both, but he was too tired.

"Try to sleep," he said, sitting beside her and huddling close. He could already hear her snoring gently. Crouched against the freezing wind, he closed his eyes and fell into a fitful sleep.

It could have been hours, or maybe only minutes, but something woke Max with a start. He looked out at the dead city, and his heart skipped. Over the rooftops and chimneys an incandescent wave of light was breaking. He watched, enthralled by its beauty, as it lit up the sky. Transparent and glowing, the light streamed in all directions, flowing over the rooftops like cool white lava.

"Wake up, Rose!" he said excitedly, his heart lighter. "Something's happening!"

Rose stirred beside him.

"Open your eyes, quick!" The light shimmering across the ice took his breath away. "It's a huge silver wave, coming up over the city!"

Rose nodded, still groggy from sleep, and Helios leaned against her, licking her face. "It's not a wave, silly, we're too far from the sea."

"Not that kind!" said Max. "It's a wave of light!"

Hooting, the owl careened over their heads; Max could see she was getting more agitated by the minute. Flapping determinedly she propelled herself into the air, shuddering upward. Max jumped up, tremulous and fearful. Was she going to fly away and leave him? What about her damaged wing?

He whistled to call her back, then stopped. His owl, he realized, had to follow her owl instincts. All he could do was let her go and trust she would be safe. He watched with pride as she flew off, heading straight into the wave of light. She's so achingly beautiful, he thought, there's no other owl like her in the world.

Rose sat hugging Helios. "It better not be an avalanche coming, that's all I can say."

The sleet turned to snow, falling in thick flakes. Max could hear silvery voices, whispering inside his head. Their whispers ran through him like a shower of light and he realized what the cresting wave was.

"It's a flock of silver owls!" he cried.

Rose leapt to her feet, her face radiant. "I can see shapes, Max, amazing silver shapes!"

Tears of elation sprang to Max's eyes as he watched his silver owl soar higher and join the other owls. Icy flames sparked at her wing tips. And her eyes, he could see, gave off a fearsome golden light. Wheeling skyward, the others followed her lead, forming a vast, glistening arc above the city.

For all his life, Max realized, he had been waiting for this moment.

Behind them, Max heard a low growl and something cold touched the base of his spine. He turned. Crouched on an overhead step, a plague wolf stared down, eyes ablaze, dirty foam frothing at its mouth.

Max's stomach convulsed. There was nowhere to run—they were trapped. "Rose," he whispered, "there's—"

"A wolf," she said. He could feel her trembling next to him. "I can smell its cruddy fur."

Helios leapt to his feet, snarling.

"No, Helios!" cried Rose, clutching the dog's leg and pulling him back. "That wolf's infected!"

Max stood paralyzed with fear, the last of his energy drained away. His only consolation was that his silver owl was safe.

"Maybe—" The words stuck in his throat. Fear clotted his brain. He was out of ideas.

The wolf's scorching red eyes bored into him. Max knew it wanted him dead. Teeth bared, the wolf sprang. For one heart-stopping moment he saw the filthy matted fur on its underbelly, its curved claws and foaming mouth. Clenching his fists, he steeled himself for the worst.

But instead of matted fur and rotting breath, Max was hit with a piercing shriek. A black shape shot out of the fog. Max threw his arms around Rose to save her, but the hissing creature flew straight at the wolf, sinking its teeth into the animal's throat.

A skræk! He watched the wolf try to shake it off, but the skræk held on, slashing the wolf with its razor-sharp teeth. Max could see blood drip onto the icy ground.

As the wolf collapsed, Max realized he was no longer standing still. He looked down and saw his boots, laces flopping, sliding across the ice, moving him and Rose toward the edge of the parapet. Alarmed, he dug in his heels, trying to get some traction, but he couldn't stop.

"Max, what's happening?" Rose clung to Helios, who was sliding along with them. "Max!"

The extra-thick treads were useless. The two children went on sliding. Max flapped his arms, trying desperately to grab on to something, but there was nothing. This can't be happening! he told himself, I can't let Rose go over!

The parapet came to an abrupt end and Max's stomach lurched

as the ground gave way beneath them. He heard Rose scream. Helios yelped in surprise as they slipped over the edge and tumbled off the fortress into space.

Max reached out and took Rose's hand as they fell. Her coat opened, billowing out around her, and on her face was a look of pure terror. The dog plummeted down, down, down, legs churning, ears sticking out like small wings.

There were so many things Max wanted to tell Rose—how much he treasured her friendship, how sorry he was not to have saved her. But it was impossible to speak: they were falling too fast. As they hurtled down into the frozen city, sadness overwhelmed him. He and Rose had traveled so far, and fought so many battles, but all that was over now. His eyes filled with tears.

It wasn't until moments later that Max realized the icy air was growing warmer. They were slowing down, no longer falling at breakneck speed. His panic turned to amazement as he caught sight of snow-covered rooftops and crooked chimneys. A fresh wind blew lightly against his face.

Pale silver feathers floated in the air around him, sticking to his mittens and jacket. Beneath them he could see the flock of silver owls, flying so closely their wings carried the three. Warmth rose from the birds' bodies, and he could smell their fresh grassy breath. Their wings beat in unison, weaving a carpet of feathers and light.

The cold left his limbs and warm blood pumped through his veins. Max felt layers of ice melting away from his frigid bones. And he glided downward, carried on the wings of owls, caught halfway between waking and dreaming.

"Rose!" he shouted, his heart alight with a wild elation. "The owls are taking us down!"

She looked at him in astonishment.

The owls slowly drifted to the ground. Their wings touched and overlapped, brushing one another like light through light. Max imagined he could hear their tiny hearts, beating rapidly. Then, with amazed delight, he saw his very own owl, flying alongside the others, her feathers shimmering with an ethereal light. From her throat came soft, silvery hoots.

In a world of extreme darkness, he knew he had found his way. The Owl Keeper was here, in this mysterious frozen city. He sighed with happiness and relief, thinking: we don't belong to this earth anymore, Rose and I—we've been touched by the silver owls and we'll never be the same.

On this coldest, bitterest day of his life, these wondrous, magical birds had saved them.

CHAPTER TWENTY-SEVEN

The owls deposited Max, Rose and the dog on a soft surface; then they took off, scattering silently in a hundred directions, and Max had no idea which way his owl had gone.

He and Rose landed the way he imagined comic-book kids would do, flopping over each other like string puppets, on a stack of bundled hay inside a snow-filled courtyard. Still in a half-trance, he rose up on his elbows, feeling a sense of perfect calm.

It seemed that while he had been aloft, carried by the owls, his life had changed in some mysterious way. He plucked a feather from his mitten and held it up. It smelled of the forest and sparkled with snow. Traces of silver light from the owls dissolved in the air around him. High overhead he could see the medieval fortress wall, with its sturdy buttresses and turrets, guarding over the city.

"Are we dead?" murmured Rose, eyes fluttering. "Are we ice-mummies?" Max could see foggy breath rising from her mouth as she spoke.

"We're not dead!" he shouted. "We're alive!" He could still feel the softness of those linked wings beneath him. "Rose, it was a flock of silver owls! My owl was there too, and they lowered us down on their wings!"

The knot in his stomach was gone. That awful churning sensation had stopped. The despair and heaviness in his chest had lifted. Max felt transformed.

Rose sat up, wiggling her toes inside Max's socks. "That was owls?" Her hair looked smooth and glossy, sparkling with new-fallen snow.

Helios lay on his back, paws in the air, but Max knew he was alive because his nose was wiggling. It looked as if the dog had a smile on his face.

From the top of the hay bales, Max watched snow whirl past bricks and stone and splintered timbers, settling on branches and walls and low stone troughs. Snow sifted down on collapsed walls and boarded-up warehouses, on rusted metal scraps and fallen chunks of masonry.

He wondered what sort of city this had been. Who had lived here and why had they left? He wished his parents were with him now. What would they think of this silent, ice-cold city? Would they be willing to start a new life here?

He found his jacket in the hay and shrugged it on, all the while studying the ancient stone columns, the damaged statues, the cavernous holes. Trees, black and leafless, pushed up through the ice-covered ground. How did anything manage to grow here?

Once again, he realized, the High Echelon had lied, telling people that if they went to the Frozen Zone they would die. Why did the government want to keep this place a secret? He was here and *he* wasn't dead.

Rose slid off the hay bales, followed by Helios. "Max, I can see again!" she cried in an overexcited voice, shaking snow from her hair. "Why does my sight come and go like that? Why can't my eyes go back to normal?"

"Don't worry, Rose," said Max. "The Owl Keeper will help you, once we find him." He wasn't being totally honest, he knew. He had no idea what the Owl Keeper could do for her, if anything.

Rose stood looking around at the courtyard. "Well, where is the Owl Keeper? I don't see any magic tower." She reached down to pull up her socks. "Where's your silver owl, Max?"

"She flew off with the others," he said, telling himself not to worry. "She'll be back, I know she will."

"Your owl better hurry up, that's all I can say—the Owl Keeper's waiting!" Rose frowned. "Max, what if she's got a new life now—her owl life up in the sky again?"

Max reached into his empty pocket; it was still warm. What if his owl didn't come back? It was too painful to think she might leave him. But what if the pull of the other owls was too great? Then what would he do? Maybe, he thought, her life down here with him really was over.

"On the other hand, that owl's your friend," Rose was quick to say as she wandered off. "She can have two different lives, right? One with you and one with the owls. Don't worry, she'll be back."

"I guess," said Max glumly. But he didn't want to share his owl with anyone else, not even the other owls.

Then he glimpsed a shape, moving through the trees, obscured by falling snow. He felt a prickling between his shoulder blades, a creeping fear. What was it? It looked too small to be a Dark Brigadier. He stiffened, suddenly alert. Was it a plague wolf? A Misshapen?

"What's this piece of junk?" shouted Rose, stomping around, kicking things that got in her way with her big green boot. She gave a loud sniff, kicking at a pile of dirty rags. "*Whooeee,* smells pretty nasty!"

Curious, Max ran over. Shooing Helios away, he bent down and breathed in a revolting smell. He recognized instantly what it was. A dull ache stabbed at his heart. There was no mistaking the crumpled wings and slimy skin, the half-formed face that had no eyes: a dead skræk, wrapped in layers of ice.

"Rose, it's my skræk!" he cried, forgetting all about the shape in the mist.

"*Your* skræk? Since when do you own a skræk?"

"It's dead—dead and frozen," he said, feeling a strange mix of compassion and revulsion. He could see the creature's head was twisted at an angle. Tears sprang to his eyes. "Rose, this skræk saved us! It attacked the wolf and saved our lives!" Blood and foam trickled out between its tiny sharp teeth. Plague, he thought grimly.

"Skræks aren't on our side, Max." Rose hopped off on the one boot, Helios at her heels. "They're the enemy."

"Not this one! He saved our lives and it cost him his life!" Max nudged the creature with his boot. Its pointy head flopped to one side, revealing a sun tattoo and a number. "This *is* the skræk from The Ruins! Look, Rose, number 176!"

He knew it was childish to cry, especially over such a gruesome creature, but a few tears escaped anyway. "This skræk was my friend and I didn't even know it."

"Okay, have it your way, Max, but you'd better bury it fast. That thing's got plague!"

Max wandered around the courtyard, looking through a row of abandoned market stalls, searching for a shovel to dig through the frozen earth. He had to give the skræk a proper burial: it was, after all, a fallen warrior—it had sacrificed its life for two humans and a dog.

As he turned a corner, a figure flitted at the edge of his vision. He ground to a halt. The figure stopped too and stood unmoving by a gnarled tree. Max could see it was small and shaped not like a wolf but like a miniature human. That made him feel slightly braver.

"Come out of there!" he shouted, his voice shaking. "I see you, so don't try to hide!"

"You's not ghosties, is you?"

Max nearly jumped out of his skin when he saw a tiny girl step forward. She wore a white woolen cape and a white dress with scalloped edges that trailed through the snow. White-blond hair flowed down her back.

Except for Rose, Max hadn't had any contact with girls in years. This one looked extremely tiny and fragile. She seemed the opposite of Rose, and much better looked-after.

"Do we look like ghosts?" he said, shaken. "Who are you? Why are you sneaking around?"

"Who are you talking to?" shouted Rose, running over.

"Some little kid!" Max rubbed his eyes. What if this child was one of the High Echelon's weird experiments?

"You's not one of them," the girl said to Max. Her voice was high and whispery. "You's real."

Max stared at her, puzzled. "What are you talking about? Who's *them*?" he asked nervously.

She waved her small hands. "Them that moves in fog, all furry and pale." Her hands reminded Max of starfish he'd seen in Gran's *Book of the Sea*.

"Skræks?" Just saying the word made him shudder. What if the government had laboratories here? What if they were manufacturing skræks and other bizarre things? That would explain why they'd declared the Frozen Zone off-limits.

"She's talking about the owls," said Rose, turning to address the child. "They make *whoo-hoo* sounds, right? They move like ghosties in the fog, right?"

"Yes," whispered the girl, nodding. "That's them."

Max watched the girl's eyes drift over to the dead skræk. She gave a frightened squeal and her face went pale. "What's that? Smelly. That's smelly." She pointed. "Is it biting?"

"Don't worry," said Max, trying to reassure her. "It's frozen solid. It's a dead skræk and I'm going to bury it."

"Don't touch it!" warned Rose. "It's got plague."

The girl looked at Rose and her lower lip trembled. "Scary," she whispered.

Max was afraid the girl was going to cry. He could see she was timid and easily upset. She looked like a worrier, the way he used to be. Or did she have a reason to be scared? he wondered uneasily. What if hideous, menacing creatures roamed this place?

"See that tower?" He pointed to the wall that ringed the city. Maybe if he explained what had happened, the girl wouldn't be so frightened. "A wolf chased us down the steps and this skræk killed the wolf and saved our lives. So it was a good skræk."

"Scary! Biting!" whispered the girl, shaking all over. It was obvious she knew what the creature was.

"That's a happy ending, right?" asked Rose.

The girl chewed on a long strand of hair, considering. Meanwhile, Helios, who had been sleeping under a bench, woke up and started to bark.

The girl's eyes darted around. "Wolfie!" She gave a terrified scream as the dog raced toward them.

Poor kid, thought Max, she's scared to death.

Rose laughed. "Helios isn't a wolfie!" The dog jumped up on Rose and licked her face. "This is my dog and he wouldn't bite a fly!"

"Scared." The little girl backed away, her frilly dress dragging in the snow. "I's scared."

CHAPTER TWENTY-EIGHT

"**M**iranda!" shouted a gravelly voice. Through the falling snow Max saw a short, stocky man in a fur coat, a rifle strapped to his back. He stumped toward them, the wind lifting his thin white hair.

"Who's that old geezer?" whispered Rose.

"No idea," said Max. Seeing the rifle made him jumpy. He hoped this was someone they could trust, someone who carried a gun to protect the Frozen Zone from plague wolves and skræks.

"Miranda Juniper Ashe!" growled the man. "Where you been, youngling?"

Max studied the old man's watery eyes, the stubble on his leathery face. He couldn't decide if this was a friend or an enemy. What if he and Rose got into trouble with the old man for trespassing? What would happen to them then? Was there a Children's Prison nearby? he wondered.

"You shouldn't be out here alone, Miranda!" rasped the old man. "Now come to Grampy." He was so intent on retrieving his granddaughter he didn't notice Max and Rose.

Miranda scampered behind a tree, hiding. "Not alone!" she chirped.

"No playing tricks, youngling, I'm far too old for tricks." The man gave a hoarse cough.

"They jumped out the tower and brung scary creatures!" The girl's voice was low and whispery, but loud enough that Max could hear. "They brung a biting-flying thing, and a wolfie, too!"

The man turned stiffly, his mouth forming an *O* as he caught sight of Max and Rose for the first time. He stared at them long and hard, and Max broke out in a cold sweat. Was the man going to shoot them?

"What are you doing here?" he demanded. "How did you get here?"

Before Max could answer, the girl tugged on her grandfather's sleeve. "Grampy, look! A biting-flying thing!" She pointed to the skræk. "Smelly! Dead!"

The man strode over and stared down at it. "Well, I'll be skeeved! Looks like its neck is twisted right around." He looked up at Max and Rose, pressing together his thick white eyebrows. "What's all this about, eh? We don't take kindly to Outsiders bringing skræks into our city. We don't take kindly to Outsiders period. And what's this about a wolf?"

"Helios isn't a wolf!" Max blurted out, worried that the man might be trigger-happy. He could see the dog at the far end of the courtyard, rolling in the snow. "Please don't shoot him, he belongs to my friend Rose!"

Head thrown back, Rose stepped forward. "Anyone touches my dog," she said in an imperious voice, "I'll cut out their eyes and strangle them dead."

Max had to hand it to Rose: she was a force to be contended with.

The old man suppressed a guffaw.

"Who are you anyway, mister?" demanded Rose in her tough-girl voice. She narrowed her eyes to see the man better. "What are you doing here?"

"*I'm* the one should be asking that question!" the man thundered.

"I'm Maxwell Unger, sir," offered Max, before Rose could say anything. He hoped that if he acted respectful the man might simmer down. Rose was impulsive—she tended to get people worked up. "And this is my friend Artemis Rose Eccles."

"Call me Wexford," said the man, but offered no further details.

"We've come from Cavernstone Grey," Max went on. "We were chased by skræks and plague wolves and the Dark Brigade."

"The High Echelon wants us dead!" added Rose. "And we're starving hungry because all we've had to eat are rotten peaches and stale cookies."

Wexford scratched his head. "Where's the rest of you?"

"We're all there is," said Max, keeping one eye on the rifle. "Just the two of us."

"Don't forget Helios," Rose chimed in. "That's my dog."

Max sensed the old man's thoughts ticking away, adding things up.

"Who sent you?" Wexford wanted to know. "Nobody arrives here by accident. The High Echelon calls it the Frozen Zone, to scare folks off. Not many folks know this city is a refuge."

"We ran away," said Max. "We followed a path and ended up here." Better not mention the secret message, he told himself, or the silver owls—just in case Wexford was planning to double-cross them.

"We fell from a parapet," boasted Rose. "A fortress way high up."

"Oh me cracking bones!" Wexford squinted skyward through the snow, then turned his gaze back to Rose. Disbelief clouded his features. "A long way to fall, from the battlements."

"That's the battlements? Up there?" asked Max.

Wexford nodded. "Old as the hills, that fortress, older than yours truly!" He made a gargling noise that Max assumed was a chuckle.

"The High Echelon says if people come here they turn into ice-mummies," said Rose.

"Humph, typical propaganda," muttered Wexford.

"Ice-mummies?" tittered Miranda, swinging on his arm.

"That's when your bones and eyeballs turn to ice," said Rose, seriously.

Laughing, the little girl fell into the snow.

Wexford rubbed his prickly chin. "Seems to me, if you fell from the battlements and you're still alive, no bones broken, there's a reason. The owls let you pass, is why."

"You mean . . . the *silver owls*?" said Max, suddenly heartened. "They live here?"

"Live here? They guard this city day and night!" The man's rheumy eyes brightened. "We'd not be alive otherwise. Oh, them silver owls can be mighty fierce."

"The silver owls rescued us!" said Max, relieved that Wexford wasn't going to turn them over to the authorities. "What's the name of this place? Is it Silvern?"

"This is Port Sunlight, oldest resort in the country," came the reply, and Max felt a stab of disappointment. "Course it ain't no summer picnic now. The climate turned arctic when the High Echelon messed with the weather."

"Is they ice-mummies, Grampy?" giggled the little girl. "They says they's not ghosties."

"No, Miranda, they're neither—though you might wonder, by the looks of them. Now get up out of the snow." Taking the girl's hand, he turned to Max and Rose. "Follow me, we'd best get something warm into you." He stared at Rose's soaking-wet sock. "Looks like you've lost a boot."

"A plague wolf got it," said Rose. "That's not all I lost either! An evil doctor shot an arrow at me and wrecked my eyesight."

"Oh me cracking bones!" replied Wexford, shaking his head.

"Uh . . . could you give me a minute?" said Max, glancing over at the skræk. "I just need to bury my friend." He had to, he reasoned; it wouldn't be right to leave the skræk exposed on the ground.

"Nobody has them things for *friends*!" Wexford spit out of the side of his mouth. "Them things are killers made by lunatic scientists."

"Yeah, but this one's special," Rose said. "It owed Max a favor, so it killed a plague wolf to save our lives."

Wexford whistled through his teeth.

Scarf wound around his mouth to mask the stench, Max chipped at the ice with a broken spade. The ground was frozen, so he built a small igloo instead of digging a hole. When the igloo was ready, he scooped up the skræk with the spade. Its wings were stiff and stuck out at right angles. Looking at the creature made him want to gag. He could see veins snarled beneath its skin, its blood still and brackish.

"Thank you for saving us, fallen warrior," he whispered solemnly. "You were gallant and stalwart and lionhearted, and a cut above the others. Thus I commit you to this igloo." He thought a moment, then added, "I'll never, ever forget you."

Few words, he thought, but heartfelt; they would have to do. His queasiness gone, he studied the knotted corpse, bleak and frozen and riddled with plague. What kind of being was it? Did it have thoughts? Emotions? Was this skræk somehow different from the other skræks?

He noticed something strange, and looked closer at the skræk. To his surprise, he saw that the sun tattoo was losing its golden color. He leaned forward, curious. The number *176* grew dimmer, fading to a pale bruise, as did the tattoo. Then they were gone.

Somewhat shaken, Max lowered the spade and dropped the

skræk into the hollowed-out igloo. In death it looked sad and harmless. He threw the spade aside, then bent down and peered inside. The skræk's wings were beginning to crumble. Max stared in fascinated horror as its claws shriveled and its head caved in, scattering slivers of teeth. The twisted body grew smaller, until only a husk remained. Then the husk split open, revealing a tiny, fragile heart, suffusing the igloo with a luminous light.

Max blinked, and the heart crumbled to dust.

CHAPTER TWENTY-NINE

With Miranda in tow, Wexford guided Max and Rose through the courtyard and down a narrow, looping street. Minutes later, he paused outside a run-down wooden building six stories high, with peaky dormers, a tilted brick chimney, and green paint flaking off the veranda. Built into one side of the building was a large makeshift greenhouse. Max peered in through a scratched sheet of glass and saw a row of leggy tomato plants. The sight of something green and growing cheered him up a bit.

Above the front door hung a weathered wooden sign that read SUMMER WINDS HOTEL. Beneath it was a painting of a woman in a long dress looking out to sea. Why call it Summer Winds, wondered Max, when summer doesn't even exist anymore? Then again, he reasoned, maybe they kept the sign as a reminder of better times.

"Was once a fancy place, this," said Wexford, fumbling with the key. "Port Sunlight was one heck of a jumped-up town when I was a youngling. Sunny climate, warm breezes, a paradise! Ach, you'd never know it now."

Inside the hotel, Wexford put away his rifle in a cabinet and hoisted Miranda onto his shoulders. Max and Rose trailed behind as they shuffled through an immense gloomy hall, past splintered mirrors and murals eaten away by time, on threadbare carpets and uneven floors, past windows stuffed with cardboard to keep out the cold.

Max kept thinking about his room at home: the coziness of his goose down quilt, the owl book under the closet floorboards, his collection of odd-shaped stones. Everything neat and tidy, each thing in its place. Don't dwell too much on it, he told himself; don't hold on to the memories. Your old life is gone.

At the end of the hall, Wexford threw open a lacquered blue door. Welcoming smells of cabbage and boiled meat hung in the air, mixed with smoke and melting wax. Max could hear his stomach rumble with hunger as he stepped inside. Candles dripped from iron sconces. Smoke swirled around timbered beams. On one side of the room a gigantic brick hearth surrounded a blazing fire.

"Here's newcomers," announced Wexford. "Fell from the battlements, they did. Silver owls let them pass!"

A hush fell over the room. Faces creased with dirt looked up with curious expressions, eyes red-rimmed from the smoke. Wrapped in furs and blankets, the adults sat at long tables, eating from wooden bowls. Max's mouth began to water. Helios scuttled over to the fire and flopped down as if he'd lived there all his life.

"We's brung wolfie!" said Miranda.

"It ain't no wolf," sputtered Wexford. "It's just an old hound." Coughing and hacking, he set the girl on the floor and she ran straight to Helios.

Max looked around the room, suddenly self-conscious. He hadn't expected so many people. There were, he guessed, three or four dozen adults, several children his own age, and some smaller ones, bundled in thick sweaters and hats, sitting on the floor near the fire shooting marbles.

"Ach, dust in me throat," croaked Wexford, spitting into the hearth. "I feel like a bit of chewed string, chasing after that youngling." He strode to the center of the room, addressing the ragtag crowd. "These here two younglings is Rose and Max. They says they come from Cavernstone Grey. They says they run away from the High Echelon."

"And they falled off the tower!" Miranda piped up. She looked around brightly at the children by the fire. "But they's not ghosties." The children giggled.

"We can see they're not, Miranda," said a severe-looking woman in half-moon glasses and a purple woolen shawl. "We can see that plain as day." She ladled soup from a stone urn, and she motioned for Max and Rose to sit down at the table. Max recognized her from somewhere, but he was too tired to think past the soup.

Seated on a wooden bench, he gazed into the bowl. Cabbage leaves floated on top of a rich broth; there were chunks of carrots, onions, potatoes, and meat, and some leafy vegetables he had never seen before. It smelled heavenly.

"We've been running for our lives," said Rose, already busy slurping her soup. "We were chased by plague wolves and skræks and the Dark Brigade, and Misshapens, too!"

Max wolfed down the steaming broth, only half listening to Rose. It was the most delicious soup he had ever tasted. He noticed that Rose was wide awake now and she couldn't stop talking.

"Max's guardian tried to make us eat poison muffins," she went on. "The old pit viper wanted me dead, but she got turned into a skræk. Then there was this evil doctor who shot a poisoned arrow and blinded me!"

There were murmurs and groans, a yelp of disgust from one of the teenagers. Max stared into his soup, annoyed. Somebody needs to wind her down, he thought.

"I'm not really blind," Rose went on, "just sometimes a white fog comes down and all I can see are shapes that look like ghosts." She paused, gazing around at the others. "Are all of you runaways, too?" she asked.

"We're all in the battle against the High Echelon, if that's what you mean," said the austere woman in the shawl. "I'm Vivian Ashe, by the way. The grumpy old man who found you is my husband, Wexford. We grew up in the Easterly Reaches and he visited Port Sunlight as a child."

Max glanced up from his soup, wiping broth from the corners

of his mouth. He vaguely recalled seeing a map of the Easterly Reaches, which was located somewhere near the coast.

"Now we're here as refugees, like everyone else," the woman continued. "We've come from all parts of the country, fleeing the High Echelon. We've settled in here despite the cold weather, building greenhouses in the city, working hard and growing our own food—"

"The High Echelon says the Frozen Zone's a wasteland," grumbled Wexford, tossing a bone to Helios. "Government claims the silver owls are extinct. Lies and half-truths, all what the High Echelon says! We're safe here, see, the silver owls keep watch from aeries that ring the city. Anyone tries to breach the walls, the owls attack."

Max knew what aeries were: hollowed-out places in walls and the sides of cliffs where birds lived. He felt an ache in his heart, remembering his own owl. Where was she now? He was about to mention her when Vivian spoke up.

"Port Sunlight will never fall," she declared. "The silver owls will defend us to the death."

Max watched her remove her glasses and dab at her eyes with the shawl. He realized she was crying.

"We're waiting for our daughter, Rosalyn," Vivian continued. "She's Miranda's mother and works in a factory ironing uniforms. Her husband was sent to jail."

"A fine kettle of fish," muttered Wexford.

"My granny's in jail," said Max, who was beginning to feel a kinship with these people. Like him, they had been uprooted, separated from the ones they loved. How he wished his mother and father were here. "Rose's parents are in prison too, right, Rose?"

He looked over and saw Rose's head resting on her elbows as she snored gently beside her empty bowl. He didn't have the heart to wake her.

Wexford cleared his throat. "Well, Max and Rose, you're welcome to stay here as long as you like." He strode over to the fire and spit into the flames, making them crackle and leap. "And it looks to me like you could use a good night's sleep. You both look like the devil."

Max wanted to ask about the Owl Keeper and the tower and the ancient town of Silvern, but he was too tired to say another word. It was as if his eyelids had lead weights on top of them.

Miranda sprang up. "Is they devils, Grampy?"

"No," said Wexford, "they's not devils." He turned to Max, the hard look on his face softening. "They're strangers, Miranda—strangers same as us."

Barely awake, Max smiled to himself, thinking how pleased Gran would be, knowing he had found a place so warm and welcoming, a place where he might even belong.

The next morning Max crawled out from under a heap of scratchy blankets. The wind whistled through a crack in the window. He'd slept more soundly than he'd slept in years, and there had been no terrifying nightmares. The room was so cold he could see his breath, and the wallpaper was loose and flapping, but none of that mattered to Max. He felt safe and cared for and, yes, happy. It was a feeling he wasn't used to.

Outside it was still dark, though he could see a pale light spreading across the eastern sky. He threw on his jeans and sweater and stepped into a hallway papered in summer flowers. Wandering along, he came to a grand staircase covered in shabby carpet and followed it down to a dreary hallway. There he spotted the lacquered blue door.

Max lifted the latch, wondering what the great hall looked like in early morning with no one around. He pushed the door open and tiptoed inside. Beside the enormous brick fireplace crouched a figure in a tattered bathrobe, stirring the embers with a stick. Something that smelled delicious bubbled inside an enormous pot that hung over the embers.

The woman raised her head as the door closed behind him. "Hello, Max," said Vivian Ashe, rising to her feet. He noticed she was tall and willowy, with an air of old-fashioned genteelness. "Did you sleep well?"

"Yes, thanks," he answered. Why did she look so familiar? Unable to contain his curiosity, he blurted out, "I've seen you before, I know I have!"

Vivian fixed him with her stern smile. "I worked in the prison system thirty years and learned a thing or two there. That was the reason I turned against the High Echelon. I trust you've never spent any time in a prison?"

"Never," said Max, thinking how things might have turned out differently. Instead of this hotel, he could be locked inside a windowless cell in Children's Prison.

"Fancy some bitter chocolate?" She dropped a gold-wrapped cube into his hand. Max looked at it suspiciously, recalling the times Mrs. Crumlin had given him poisoned chocolate drinks. "It comes from your town, Cavernstone Grey: 'The finest chocolates in the country,' as the advertisement goes." Vivian's eyes seemed to sparkle. "I've never been to Cavernstone Grey, however, so I can't think how our paths would have crossed." Reaching into her robe, she pulled out her glasses.

My mom and dad could have made this, Max thought sadly, popping the chocolate into his mouth. It tasted sweet and smoky. "My parents work at Cavernstone Hall," he said, suddenly homesick. "That's the factory that makes these chocolates." If only he knew whether or not they were safe. He worried that his mother had been punished because he'd used her smart card to get inside The Ruins.

Vivian slipped on her glasses. Max took one look at the wire frames and half-moon lenses and realized where he'd seen her before. "Wavy Gray!" he cried. "You're the lady on the Cavernstone Grey Hot Cocoa carton!"

Vivian's eyes widened in surprise. "Why, yes, I am—though very few people know it." She handed him another chocolate. "The artist who did the illustration was an inmate at the prison where I worked. Very talented, he was. Is it a good likeness, do you think?"

"Oh yes!" Max replied. He wondered if Vivian Ashe knew that there were two different kinds of hot cocoa. Not wanting to upset her, he decided not to mention it just yet.

"Why have you come here?" she asked. "Was it to find the silver owls?"

"We're looking for the Owl Keeper," said Max simply. "Rose

and I have to deliver something important to a tower in an ancient city called Silvern. Have you heard of it? The Sages and silver owls fought the Alazarin Oro there hundreds of years ago, but now the Dark has come again. Gran always told me that an Owl Keeper would appear to join the silver owls and Sages, to defeat the evil forces."

"Ah, your grandmother taught you well," said Vivian, nodding with approval. "Silvern was the holy city of the Sages. But centuries after that terrible battle, Port Sunlight was built over the ruins of Silvern. You are in Silvern, Max; this is the place you've been searching for."

"Port Sunlight is *Silvern*? The battle happened *here*?" he cried. A thrill of excitement rushed through him. Then he'd come to the right place after all!

"The fulfillment of the Silver Prophecy is what the High Echelon fears most." Vivian knelt and picked up a black leather bellows, pointing it at the embers and pumping. "That is why the High Echelon has spread the idea that the owls are extinct," she explained as she fanned the flames.

Her words sent a chill through Max. "I knew they weren't extinct, but are they really trying to kill them?" he asked. "My gran told me that the silver owls have strong magic. They'd be able to protect themselves, right?"

Vivian stared into the glowing fire. "The silver owls are powerful, it's true, but they've lost something that was integral to their very being. You see, the silver owls have gone silent. They've lost the ability to sing their magic songs."

"Why can't the Owl Keeper help the silver owls?" asked Max,

his heart thumping. Though, the more he thought about it, the more different the silver owls he'd met earlier seemed from his own. They were far less vibrant than his little owl. They were tough and scrappy, and they'd carried him and Rose on their wings, yet all the while they'd been subdued—and eerily silent.

"I am no Sage or seeress," said Vivian slowly. "I cannot say if the Owl Keeper can help the owls or not."

"But that's the reason we came! The silver owls have to carry out the Prophecy!" cried Max, panicked to think it might not happen after all. "Listen, I have to talk to the Owl Keeper! I have to go there right away!"

"There is a keeper, but"—Vivian gazed at him over the half-moon lenses—"Miranda knows the way to the owl tower. She and the keeper are rather good friends."

"Miranda?" said Max, disappointed. He couldn't think of a more unlikely guide. "She's just a goofy little kid! She thinks the owls are ghosties!"

Vivian chuckled. "Max, you know the silver owls are not ghosts! They protect this ancient city and the people who took refuge here. They are smoke and fire and stars and wind, all rolled into one. You might say they're heaven and earth and every brave heart that ever lived combined. They are, in a nutshell, hope."

Max stared into the flames, lost in the mystery of the owls, wondering at their goodness and fearlessness. What a thing it was, he thought, to live in a time such as this.

Vivian leaned forward, staring at him intently. "I understand you are a Night Seer. Your friend Rose mentioned it to my husband. May I see your tattoo?"

Max sighed, feeling deeply irritated with Rose. She couldn't keep a secret if her life depended on it. "I guess so," he mumbled, not wanting to say no to this fascinating woman who was the real Wavy Gray.

Vivian pushed a clump of his brown hair to one side and prodded his neck with her fingertips. He hated that tattoo. For him it would always be a grim reminder of the skræks and the High Echelon, and the horrible future they'd planned for him.

"There's no tattoo here," she murmured at last.

"It's a yellow sun," said Max. "You can't miss it." Maybe she needs new glasses, he told himself, maybe she should trade the half-moons for whole ones.

"What I see," said Vivian, "is the outline of an owl."

He gasped. "The Mark of the Owl?" Max reached back and felt a raised shape on his neck. A delicious shiver went through him. "It's gone!" he whispered. "The sun tattoo's gone!" It was like a terrible curse being lifted.

"Why are you surprised? After all, you fell through the silver owls and, as you know, they possess strange, unknowable powers." Eyes dancing, Vivian offered him the last bitter chocolate from Cavernstone Grey. "They have given back to you the owl mark you were born with. You carry once again the Night Seer's symbol of generations past."

CHAPTER THIRTY

Max raced upstairs to the sixth floor and burst into Rose's room, where she stood braiding Miranda's hair. He saw the dog dozing on a tatty rug. Miranda's braids were coming out crooked, but the little girl didn't seem to notice. Helios awoke and padded over to Max. His fur gleamed, as if someone had given him a good brushing.

"My sun tattoo's gone!" shouted Max. "The High Echelon doesn't own me anymore!" He felt somehow stronger, more centered, more *himself*. Helios sprang up, licking his ear with a kind of doggy happiness. "And the Owl Keeper's here, Rose! So come on, we've got to—"

For the first time since entering the room, he actually looked at Rose. Suddenly tongue-tied, all Max could do was stare. Rose looked unfamiliar and oddly girly in a clean white filmy dress. Beneath its lace hem were two freshly bandaged knees. On her feet were white shoes, paper-thin, with sequins spattered across the tops. Her sweet proud face was shining and her silken hair fell in waves of pale fire.

"What?" said Rose. Her voice sounded softer. "What are you talking about?"

She didn't look like the Rose he knew, who had mussed-up hair, scabby knees and a dirty, torn overcoat two sizes too big. It struck him that this girl was, well, *pretty*.

"Vivian said the silver owls zapped my tattoo," Max muttered at last, jamming his hands in his pockets and looking at the floor. "They used their magic when they brought us down." He touched the back of his neck, tracing the owl birthmark with his forefinger. "I have my owl mark back!"

Rose spun around, nearly knocking over Miranda. "What about me? It wouldn't be fair if they erased your tattoo and not mine!" She lifted her hair and searched for it. "Miranda, quick!" She lowered her head. "Do you see a yellow diamond on my neck?"

"No," answered the girl. "I doesn't see a diamond. I sees a owlie."

Smiling, Rose looked up at Max. "The Mark of the Owl! I've got mine back, too!"

Miranda skipped in a circle, then skipped over to Max and shyly offered her hand. Rose took her other hand and, laughing, they danced in ragged, earthy joy, Helios leaping beside them, until they all became so dizzy that they collapsed, breathless, on the floor.

Rose stood up first. "You seem different, Max," she said, brushing off her dress.

Max pulled Miranda to her feet. "How do you mean, *different*?" How clearly, he wondered, was she seeing him?

He pushed a lock of brown hair from his eyes. After all, he was wearing his same old mail-order boots and jacket, and he badly needed a haircut. He wasn't spiffed up the way she was.

"Something about the shape of you, Max. You're standing extra straight and tall, with your shoulders pulled back, not slumped over like before. Yeah, you're different."

Max mulled over her words. He supposed she had a point. It occurred to him that he felt straighter and taller on the *inside* as well. And braver, too.

"Rose?" he said quietly. "Can you see me?"

She shrugged and looked down at the floor. "Sort of. It comes and goes, and sometimes I just see shadows."

Max felt a sudden tightness in his throat. "Oh, Rose," he said, throwing his arms around her.

"I don't want to lose my sight," she whispered in his ear. "Help me, Max."

"I will. I promise." Max gritted his teeth, trying to hold back his tears. He knew crying wasn't going to help Rose, but maybe the Owl Keeper could do something for her.

"Get your coats," he said to Rose and Miranda. "We're going to the Owl Keeper."

"Now?" asked Rose, wiping away tears with the back of her hand.

Miranda twirled around, braids sticking straight out. "I knows, I knows, I knows," she sang, "I knows where the Owl Keeper lives!"

"You do?" said Rose. "Will you take us?"

"Yes, I will, I will—" Helios pranced over to lick her face and Miranda tipped over in a fit of giggles.

Through a window of fractured glass, Max could see snow falling outside. He heard a distant rumble that sounded like thunder. Reaching into his pocket, he tugged out Gran's shell. There was no sign of Dr. Tredegar's blood on it. Maybe the silver owls had used their magic on the shell, too.

His thoughts turned to Gran, and he felt a deep sadness wondering if he'd ever see her again. What about his mother and father, toiling away in the chocolate factory? And Rose's parents, imprisoned in faraway cells? What about his silver owl, why hadn't she returned? And Rose's eyes—had they been damaged permanently?

Max knew that not all mysteries could be solved, and not all stories had happy endings, but the shell he held in his hand glowed with a dreamy light, easing his pain, giving him the tiniest shred of hope.

At eleven o'clock that morning, Max, Rose and Miranda set off from the hotel, carrying backpacks filled with poppy seed cakes, goat cheese and a flask of cider. Feeling somewhat apprehensive, Max raced with the others along the frost-covered streets, Helios yipping at their heels. Snow gusted, whirling around them. They ran on, unafraid of the thunder booming in the distance. A brisk wind struck their faces, and every few steps, Max whistled for his owl.

In courtyards and along the streets, tall trees rushed up from the earth, waving skeletal branches. The ground was cracked and frozen, the buildings half-buried in ice, yet to Max the city felt remarkably alive. He looked around in wonder, marveling, as they threaded past makeshift settlements and blazing fires, trudging past people in stalls hawking quince muffins and fire-roasted chestnuts. Until now he'd had no idea that the city was so populated! Shaggy animals bleated, causing Helios to stay close to Rose, refusing to leave her side.

Families gathered in noisy clumps, warming themselves beside open fires, roasting meat on huge spits, waving and shouting as the children ran past. A stately long-legged creature with a swishing tail and braided mane trotted by, pulling a caravan piled high with suitcases.

"A horse!" cried Max, astounded by its size and elegance. He had only ever seen horses in books. Port Sunlight, he was beginning to realize, wasn't dead at all.

Miranda skipped confidently along in her white fur-lined cape and high-buttoned boots. Max thought she looked like a time traveler from another century. Twirling, Miranda ushered Max and Rose along a narrow street that wound out of the city. Max called again for his owl, but there was no reply. Leaving the houses and buildings behind, they crossed a road covered with snow.

"Your grandparents let you come all this way alone?" Max asked Miranda. She seemed too little to be on her own.

"I comes with my gramma." Miranda skittered across the ice and called back to them. "Hurry! We's almost there!" Clambering onto a stone wall, she crab-walked out of sight. "I sees it! The tower!"

Max and Rose followed Miranda over the wall, dropping into knee-deep snow on the other side. Impatient, Miranda hopped up and down a few yards ahead of them.

"Come!" she called, waving her arms. Barking wildly, Helios bounded after her.

Through a tunnel of pale trees, Max saw a cobbled path glimmering with ice and snow. He and Rose plunged through the snow and onto the path. Branches bent over them, frosted with crystals, as they trudged across the glazed cobblestones.

Max looked up and saw the smoky outline of a tree and, behind it, a tower. The air smelled of chimney smoke.

"The owl tower!" he breathed.

The tree was ancient and wide and scarred. It seemed to burst out of the frozen ground, silver branches waving at the sky. The tree reminded Max of his beloved owl tree back home, though it was a much larger version.

"Look at the leaves, Rose! They're silver!"

"Silver leaves on a winter tree!" Rose's hushed voice floated over. "Max, I have a feeling about this place. I think it's enchanted."

True enough, he thought. Nothing about the place was the least bit ordinary. As they neared the tower, the silver leaves shuddered in the wind, lifting off the branches and into the air. Astonished, Max watched them scatter in all directions. They weren't leaves at all.

"Silver owls!" he breathed. He watched the owls fly above the tree, darting and skimming amid the top branches. Was his owl there with the others? "Can you see them, Rose?"

"Oh no, everything's gone white again!" she said, and Max could hear the sorrow in her voice. "But I can imagine what they look like."

Max felt a pain in his heart. Rose was so brave.

Max hooted and called, but still there was no sign of his owl. Lightning flared—pure white flashes across the sky—throwing the scene into disarray. He saw Miranda and Helios at the top of the path, leaping in the snow. And with sudden clarity he realized that the Owl Keeper and silver owls belonged not only to him but to Rose as well. It was a tale of danger and friendship and astonishing adventures, and it bound them together.

Hands linked, they ran up the path to the tower. Max saw the huge wooden door fly open, spilling light across the cobblestones. With mounting apprehension, he glimpsed a tall shadow framed in the entrance.

The Owl Keeper stood waiting for them.

CHAPTER THIRTY-ONE

Transfixed, Max stared up at the tower. It seemed to expand as he climbed the path, filling the sky with incandescent light. He had never seen a building so strange or intriguing.

The owl tower was a massive structure, exactly as his grandmother had described: six stories high and built of polished stone, with balconies and dormers and a steep thatched roof that rose to a point. Smoke billowed out of a tall brick chimney. Behind the mullioned windows on the lower floors a warm, welcoming light glowed. Just below the roof Max could see tiny round holes through which silver owls flew in and out.

"We goes to the Owl Keeper!" yelled Miranda, running up to Rose and taking her hand.

Max hung back, hands in pockets, feeling shy. He gazed at the tower, the owls, the silver tree, wary and uncertain as a young child. He called again for his silver owl and his heart sank when he heard no answer. All he could hear was the echo of his pulse in his ears.

Rose and Miranda ran off, Helios loping behind them. The Owl Keeper stood waiting, silhouetted beneath the tree, rough woven cloak snapping in the wind. A line of silver owls swooped down, forming a brilliant arc, and one small owl broke away and flew off. Max felt suddenly lonely, thinking of his own owl.

Dwarfed by the massive tree, Miranda and Rose ran to the Owl Keeper, dresses trailing in the snow. Chittering merrily, Miranda skipped off with the Helios, shouting to the silver owls, while Rose stood talking to the Owl Keeper.

Snow flicked past on the wind as Max headed up to the tower. Would the Owl Keeper be angry because he hadn't brought his silver owl? Not *his* owl, he thought ruefully, the silver owl had never been *his*—he had no claim to her.

He tramped along the path, bristling with anticipation. He could see Rose, hat strings fluttering, deep in conversation with the Owl Keeper. Drawing closer, he noticed worn carvings on the sides of the tower—circles, spirals and zigzags—ancient as the spells in the stories his gran had told him. Wonder and anticipation stirred within him.

The Owl Keeper held up a glowing shell. It was shaped the same as Gran's shell, though slightly larger, and the sight of it somehow reassured Max. Yet as he hurried on, irrational fears took hold of him. Was Rose safe? What was happening? The Owl Keeper looked so strange and wild, yet so oddly familiar.

The hands of the Owl Keeper grew luminous as light streamed from the shell into Rose's eyes. Max could see the Owl Keeper growing more and more transparent, dissolving into light and air. His arms broke out in goose bumps. Snow fell in dizzying currents, landing on his nose and eyelashes, dusting the path. He sensed that the ground beneath his feet had become enchanted, brimming with magic and power.

As he stepped off the path, powdery snow flew around him; he heard a familiar hooting and the whoosh of beating wings overhead. In a flash his silver owl swooped down, landing on his shoulder, nudging her beak against his face. She looked at Max with eyes that were sad and wise and ancient, as if to say, *I'm home.*

Max gave a long, happy sigh. His owl had returned.

Beneath the tree, the Owl Keeper raised one arm above Rose, and with a shock Max realized the Owl Keeper was a woman! The silver owl cried out and Max stared in disbelief, eyes fixed on the sharp profile and blowing hair, the shell glowing around the Owl Keeper's neck. Lightning flashed and he saw her face as she turned: long and craggy, framed in a swirl of snow-white hair, so striking it seemed carved out of ice. In that instant she appeared goddesslike, immortal.

The Owl Keeper caught sight of Max as he sprinted madly toward her. Calling his name, she waved her arms, beckoning him. He ran so fast his woolen cap flew off. Then he was there, standing before the Owl Keeper, unable to believe his eyes. The silver owl hooted joyously from his shoulder.

"Gran!" Max fell into her arms, sobbing. "It's really you!" Tears blurred his vision.

"Oh, Max, you're here at last! I've waited so long!" His grand-mother held him close and Max smelled the musty scent of old books. "And your parents? Are they—"

"They're still in Cavernstone Grey!" Sobs racked his body. To his embarrassment, they wouldn't stop. "Oh, Gran, I ran away without telling them and now they're moving to the dome! What if I never see them again?"

"Oh, Max." She held him closer, and he knew she was crying too. "We'll find your parents, we'll get them back somehow—I promise." She brushed away his tears, then stepped back, snow crunching beneath her boots, looking taller than he remembered. "Oh my, what a great distance you've traveled—and look how you've grown!"

Max studied his grandmother's face. "I can't believe I found you!" he cried, afraid to blink and find her gone. "I can't believe you're real!" He turned to Rose. "This is my gran, Rose!"

Rose's voice was low and breathy. "I thought you went to prison. Did you escape?" In her eyes Max could see a look of stunned admiration—eyes, he realized, that were once again clear and watchful.

"Yes, I managed to escape," Gran replied. "But that's a story for another day."

Gran's eyes, Max noticed, were a pale silvery blue—like old glass, he thought, glinting in the sunlight. He remembered her eyes being a much darker, stonier shade of blue. Had the light from the silver owls changed her eyes? How could that be?

"You sent the silver owl to me, didn't you, Gran?" he said, holding his little owl against his chest. "I thought she was the last silver owl in the world!"

"Yeah," piped up Rose. "Me too."

"In a sense, she *is* the last silver owl," said Gran, reaching out to smooth the owl's feathers. "She is the last remaining owl who remembers the ancient OwlSong. The other silver owls are still alive, but they have fallen silent. Hunted down and attacked by the dark forces, their powers are diminished, and they have lost their ability to sing the OwlSong." Gently she stroked the owl's curved beak. "One dark night I heard this small owl singing outside the window of my prison cell. I knew then there was still hope. I wrote a message to you for her to deliver, knowing she was brave and loyal and determined—like you, Max."

Max beamed. Gran had paid him the highest compliment, comparing him to the silver owl. He thought how wise and kind Gran was, how he had missed her all these years.

"She turned up in the owl tree with a broken wing, all covered with snow," he told Gran. "I was afraid of her at first, but then we became friends. She really is a brave owl." At this the owl fluffed her feathers a bit. Max looked up at Gran. "She helped us find our way here."

"I've no doubt the path was long and treacherous, but you never gave up, did you? You kept going."

Max kicked at the snow, uncertain of how to respond. He hadn't done any of it on his own. "I'm only here because of Rose and the silver owl," he said. "The owl fought off skræks and plague wolves, and Rose saved us from the Misshapens! Lots of times Rose couldn't see, but she believed we'd find our way; she said the path would take us here and she was right."

"Hmmm," mused Gran. "*'Blind child comes leading . . .'* I am honored to meet you, Rose." She bent down and hugged her.

"I never thought I'd ever meet you," whispered Rose, hugging her back.

Gran turned to Max. "You had everything of which the Silver Prophecy speaks—Rose, the silver owl, your own courageous heart—and together they led you here."

"Max says he isn't brave, but that's not true. He's braver than any person I know." Rose jutted out her sharp chin. "He fought off the Misshapens and plague wolves and skræks, and a lunatic doctor! It was really scary, but he got us here in the end."

Embarrassed, Max stared at the tops of his boots. No one had said such nice things about him in a long time.

"Just because there were times you were frightened doesn't mean you weren't brave," said Gran, placing a hand on Max's shoulder. "Without doubt, it is the greatest act of courage that is often the most fearful."

He smiled up at Gran, thinking how she had been his first teacher in these matters. Everything he knew about bravery he had learned from her.

"You's different, Rose!" Miranda squealed. Max looked over to see the young girl covered head to foot in snow, her cheeks glowing red. "Your eyes is bright!"

It was true: Rose's eyes were luminous. Max could see they shone with a silvery green light.

"Rose told me she was struck by a poisoned arrow," said Gran.

"She feared she was going blind. I thought of the Seraph Shell—a sacred shell with magical properties—and I transferred some of its healing power into Rose's eyes."

Max glanced at Rose again. She looked radiant, but even so, all these things Gran was saying sounded a bit highbrow and mystical to him.

Rose gave a lopsided smile. "Now I can see auras. I see them everywhere! Your aura is beautiful, Granny Unger."

Gran smiled. "Thank you, Rose."

"Mrs. Crumlin and Dr. Tredegar plotted against us!" said Max, feeling the old rage build up inside him. "Tredegar told my parents I was allergic to the sun, but it wasn't true!"

"Everything that quack told you was a pack of lies," said Rose with a sniff, "and that witchy old Crumlin brewing you up poisoned hot cocoa!"

"They tried to make me forget about you, Gran!" said Max. "They gave me drugs to make me think everything I learned about the Sages and silver owls were fairy tales!"

Gran held up one hand. "I think you'd better slow down, both of you. My head is spinning—"

But Max couldn't stop talking. "Mrs. Crumlin was a spy for the High Echelon! She turned you in, Gran! She and Tredegar tried to trick me into becoming a Skræk Master!"

Rose gave a little cry. "Max, you never told me! And skræks kill *silver owls*!"

The silver owl shuddered. Max, aware of her distress, stroked her, calming her down.

Gran gave a ragged sigh. "I knew your life would not be an easy one, Max. I knew from the moment you were born."

Max watched snow sift down, melting on Gran's hair and cloak. Overhead, a ray of sunlight broke through the clouds. He studied his grandmother's face, expecting to find bitterness or regret from her years spent in prison, so far from the people she loved, yet he saw only a calm serenity. She was still Gran from long ago, of course, yet he knew she was far more: healer, enchantress, a keeper of owls.

Was she *the* Owl Keeper? He wasn't sure.

"I knew you were a Night Seer, Max," Gran continued, "capable of great things." She tousled his shaggy hair, something she used to do when he was small. "If only I could have kept that fact from the authorities. Unfortunately that was impossible: you were identified by the High Echelon at birth."

Capable of great things? Max blushed, hearing such an extravagant phrase used to describe him.

"Why does the High Echelon hate Night Seers so much?" asked Rose.

"Centuries ago the Night Seers were half-magical beings who lived in the forests," explained Gran. "They had a special bond with the silver owls because they spoke the language of the owls. The High Echelon has been trying to break this connection by sending Night Seers to work underground, where they won't be able to communicate with the silver owls."

"I hate the High Echelon," declared Max, clenching his fists, thinking of the heartache and pain they had caused.

"I'm a Night Seer too," boasted Rose. "Can you tell, Granny Unger?"

"Oh yes, Rose, I can. It is a marvelous gift." Gran glanced over at Miranda, who was leaping in the air trying to catch a silver owl. "This child is also a Night Seer, though perhaps she is unaware."

"I's what?" Miranda stopped dead in her tracks, flicking her tongue over her lips and frowning.

"It's nothing to be afraid of," said Max, seeing the girl's worried expression.

"You're a Night Seer, not a ghostie or an ice-mummy!" added Rose. "It's a talent you were born with."

Miranda's too young to know what it means to be a Night Seer, thought Max, watching the little girl clap her hands and throw her hat into the air. Helios leapt straight up, ears flopping like a comic-book dog, catching Miranda's hat in his mouth. But one day . . . one day, he told himself, she'll find out how special she is.

CHAPTER THIRTY-TWO

Max heard the groaning of the massive wooden door as it swung open to reveal the entryway to the owl tower.

The tall woman with flowing white hair ushered the three children and their dog inside. Eyes bright, the silver owl hovered close to Max. She had a certain look, he noticed, as if she was returning home from a long journey. Had she been to this tower before? he wondered.

The winter sun danced through diamond-paned windows, setting the rooms and passageways alight. Max was charmed by everything: the courtyard of brick and cobblestones; the tables and sideboards of gleaming rosewood; the blazing lamps and fires; the cavernous kitchen that smelled of lemon and nutmeg, a jade tree growing up through the middle. He felt instantly at home beneath the high arched ceilings inlaid with stars and in the rooms painted in shades of blue and poppy and emerald.

What impressed him most were the hundreds of books that Gran kept here—more books than Max had ever dreamed existed. Everywhere he looked there were bookshelves reaching to the ceilings, lining the walls and hallways, tucked beneath eaves, set into niches and vaults.

"Books salvaged from libraries, before the burnings," explained Gran, looking pleased that Max was so taken with them. "I had assistance getting them here, of course. Books weigh far more than one might imagine."

She guided Max, Rose and Miranda down corridors, pointing out stone terraces and balconies, tapestries and roofed halls, and secret places beneath the dormers. It didn't seem to bother Gran that Helios was dripping snow everywhere, shaking wet flakes from his fur as he trotted about sniffing around the hearth fires and woven carpets.

"Here in the owl tower you will find an ancient magic," said Gran as she led them from room to room. "It runs true and deep, kept alive by Sages and silver owls for centuries."

Max looked around, sensing that very magic in the snow-covered ground the tower was built on, in the dreamy light of the stones; he felt it in the blues and greens of the windows, and in the vast silver tree with its enigmatic owls.

Gran led them through a room of hanging dried peppers, down

a long passageway and up a spiral staircase to a circular room where silver feathers floated in the air. There were nests and roosts and hollowed-out spaces deep within the stone. Directly below the eaves, Max could see small round windows, carved just big enough for owls to fit through.

"This is where the silver owls sleep," explained Gran. "They arrive here in a weakened state, some of them barely alive. I do all I can to restore their strength and energy, which they need to guard the city. But despite all I've done, they make no sound. They have forgotten the OwlSong."

She passed around a battered leather book with rough-edged pages. "I keep track of their progress—a daunting task, since new silver owls are arriving daily. Sadly, some are so weakened"—her voice caught—"they do not survive. I've buried them in a small graveyard behind the tower."

"Oh, those poor little things," said Rose quietly.

The owl quaked against Max and he held her closer, feeling protective. A lump formed in his throat as he listened to her shaky sounds of sorrow.

Gran pointed out leather-bound books on the feeding of owls. She showed the children a medical chest for owl ailments, bottles of clary sage oil to keep feathers sleek, tweezers for extracting thorns and thistles. Max watched Miranda scrutinize each bottle, each implement.

"Perhaps when Miranda is older," said Gran, "she can help look after the owls." She called to the little girl. "Those are tools for repairing aeries, Miranda, and different kinds of wood for constructing owl roosts."

Miranda nodded solemnly.

Afterward, in the old-fashioned kitchen with hanging copper pots, the children sat at a round table spread with durum wheat bread, pots of honey, and fruit piled into ceramic bowls.

Max watched Gran make buttered toast and sprinkle it with cinnamon and sugar—his favorite. She carried it on a tray to the table, along with pewter mugs of honey-clove tea. Helios stretched out before a blazing fire; the silver owl fluttered down and landed on the dog's back. Moments later, both owl and dog were asleep.

"When you were in jail," said Rose, munching, "maybe you bumped into my mother? She's real tall and her name is Violet Silvertree-Eccles—that's hyphenated—and she writes me letters from a high-security prison in the Low Dreadlands." She swallowed. "Well, she used to."

Max felt a pang in his heart. What if Rose got her hopes too high and they came crashing down? He was furious with himself for telling her that the Owl Keeper could fix everything. It had been a thoughtless thing to say, since he knew virtually nothing about the Owl Keeper's powers.

"I'm afraid I never met your mother," said Gran. "I was in the eastern hills, you see, a stone prison with six cells. Fortunately I wasn't there long."

"Oh," said Rose, disappointed. Max knew Rose well enough by now to tell that she was devastated. But, as usual, she put up a brave front.

"I know her by reputation, of course," Gran added on a more hopeful note.

Rose's face brightened. "You do?"

"We heard a rumor via the underground that Violet Silvertree-Eccles led a prison uprising in the Low Dreadlands not long ago," Gran went on. Max leaned forward, listening intently. "Many political prisoners escaped."

"My mother too? She got away?" Rose looked hopeful. "Max, do you know what that means? My mom could show up any day now looking for me and we'll go spring my dad out of jail! You can come with us if you want!"

Max exchanged a worried look with Gran.

"Don't get your hopes too high—not yet, my dear Rose." Gran placed a sympathetic hand on Rose's arm. "In time we'll know more details, but until then . . ."

Rose stared down at her toast, suddenly quiet, and Max felt terrible. Then his thoughts turned to his own parents. "I never said goodbye to my mom and dad," he told Gran in a quavering voice. "They don't know where I am, they don't even know if they'll see me again!" The thought of his parents going off to the domes without him filled him with sorrow and regret.

"Oh dear, you poor, poor children." Eyes glistening with tears, Gran reached over and took Max's hand. "Your father is my only son—I miss him and Nora terribly. This is why the Owl Keeper has been summoned: we are in the time of Absolute Dark, as foretold in the Silver Prophecies, when evil stalks the land and families are torn apart."

"Is that why you hid the poem for Max to find?" asked Rose with a sniffle. "So he'd bring the silver owl?"

Gran nodded. "Five years ago, when I knew I'd soon be arrested,

I hid the Silver Prophecy in your closet, Max, away from prying eyes such as that Mrs. Crumlin's. I trusted you would find it when the time was right."

"Actually, *I* was the one who found it," said Rose loftily. Max couldn't help smiling, thinking how typical a Rose remark that was.

He looked over at the silver owl and saw her open her eyes. She launched herself off the sleeping dog and landed on the table next to his mug of honey-clove tea. Miranda reached over, offering the owl a crust of toast.

"Nobody told us *you* were the Owl Keeper, Granny Unger!" said Rose. "That was a really big surprise!"

"Ah, but you are mistaken, my dears." Gran gave an enigmatic smile. "I have been tending to the owls until the Owl Keeper arrives." She leaned toward the owl, stroking her feathers with the tips of her long fingers.

Max sat back in his chair, astounded. How could Gran *not* be the Owl Keeper? Hadn't she kept the tower going all this time and cared for the silver owls? Wasn't she the wisest person he had ever known in his life?

Miranda crammed another slice of toast into her mouth. "You's not the Owl Keeper? My grampy says you is."

"Then if it's not you"—Rose tapped her knife against her plate—"who the heck is it?"

Granny stood, eyes shining, her bright garments swirling around her. "As the time of the Owl Keeper nears, Sages and silver owls are making their way to Silvern. It is a long and arduous journey, but Absolute Dark is upon us and we can wait no longer.

The powers of evil have multiplied, spreading dark tendrils throughout the country. But now, at long last"—she looked pointedly at Max—"the Owl Keeper is here."

Max dropped his toast. Disconcerted, he stared at Gran. Why was she looking at him like that?

"I sent the silver owl to bring you here, Maxwell Unger, because *you* are the Owl Keeper. You were born with a gift, a power. This has been your destiny since the day of your birth; you cannot turn away from it, Maxwell Unger. The power has been bestowed. All you can do is accept it."

The small owl gave a silvery hoot, fluttering to Max's shoulder. His blood quickened. "I—I don't understand," he whispered, pushing his hair out of his eyes.

"Nothing of consequence can happen here without the Owl Keeper," said Gran. "The Owl Keeper's task is to bring together Sages and silver owls to destroy the dark forces. He must make the tower indestructible. The Owl Keeper combines the warriorlike qualities of the silver owls with the wisdom of the Sages. He is of the Ancients—he is the spiritual force that holds everything together."

The room fell silent.

"Hold on, you're making a big mistake!" said Max, unnerved by the way Rose and Miranda were staring at him. "I'm not special, I'm just a kid! I don't know how to fight against the dark powers!"

"According to the Prophecy, the Owl Keeper is a Night Seer, small in size and generous of heart." Gran smiled. "He—or she—must be born at exactly seven minutes past midnight, on the seventh day of the seventh month, during an eclipse of the moon— or moons, as the case may be. His love for owls has no bounds."

Max dug his fists into his eyes, trying to make sense of her words. Inside his chest his heart thumped wildly. Was Gran losing her mind? Elderly people often got befuddled, he knew, so maybe she was mixing her stories up.

"The Prophecy says the Owl Keeper will undertake a long and dangerous journey," she continued. "Along the way he will be tested, forced to choose between the Silver Teachings and the hollow promises of the Dark."

Max felt delirious. A thousand urgent questions swarmed through his head. His owl rubbed her beak against his face, trying to get his attention, but he was too distracted to respond.

"Is that true, Max?" Rose leapt up, her green eyes flashing. "Born during a moon eclipse at seven past midnight?" He saw a wild, overexcited look on her face. "The seventh day of the seventh month?"

"Yeah, but—" The Owl Keeper isn't me, thought Max, it's somebody brave and magical who can save the world. "What if the Prophecy's wrong?"

"Not very likely," said Rose. "When it comes to six-hundred-year-old prophecies, they don't mess up!" She waved her arms around dramatically. "I can't believe it! All the time we were looking for *you*! *You're* the Owl Keeper, Max, and we didn't even know it!" She and Miranda began to laugh.

"That's ridiculous," Max growled, his ears smarting from the sound of their laughter.

"The High Echelon wanted more than anything to take this gift away from you," said his grandmother softly. "That was why they intended to make you Skræk Master."

Max winced, remembering.

"They knew all about the Silver Prophecy, you see, and the circumstances of your birth. It was your innocence they were after, your pure heart. By taking your soul on the day you turned twelve, depriving you of your destiny as Owl Keeper, they planned to turn the Prophecy on its head—ensuring that this time nothing would stop the forces of the Dark."

Frowning, Max sat very still, absorbing Gran's words. He remembered the odd phrases Mrs. Crumlin had used, like *tabula rasa* and *untainted by civilization*.

Rose and Miranda looked at him expectantly. Were they waiting for him to do something stupendous and magical? They'll be disappointed, he told himself. He knew without a doubt that he was just plain old Max Unger. Even so, he couldn't escape Gran's unwavering gaze. Her eyes were wise and honest, and he knew she would never deceive him.

Stretching to her full height, the silver owl flapped her wings and puffed up her chest. How proud she looks, thought Max, how regal. He smoothed her glistening feathers and stroked the top of her head. From inside her throat came soft, urgent noises.

"Listen to her, Max!" shouted Rose. "Your owl knows who you are! Can't you see she's telling you?"

From the silver owl's beak fell soft, silvery notes, spiraling up into Max's ears. He seemed to hear her sing: *You are the Owl Keeper and this tower is your home.*

CHAPTER THIRTY-THREE

Max, Rose and Miranda stood in a bare moonlit room, watching Gran burrow through an old trunk. The silver owl sat motionless on Max's shoulder as Gran lifted out a cloak of shimmering fabric.

"This cloak belonged to Fuchsia, the first Owl Keeper," she explained, shaking it out. Dust and silver feathers drifted to the floor. "Every Owl Keeper has worn it since." She handed it to Max. "Go ahead, try it on."

It was similar to the cloak Gran wore, only this one had owls stitched in silver thread along the edges. Max fingered the cloak. It was luminescent and the fabric was soft and velvety, the way he imagined the petals of the deadly purple sphinx to be. He threw it over his shoulders and heard a muffled giggle behind him: Rose. When he looked down, he saw the cloak puddled around his ankles.

"You'll grow into it, don't worry," said Gran, adjusting the shoulders. Her eyes grew solemn as she pressed a shiny object into the palm of his hand. "This, too, is for you: the clasp to your cloak, forged by Sages in the holy town of Silvern. For generations it has been handed down to each new Owl Keeper."

Max stared at a brooch wrought of delicate silver, fashioned into the shape of an owl. It glimmered in his hand, casting a soft, steady light. "Gran, I don't know what to say. This is all so . . . well, I just can't quite believe it. It seems incredible."

"As are you, young Owl Keeper." Her lips grazed his head, soft as moth wings, reminding him of his mother's last kiss. Sorrow and joy pulled at his heart.

"Follow me." Gliding toward a rough-cut stairway, Gran motioned to the children. "We go to a hidden room at the heart of the tower: the Chamber of Silver Scrolls."

Silent with wonder, Max and the others followed her up the narrow stairs to a door of golden oak with an owl carved at the center. Gran extracted an elaborate key from her robes. "It was in this room, centuries ago, that the first Sages encountered the silver owls and set them free from their spell of stone." Turning the key in the lock, she pushed on the door and it swung open.

Max peered into a vast, windowless room lined with stone niches along the walls. He could almost envision those enchanted silver owls, waiting in frozen silence for the spell to be lifted.

Candles flickered from iron sconces, and at the far end a fire blazed, sending sparks up a huge brick chimney. On each side of the chimney, enormous stone shelves were built into the walls, rising from the floor to the ceiling. Max could see that the shelves were empty—all except one. Gran strode over to it, reached inside and extracted a rolled-up parchment bound with silver thread. She held it up for the others to see.

"A Silver Scroll!" breathed Max. His owl leaned into him, bristling with excitement. The Scroll looked so mystical, he thought, but fragile, too, as though in an instant it could fall to dust.

"The Sages composed the Silver Scrolls centuries ago in a forbidden runic language. That was their task, and still is, you see: to keep the Old Knowledge alive so that no one forgets the old traditions, nor the Sages' philosophy of peace and nonviolence," explained Gran. "During the Great Destruction, the Scrolls were scattered and lost. Defying the government's edicts, the Sages have been secretly gathering up the Scrolls, a difficult and dangerous endeavor."

"Where are the Sages?" asked Rose. "And where are the Scrolls?"

"They are on their way, my child," said Gran, smiling. "They will be here."

It was almost midnight when Gran led the children out of the Chamber of Silver Scrolls. They trooped through a maze of corridors and followed her up a winding marble staircase to the upper half of the owl tower. Somewhat unsure of his new role, Max took care not to trip on the hem of his robe, which somehow seemed to fit him better than when he had first put it on.

At last they stood before a plain wooden door with images of fierce owls carved along its edges. Bearing down on the latch, Gran told Max to go ahead. "The Owl Keeper," she said, "must be the first to enter."

Swallowing hard, Max stepped inside, the others stumbling in behind him. His silver owl made a low keening sound as he looked around in shocked dismay. Unlike the warm, welcoming rooms below, this part of the tower was cold and dank, with thick shadows and cobwebs floating on the murky air. He caught his breath when he looked up at the thatched ceiling: every inch seemed to be covered in silver owls.

Multiple twisted staircases ran at breathless angles along the high curved walls, and beneath the eaves Max could see small gaps for the silver owls. He gazed out through the thin arched windows and saw the two moons rising.

"See where the roof comes to a point?" said Gran, pointing. "And the small balcony just below it?"

Max looked straight up. He could see a platform attached to the rafters, just below the apex of the tower. A dangerous-looking staircase twisted its way up to it. Max felt his heart leap into his mouth. He had to go all the way up *there*? Would that crumbling wooden staircase hold him?

"At seven past midnight, the time of your birth, when you turn twelve years of age," Gran went on, "the silver owl must begin her OwlSong."

Max pressed his silver owl to his chest, against the soft folds of the cloak, drawing strength from her presence.

In a low voice, Gran spoke. "Remember, Owl Keeper: the silver owl is your muse. And she is muse to all the silver owls. You must carry her to the highest point of the tower, where the moonbeams cross and merge. Only then can she begin her OwlSong."

Gran, Rose and Miranda stood silent before him, regarding Max with expressions of excitement and joy, and a bit of worry as well. He gave each one a swift hug. Heart pounding, he turned to the stairs and started up. The staircase twisted at sharp angles, creaking underfoot. He felt cobwebs land on his face, and dust flew up, making him sneeze. He climbed higher, gripping the stone rail in case the steps gave way, not daring to look down.

Halfway up, Max noticed his silver owl shining brighter. The higher he went, the brighter she became, her golden eyes illuminating the way. He stumbled once, but quickly caught himself and continued on, calmed by the light from his owl, strengthened by her glowing energy.

At last he reached the top of the tower. Wary of looking down, he stepped from the staircase onto the balcony, his heart pounding. He looked up, startled to see hundreds of pale spectral shapes moving about. The silver owls! Suddenly they fell still, not one of them moving, fixing their golden eyes on the small silver owl.

Max had no doubt his timing was perfect: he knew intuitively that it was exactly seven minutes past midnight. Through the windows fell light from the two moons—thick beams of silver and crimson, crossing through each other as they illuminated the balcony.

Dazzled by the light, Max lifted his owl, her silver feathers nearly blinding him. At once she began to emit a low, unearthly thrumming—a sound so resonant he felt it in every nerve of his body, a vibration so deep it rippled through the air around him. Mesmerized, he listened, a deep serenity enveloping him.

The silver owl shimmered as if spun from moonlight, emblazoned with silver light, burning with a wild silver fire. Her OwlSong rose up and up, filling every corner of the tower, resonating off the ancient walls. Max realized that this was the pitch-perfect point, the exact confluence of light and space and sound within the tower. The owl's ethereal humming grew deeper, huskier, glancing off the stone tower, resounding for miles.

Then Max could hear, one by one, the silver owls overhead joining in.

He imagined all the lost silver owls, perched in trees and dark places, turning their heads and blinking their eyes, awakened by this small silver owl. On hearing her song, they would begin to sing as well, weaving their OwlSongs together. They would grow brighter, stronger, their faded feathers turning to silver, their golden eyes alert. OwlSong would resonate across the regions, creating a protective force of good, shifting the balance of power away from the evil forces.

Max surveyed the glowing room, and a rush of sheer joy flooded his heart. Not only was this tower made of stone and brick and wood, he thought, it was imbued with a magic beyond imagining.

Then he turned to his silver owl, looking at her with a pure, unshakable love. Transformed, this somewhat broken bird with her crooked wing and damaged eye had become a ferocious, magical, light-filled creature, calling the silver owls to her side, ready to vanquish the powers of the Dark.

As the two moons crossed over the sky, Gran and the three children ventured out of the tower. Hands linked, they stood beneath the enormous owl tree, staring out at the darkness, silver owls flying in and out of the tower, the snow falling hard and fast.

"Ghosties!" shrieked Miranda.

"Not ghosties—they're silver owls!" cried Rose.

"Look, my dears, they are coming," said Gran. "The Sages are on their way here! I can feel their presence."

Max's silver owl fluttered above his shoulder, making low noises in her throat. He didn't catch quite everything she said, but he was getting better at understanding her language. She was describing the silver owls as fierce warriors, explaining how they would align themselves with the wise Sages and keep the Darkness at bay.

"A mystery, this life," mused Gran. "Yet somehow we muddle through. Rose and Max, you have found your way. You hung on to hope, you kept hope alive."

Max looked into Gran's amazing blue eyes. They were the color he imagined the sea to be on a bright summer's day.

"Hope!" cried Miranda, breaking away and leaping with Helios in the snow.

Gran lifted her exquisite shell, which hung by a silver chain from her neck. Max could see it glowing like a distant star. "To you, Artemis Rose Eccles, I give the Seraph Shell." Gran placed the chain with its shell over Rose's head. "Thus begins your apprenticeship in healing."

Max grinned, seeing Rose's delighted expression. It was, he thought, the perfect gift for her.

"It's beautiful," she said under her breath.

"You's beautiful!" Miranda shouted to Rose. "You's glowing like the shell!"

Lightning flashed for a single mad instant. A thousand owls cried out. Elegant and wild, the silver owls came swooping down, feathers flying in the cold air, looping and wheeling around Max. He laughed out loud in sheer delight, raising his arms as if to embrace them.

For a moment, time crunched to a halt and he watched the years go in reverse, backward over the centuries, to a time when Port Sunlight was Silvern. In his mind's eye he saw the owls awaken from their trance, shaking off the dust of the stone tower, rising like silver flames into the air.

He felt the wind change direction and the owls spiraled upward, soaring into the lightening sky. His silver owl beat her wings and flew after them, high above the branches of the magnificent owl tree. Struck by the owls' grace and symmetry, Max watched them spread in all directions, warming the stones of the city, keeping watch over the owl tower and the fortress walls, holding back the Darkness.

"Here they come!" cried Gran excitedly. "Look, down there on the path, the Sages are coming!"

The children cheered. Max could see stately robed figures

making their way up the cobbled path, each one carrying bundles of rolled-up Scrolls in their arms.

Snow kept falling, falling. The children shivered in the cold light of dawn. Max brushed a twig from Rose's hair. He thought of magic and hope and mystical places, and of Rose beneath the owl tree, the first time he'd ever seen her.

"Remember what you said, Rose?" he whispered. "How sometimes, for a moment, earth and heaven meet?"

"I remember," she whispered back, looking at him with those enormous green eyes.

"I think," he said, "that this is one of those times."

ACKNOWLEDGMENTS

To the loyal muses in my writers' group: Pat Lowery Collins, Laurie Jacobs, Donna McArdle, Lenice Strohmeier, Christopher Doyle and Patricia Bridgman. My grateful thanks for your insightful critiques and encouragement while you read and listened to the many versions of this book. Thanks also to my other muses—Ian and Derek Jones, Heather Wilks-Jones, Rhys Laws (the book's first young reader), and my late friend and mentor Jo Ann Stover.

To my agent, Stephen Fraser, with heartfelt thanks for believing in *The Owl Keeper*! Your persistence and unwavering enthusiasm are deeply appreciated. As promised, you found the perfect home for this book.

To my editor, Krista Marino: a special thank-you for your brilliant editing, creative suggestions and dedication to the vision of this book. Your enthusiasm kindled the spirits of Max, Rose and the silver owl as they burned brighter over time.

A final thanks to my husband, Peter, for his sharp perception and editorial skills—and especially for our midnight OwlSong conversations.

CHRISTINE BRODIEN-JONES has always been fascinated by the mysterious "other worlds" that we inhabit as children. Her novel *The Owl Keeper* began with an image of two children beside a river in a forest without colors. Intrigued by this "other world," she followed the children inside. Brodien-Jones studied writing at Emerson College in Boston and has been a journalist, an editor, and a teacher. She now splits her time between Gloucester, Massachusetts, and Deer Isle, Maine.